# SANTA FE PASSAGE

*Also by Clay Fisher*
*in Large Print:*

Outcasts of Canyon Creek

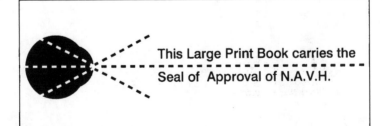

This Large Print Book carries the
Seal of Approval of N.A.V.H.

# SANTA FE PASSAGE

## Clay Fisher

Published in 2002 by arrangement with Golden West Literary
Agency.

Wheeler Large Print Western Series.

The text of this Large Print edition is unabridged.
Other aspects of the book may vary from the original edition.

Set in 16 pt. Plantin.

Printed in the United States on permanent paper.

**Library of Congress Cataloging-in-Publication Data**

Fisher, Clay, 1912–
    Santa Fe passage / by Clay Fisher.
      p. cm.
    ISBN 1-58724-335-0 (lg. print : sc : alk. paper)
    1. Wagon trains — Fiction.  2. Large type books.  I. Title.
PS3551.L393 S26 2002
   813´.54—dc21                   2002033165

# SANTA FE PASSAGE

# 1

Coming slowly in out of the main current to nose gingerly among the clot of mongrel craft tied up along the levee, the trim packet flashed her stern paddles disdainfully. Choose as she might, she could do no better than a narrow berth between a pig-stinking Ohio hog barge and a broad-beamed old slut of a Natchez cotton steamer. Accordingly, the *Prairie Belle* backed haughtily, chuffed an irritated cloud of blue woodsmoke from her twin stacks, and prepared to slide daintily in through the opening.

Leaning on the rail of her Texas deck, just forward of the glassed-in holiness of the pilot's house, Kirby Randolph thought he knew how the *Belle* felt. And looking past the swarming levee at the rutted-mud charms of the town beyond, he shared her feelings.

Yonder there, fronting on the river, eye-hurtful in its yellow paint and double-storied galleries, squatted old René Chouteau's mansion. Past that, up Walnut Street, the cathedral glared defiantly, its Moorish nave rupturing the clean sky. Back of the cathedral lay the old town, Carondelet, called "Vide Poche" by the old-timers, after the traditionally empty pockets of its French-Canadian inhabitants. Still farther up the hill, naked in the splendor of its mud square, floated the bulbous dome of the old courthouse. In between and around these awkward landmarks sprawled the huddle of log hostelries, canvas saloons and clay huts that was St. Louis in 1839.

"She's a sure enough ugly old bitch," muttered Kirby, turning from the rail. "Funny how a feller cain't hardly wait to get his arms around her."

Going below, he threaded his way through the welter of materiel and humanity littering the boiler deck. Everywhere were shaggy bales of buffalo robes, neat bundles of beaver plews, ragged cords of dried buffalo beef and immense rolls of Indian-tanned doeskins. Prowling what free deck space remained, the chaperons of this polyglot lading easily equaled their merchandise in outlandish character.

Forcing his way through the sweating crowd, Kirby wondered if the *Belle* hadn't made a mistake by not going gallantly to the bottom somewhere up around the mouth of the Cannonball, taking the whole smelly crew with her. A quick look at the Ohio pig boat coming alongside with its squealing, milling burden convinced him that for all her elegant airs, the *Prairie Belle* was trafficking in the same trade. "Only difference," he grunted to himself, "is thet these pigs on this h'yar boat has got only two legs."

"Talkin' to yerse'f agin, Kirby?" The question came from a bright-eyed little man perched like a scrawny bird on a bale of green robes. He was perhaps fifty, lean and gray as a fox, wearing the grease-blackened buckskins and carrying the heavy Hawkens rifle of the mountain man. This was Sam Beekman, prairie mate of Lisa and Chouteau in the old days, dean of the current young crop of plew hunters.

"Jest thinkin' we ain't much different than them damn pigs," vouchsafed the younger man, jerking his head toward the close-packed hunters and trappers, "savin' we got only two legs. Same amount of squealin' and millin' around, appears to me."

"Wal, now, I mighten take leave to differ with ye on thet. I allow —"

"Plank's down!" the cry of the ropemen in the bow of the *Prairie Belle* announced her tie-up, interrupting the mountain men's conversation. Kirby and Sam let themselves be carried along the deck and down the plank in the rush of the men to be off the boat. On the levee the two friends parted, Sam to see that his furs got safely off the *Belle*, Kirby to head for the Sublette Trading Company's office up on Courthouse Square.

"Reckon I'll see ye over to the Rocky Mountain House," nodded Sam. "Leastways, soon's ye've had yer talk with Sublette and see'd thet slinky yeller gal of yern down to Vide Poche."

"Reckon ye will," answered Kirby, his mind

9

already racing up the narrow street behind the cathedral. "I'll be along directly."

With a backhand wave to the old man, Kirby swung up Walnut Street to the Square, walking with the loose, bent-kneed gait which stamped his breed wherever it might stride. From the shoulder-length black hair, unwashed since the summer before, to the beaded toes of the Arapahoe hunting moccasins, he was the picture of the professional frontiersman: dirty, wild-haired, hard-eyed; lean, long-muscled, deceptively slow in motion.

Going around the Square to Sublette's, he marveled at the way the town had boomed. It struck him there must be nearly two thousand people camping here the year around, now. Anywhere a man might want to look there was nothing but people. And every scandalous kind under the sun. And the noise of them! They were making more racket than a flock of magpies ripping the *boudins* out of a live buffalo.

The gaunt young trapper was glad to get off the street and into the quiet of Sublette's store. His business there amounted to no more than cashing the sight draft which had been given him for his beaver plews at the upriver rendezvous, and he was soon done with that.

Shambling along under the flaring torchlights of the Square, head down and scowling, the mountain man didn't see the flashy brougham until it was on top of him. Too late, he went jumping sideways, wilder than a spooked Sioux pony. The shoulder of the off-wheel horse clipped him in the backside, sending his lank body sprawling gutterward.

There was a seeming fractional pause in mid-air during which the front of his eye made unhappy calculation of the coming gutter's contents; a foot of liquid mud topped by a smoking meringue of warm road apples; while the tail of the eye took in a flying idea of the rig which had struck him; a custom-built Dearborn with a span of blood hackneys that would catch the eye of any Virginian, even on his way to the gutter.

Of the driver he couldn't be sure. But if "he" weren't a willowstick of a girl, about sixteen, with a bright chestnut forelock and teeth that flashed cleaner than fresh snow, he'd eat his buckskins. So much did Mr. Randolph's well-trained eyes observe before the fluid soil of old Missouri parted to receive them.

Kirby lay quietly in the mud, speculating on his immediate past and direct future. What in tarnal hell was better than six feet of grown mountain man to do about getting his behind knocked into a muddy gutter by five feet of red-haired girl? He eased his gutter companion, a long-dead cat, away from his dripping chin and reared up on one elbow. Best forget the whole thing, likely. After all, the mud wasn't any more stinking than plenty he'd slept whole nights in up on the plains. And maybe she hadn't swung the team into him on purpose. A man was always too quick to make out that accidents were insults.

Halfway up on his hands, Kirby paused, sudden-struck by the awful truth. By Tophet, that kid had *laughed*. Laughed like crazy. A man might see wrong when he was hard hit and sent sailing, but he could sure hear right. "No sir, by God!" he announced to no one in particular. "She done it a'purpose!"

"Ye goin' to spend the night in thar, Casanovy?" The query came in such tones of familiar contempt as could be safely used on a mountain man by nobody but a very old friend. Kirby's head slewed around as Sam Beekman lounged up to deliver his crotchety conclusion. "Whut in tunket ails ye, boy? Are ye drunk?"

"Sam," Kirby hauled himself to his feet, coming out of the puddle shaking himself like a wet dog, "did ye see thet female knock me in h'yar? She run me down with a rig. Young gal, no more'n a kid. Drivin' a stylish rig with two high-steppin' bays."

"Reckon I didn't," grinned Sam. "But I kin call her cut fer ye, like as not. Young gal, looks about fifteen, sixteen, mebbe. Slim as a stick, sorrel hair, good teeth, purty as a blacktail fawn. Dearborn brougham, span of blood hackneys —"

"Thet's the outfit." Kirby's words grabbed quickly at Sam's. "How come ye to know it, allowin' ye didn't see it?"

"Anybody thet hadn't spent his last three years squeezin' castor out'n beaver sacs, would," the old man growled. "Thet thar's old Marcel St. Clair's rig."

"Damn the rig," grinned Kirby, knowingly. "Who in hell's the gal?"

"Wal," the old trapper laid his back against a torch post, shot a stream of Burley at the dead cat in the gutter, "accordin' to the boys over to the Rocky Mountain House, she's *supposed* to be old Marcel's niece."

"Whut ye mean, *supposed?*" demanded Kirby, suspiciously.

"Jest thet. Boys say she's really his own kid, sired out'n some red squaw out thar to Fort St. Clair. Ye realize, don't ye, thet these h'yar St. Clairs is them as makes up one half of the top-dog Santy Fee tradin' firm of Blunt and St. Clair?"

Kirby whistled under his breath. "Wal, old salt, appears I've stepped myse'f into mighty fast company."

Sam ignored him, continued his narration. "Story goes, the gal was brung up out to Fort St. Clair in the Territory. Was runnin' a leetle free out thar, seems like. A real fuzztail, the boys say, wilder than a green-broke colt. Marcel had her brung down h'yar to put in the convent so's she could be cooled off somewhat."

Pausing, Sam took another spatshot at the cat. "Since bein' down h'yar, she ain't bin in

13

nothin' but trouble. Winged a wagon boss who took to allowin' out loud thet she was purtier than a heifer. Downed him with one of them new leetle Colt's revolvin' pistols. Boys say she carries the dang thing around in her dress somewheres. Then she buggywhupt a woman down in front of Sublette's fer callin' her a high-flyin' halfbreed hussy —"

"Did ye say 'halfbreed'?" Kirby's break-in was slow and hard.

"Now dammit, Kirby," the old trapper's continuing tones were uneasy, "ye know full well ye ain't got no call to be so snotted-up about breeds. Besides, this h'yar gal's no breed. Thet's just a lot of dirty trapper's lies!"

"I allow ye're lyin', old hoss." The tall youngster was grinning again, his weather eye warming to the old man's stout defense of the girl. "But I aim to find out, all the same. I owe thet chit somethin', white or halfbreed. Happen right now is as good a time as any to give it to her."

"Whut ye thinkin' of doin'?" the old man demanded suspiciously.

"Never ye mind." Kirby still had the grin working. "See ye at the Rocky Mountain House. And have my possibles packed fer me. I got to be movin' on down the river to find myse'f a gal."

"Wal," Sam's acceptance of the assignment was laced with the caustic soda of long association, "if ye're up to yer usual cub-bear form, I allow ye'll be comin' back from St. Clair's with a fair runnin' start fer the journey!"

The eight-foot split-log stockade around the St. Clair place gave Kirby a pause — a pause long enough for him to ease up to it, pull himself up and swing-vault over to the opposite ground. Perhaps he made a little noise landing. But then so does a snowflake make a *little* noise landing.

He hadn't more than gotten over the stockade before he saw a lantern flash down by the gate, heard the crunch of the returning carriage wheels on the drive. He went into cover like a coyote, running the length of the tree-lined drive ahead of the approaching horses, to slip into the dark of the carriage house. There, he stepped behind a parked landau, pressed back into the shadows, waited noiselessly. The beam of the carriage lamps entering the building flicked across his face to light up a grin as wide as a catfish's.

The girl brought the bays up, wrapped the lines smartly, stepped down off the driving box and out into the lamplight almost before Kirby's grin died away. As a matter of fact there were still traces of it lifting his mouth corners when he stepped up behind her.

"Evenin', ma'am," he murmured, his left arm sliding around her neck with the greeting.

The girl's gasp was cut off in its infancy as the crotch of the lean arm tightened on her throat. At the same time its stillbirth was abetted by the rough buckskin gag whipped across her mouth and cinched down on her struggling tongue hard as a spade bit.

The trapper knotted the gag, slung his kicking victim under one arm and stepped away from the carriage so as to be in the best light from its lamps. "Coo-ee, boys!" he called softly to the nervous horses, and seated himself on a convenient bundle of hay. Here, with dispatch and admirable restraint, he set about doing what he had come to do — turning the spoiled St. Clair girl over his bony knee and whaling the tar out of her.

Applying his outsize hand to the bobbing target beneath it, Kirby's pleasures were not entirely derived from the objective feelings of poetic justice. By cripes, she might be a little thing, sure enough, but she wasn't *all* little.

Still, the trapper didn't let his gift for quick physical assay mitigate the force of his visit's primary object. He'd got his in that gutter half an hour ago, and now she was getting hers.

She strained and twisted in his grasp, a perfect slim fury, but the left hand that could neck-down an eight-hundred-pound Indian pony wasn't too tried by her inspired wriggling. What terminated the spanking was the coming bob of a lantern from down the drive.

Of course! The jasper who'd let her in down at the gate just now would be coming along up to the carriage house to see to the

16

horses. He'd have to let up on her, else he wouldn't have time to give her a good look at him before he had to make his tracks. As it was, he'd probably have to drop the jasper in making it.

Easing off the hay bundle, he straightened, spinning the girl around to face him. "Take a good look, honey," his voice purred with the grin in it, "so's next time ye run over this man ye'll know him!" As the words got out of him, Kirby began to see what he was looking at.

The grin fell open with the gaping mouth.

The girl's eyes flared at him, green as a trapped she-wolf's, her nostrils spread thin and wide and whistling with the breath in them. Her hair, burning red in the smoky lamplight, spilled thick and wild to her shoulders, a heavy forelock of it shadowing the dark face and high-flushed cheeks. From the corner of the wide, full-lipped mouth, a thin trickle of blood showed bright under the twisted gag.

"Lord Almighty, ma'am —" Kirby breathed the phrase, his own gray eyes fired with the beauty of her. The movement of his belt knife, flicking up to sever the cruel buckskin, was no quicker than the one which followed the fall of the parted gag from her mouth. Kirby's arm went behind her head, his body stepping into hers before she could move. The next instant his lips, more cruel than any gag, were driven into her bleeding mouth.

Kirby tasted the fire of that kiss long after the

17

blood of it had ceased to salt his lips.

The girl shot him low down, in the left side, the little .34-caliber ball plowing up and across the last four ribs. He hadn't felt her pull the gun, had no idea where she'd gotten it from. He just knew that he felt it ease into his belly. His wild twist, sideways, timed with the hammer fall, was pure reflex.

Reflex, too, was the snake-fast strike his left hand made for her right wrist. But the backhand slash of his right hand across her face was deliberate. The blow sent her back across the piled hay, limp as a broken doll, leaving Kirby towering over her, the silver-mounted Colt smoking in his left hand, his face black with the distortion of pain and anger.

"Ye halfbreed witch!" The snarl came out of him twice as bitter for its choking softness.

Her eyes were open, staring up at him blankly. He saw them widen ahead of the strange suddenness of her warning cry. *"A-ah!"* The word sprang from her with startling force. Kirby, struck by its foreign sound in that time and place, nevertheless responded to its message without question or delay. *"A-ah!"* It was the Dakota Sioux warning word. *"A-ah!"* Beware! Sudden danger! Look out!

As the mountain man spun around, he snapped his long body over in a doubled-up crouch. The dull flash of the thrown knife hissed high past his bent shoulder, precisely where his broad back had been the instant be-

18

fore. The figure following the knife was the tallest redskin the trapper had ever seen. Dressed in the plain shirt and leggins of a Sioux hunter, the Indian loomed over Kirby like a mountain over a foothill. And Kirby stood six-three, with nothing between him and the bare earth but the thickness of an elkhide moccasin sole.

"*Onhey!*" the savage grunted, and came for him, grizzly fashion, arms circled, big head swinging, angry voice growling. *Onhey* was the Sioux word for a *coup* struck in punishment, and it meant, literally, "I kill him first!"

The white man hung in his crouch until the giant Indian was right over him, then drove his right fist up into the snarling red face, snapping his body straight up behind the blow. It was a lucky shot, taking the huge one chin-flush, dropping the reaching figure to its knees, momentarily stunned.

Ducking around the dazed Indian, Kirby's eyes sought the girl. She hadn't moved. "*Ha-ho,*" he said in Sioux. "Thank you." Then, quickly. "*Niye osni tona leci?* How many winters are you here? How old are you?"

"*Wicsemna sokowin,*" she responded, wide-eyed, "seventeen."

"*Woyuonihan!*" Kirby bowed toward her, touching his left fingertips to his forehead. "I respect you!"

With that he was gone, racing down the graded drive. Quick and light as a shadow, his tall figure faded. Behind him lanterns were beginning to bloom around the main house and, out toward the carriage house, voices to call back and forth across the darkness. Aurélie St. Clair remained motionless across the hay, her slant green eyes staring after the departed mountain man long after his lithe-swinging form had melted into the black of the driveway trees. . . .

Going over the stockade, Kirby grinned. From the hullabulloo back there at St. Clair's, he'd given himself that running start old Sam had predicted. The old buzzard had best have his stuff ready like he'd told him.

For some reason, perhaps neither clear nor important, the young mountain man felt better than he had in four years. He'd gone a mile before he remembered the wild-eyed girl had shot him with the little Colt when he'd kissed her. The only reason he remembered the wound at all was that he suddenly became aware of the fact he still had the fancy little silver gun in his left hand.

Kirby threw back his head and sucked in a big lungful of the balmy night. The war whoop that came with the night air when he spat it back out would have curled the hair of a wooden Indian. But the peaceful citizens of Mudville by the Mississippi never missed a snore.

Drunk or crazy or up to their armpits in love, mountain men were no novelty in St. Louis.

★ ★ ★

When Kirby got back to the Rocky Mountain House he detailed his adventure to Sam, laughing here and there as he went along. The old man didn't join the laughs and when Kirby had finished, he laid it on him proper. "Dammit, ye've stirred up a mud-dobber's nest, boy. It ain't likely to be so all-fired funny come sunup!"

"Whut's to be done, Sam'l?"

"Did anybody see ye? Besides the gal and the Injun?"

"Nope."

"Wal, h'yar's whut ye do. My room's number three, upstairs. Scramble up thar and clean off thet shot scratch. Sneak yer possibles down h'yar and wait out in the shed, yonder. I'll be along directly."

. . . To Kirby, stretched out on a stack of cut hay in the corral shed, it seemed hours since Sam had gone. He wondered, idly, what the old man was up to, and just how bad a tight he himself should figure he was in. There wasn't a lot of law in St. Louis, but there was enough of it that if old St. Clair wanted to get mean about having his niece mussed up, he could put Kirby away until the snow flew. The next thing he knew, Sam was shaking him awake.

"Whut took ye so long?" asked Kirby, sleepy-eyed. "Ye had time to scout a village and steal six hosses. Whar ye bin?"

"St. Clair's."

"The hell!"

"The hell, yes!" snapped Sam. "And I found me out plenty. Old Marcel he's red-hot as a ruttin' elk. Swears no lousehead mountain man is goin' to get by with assaultin' his leetle niece, Aurélie, and smackin' her Injun maid on her jawbone."

"Injun maid!" Kirby's denial was indignant. "I didn't bust me no Injun but thet Sioux buck I told ye about. And thet son of a gun was a half a foot higher than a bull buffler!"

"Thet 'son of a gun.'" The acid of Sam's statement etched the words on Kirby's eardrums, "happens to have bin a 'daughter of a gun.' Sioux squaw. Name of Ptewaquin. Appears she raised the gal out to Fort St. Clair."

"Naw! *Ptewaquin?* The Packin' Buffler? The Ox?" The younger man's questions echoed with patent admiration. "By damn, ye jest cain't beat Injuns fer namin' things!"

"Ye cain't even tie them," grumped Sam, continuing glumly. "Now, listen boy. St. Clair's gettin' out a warrant fer ye. And while I allow he'll not haunt ye to the ends of the earth, it's a gut-cinch ye've got to get out'n St. Louis."

"Is thet all, old salt?"

"Not entire, boy. Seems St. Clair heered about the gal knock-in' some innycent footwalker into a mudhole up on the Square. He's het about thet, too. Allows he's had him his bellyful. He ain't bin able to get the gal into

22

the convent nor to do a dang thing he wants did. So he's packin' her up and shippin' her to his brother's folks down to Santy Fee."

"Whut does the gal say?" Kirby's apparent disinterest failed to take with Sam. The oldster watched him closely as he answered.

"Why, she's all fer it, boy. Says St. Louie is dead and jest ain't bin covered up yet. Claims she ain't see'd but one proper man since she left Fort St. Clair. And thet was the mountain man thet tanned her bottom."

"Damn ye, Sam!" Kirby felt the thrill of the old man's words. "If ye're lyin' to me I'll strangle ye barehanded!"

"Wal, she said it!" defied his companion. "Though I allow she ain't see'd many real men, callin' ye fer a proper one."

"I allow thar's somethin' to thet," the young trapper's admission lifted cheerfully. "Whut ye aimin' I should do now, Sam?"

"Put yer plunder aboard thet bay geldin', yonder, and skeedaddle. I'll buy him fer ye, soon's ye're gone. Head down the river fer Westport. I'll foller on the *Belle*."

"Happen ye're right," nodded Kirby soberly. "Whar'll we meet?"

"Wagon grounds, west of town. By the springs. Stay out'n town to let yer beard brow a mite before ye come in. Buy yerself a beaver hat to cover up yer hair. Thet cussed streak of white what's growed in over thet Pied Noir War-axe wound would give ye away in a

23

minute. And get rid of them upriver buckskins." Sam caught up the bay while he talked,
and Kirby slapped the saddle and bags on him.
Mounting up, he leaned down to shake the old
man's hand.

"See ye down the river, Sam." Then, trying
without notable success to sound nonchalant,
"Say — most of them trains takin' out fer Santy
Fee are makin' up in Westport nowadays, ain't
they?"

"I reckon the gal will start from thar," opined
Sam, drily. "Mebbe ye kin wave her farewell as
her wagons go past the springs. Thet is if old
Marcel don't ketch ye meantime."

"How fur is Santy Fee, Sam? From
Westport."

"Oh, seven, eight hundred mile. Why fer? Ye
ain't thinkin' nothin', are ye?"

"Jest thet I ain't never bin thar."

"It's a hell of a place," grimaced Sam, letting
down the corral bars.

"Allus figgered I'd like to see it."

"Yep." His accomplice stood aside to let the
gelding pass out. "I calculate thet 'allus' of yers
took aholdt of ya rather sudden. Mebbe so
about five minutes ago!"

# 2

Sam had been in camp on the wagon grounds better than a week when he finally spotted what he was looking for: a solitary horseman jogging into the grounds from the east. The newcomer rode a good bay horse, topping him in such a way it didn't take two looks to figure out where he had learned to ride. Two breeds sat a horse that way — mountain man and Indian.

Sam relaxed, the crinkles around his eye corners multiplying into a vastly pleased grin. That was some boy, that Kirby. Not many had his stuff. The old man put back his head and let loose a whicker it would have taken a Pawnee horse tracker to tell from the come-hither nickering of an eager mare.

Down in the flat of the wagon grounds, Kirby rocked along to Old Brown's swaying walk. The morning sun was sparkling bright, he had a passable horse under him, his new clothes were the best that gold money could buy, that smoky-looking St. Clair girl was somewhere near to hand, and he felt cockier than a sassback jaybird.

These lifting thoughts were interrupted by a

sociable mare whickering somewhere off across the camp. Raising his head, the young mountain man came forth with a stud-horse whistle that was like to pull the picket pin on every filly in Westport. When Sam called back for Kirby to spot him, he waved sign that he had, and put the gelding up the rise toward his friend. Sam's sour greeting brought the meeting to sudden order.

"Whar'n hell ye bin?" The old man rapped the words. "Ye mighten as well know ye've missed the gal's train. She's done gone, boy!"

"Naw! She ain't! Ye ain't sayin' she's actually gone a'ready!" Alarm ate up the youngster's fading grin.

"She ain't, eh?"

"Dammit, Sam. It's only bin a week. I figgered —"

"Wal, ye figgered wrong. Ordinarily, it would have tooken them a week to make up the train. Ye kin see down thar on the flat whut a turrible mess it is gettin' them wagons spanned out to travel in a line."

Kirby, following his friend's thumb, looked down on the wagon grounds, nodding. For a square mile in every direction were wheeled rigs of all descriptions. And livestock! By heaven, there was no end to it. Herds and herds of it, grazing the bluestem grass clear up around the bend of Indian Creek. The young trapper, thinking he had seen some tall dirt and confusion in the big Sioux and Cheyenne buffalo camps, was amazed. "God A'mighty," he shook his head at Sam, "I cain't get over how they're swarmin' out west. Up on the river a man loses track."

"Ye ain't bin down fer six springs, boy. Things have changed. Especially toward Santy Fee. Feller over to Westport was tellin' me thet twenty trains went down the Trail last year, haulin' out goods worth close to one hundred thousand dollars."

Kirby whistled softly. "Whut's the trade mostly in, Sam?"

"Everything!" the oldster replied knowingly, superior in his grasp of the current ranges of high finance. "Jest take this mornin' fer instance. Feller told me he sold calico prints in Santy Fee last spring fer twenty dollars a yard. Calico prints thet was bought right h'yar in Westport fer less'n five!"

"Why, thet's better'n four-fer-one!" declared Kirby, wild-eyed. "Sam, by God, ye're goin' to make our pile goin' down thet trail!" The announcement jumped with the excitement of great decision dashingly taken.

Sam didn't quite dash after it. "Whut the hell ye mean, *I'm* goin' to make *our* pile goin' down thet trail?"

"Why, we're goin' to throw in together and buy the biggest goddam Conestoga in Westport, or Kansas City, whatever they're callin' this place now, load her to the sheets with calico, span mules to her and haul her

27

spang down to Santy Fee. We'll get rich!"

"Yep." The way Sam spit showed he wasn't spending their vast profits just yet. "Ye bin in St. Louie twenty-four hours and ye manage to cash yer plews fer nine dollars, get smacked into the gutter by the purtiest female west of Chicagy, whup her and fall in love while ye're whuppin', tangle rear ends with the richest old buzzard in the fur trade and skeedaddle out'n town on a quick-bought hoss!"

The old man stopped to build up his wind, launched right back into his admiring review. "Now ye've bin in Westport twenty minutes and ye've made fifty thousand dollars. Not to mention gettin' it into yer knucklehead to go shaggin' off down the Santy Fee Trail after a chit of a gal, while old Sam stays behind and labors a ten-mule freight outfit along in yer dust. Happen ye're full of hoss manure, boy!"

Kirby laughed, throwing his arm around the oldster's shoulders. Sam scowled blacker than ever, knowing he was done. When that boy laughed and cuddled up to you, you were through. "Whut about the gal, Sam? Ye know damn well I aim to ketch her. Ye mighten as well leave me have the trail, straight."

"I cain't beat ye, young un. Ye know thet. But honest to Pete I sometimes wish ye'd have chose yerse'f another mother."

"I ain't complainin', Sam. Ye're the best mother this jasper ever had!" The younger man's smile was as unaffected as a barefoot

28

hookey player's, and the old man hauled down his flag with a helpless shrug, trying to let on as mean and grudging as he could.

"Wal, she come down on the *Belle* with me. Her and the big Injun and old Marcel. They got in h'yar and found thet Blunt and St. Clair had jest put a train out fer Santy Fee and thet thar wouldn't be another startin' till June.

"But then they run onto a Spaniard who's mixed into their clan somehow, feller named Don Pedro Armijo. He's a young slicker, handsome buzzard, big fer a Mex. Nephew to old Armijo whut's Gov'ner of Santy Fee, I'm told.

"Wal, it appears this fancy rooster had bin headin' the outfit the gal jest missed, and had come back to pick hisse'f up another caravan captain. Seems his boss skinner, feller named Tuss McLawry, had hisse'f a go-round with the captain they had. Kilt him deader'n a froze buffler. Folks say Armijo claims it was a fair fight, but they's plenty of local doubt.

"Anyhow, Marcel done turned the gal over to Armijo. Last I see'd of them was Armijo and the gal and her Injun ridin' past the springs, h'yar. Headin' out to jine up with the train in Council Grove. And from the way him and the gal was grinnin' and chinnin' a feller would allow they'd knowed one another quite some spell."

"Ye say thar was jest the three of them?"

"Yep. Apparently Armijo didn't get hisse'f

thet new captain. Fact is, fur as I know, the job's still open." He watched Kirby, sidelong, as he said it.

"Sam, old saltbutt!" shouted Kirby, springing to his feet and throwing his chest out like a Dominicker rooster fixing to crow down every cockbird in the county, "ye're lookin' at the toughest, smartest, by-God wagon captain ever to work fer Blunt and St. Clair!"

"Lord A'mighty!" admired Sam. "Now ye not only made yerse'f fifty thousand dollars this mornin', but ye jest signed yerse'f on as wagon captain fer the biggest freightin' outfit in the Santy Fee trade. Dammit all, congratulations boy!"

"Thank ye, Sam'l." The young man bowed politely. "And now with yer kind permission, Mother —"

"Go to hell!" snapped Sam. "I'll buy us an outfit and foller along, damn ye. Fust camp's Round Grove. Twenty-five mile due west. All ye got to do is stay in the wagon ruts, boy. And don't let the Kaws take yer pony away from ye."

"Thanks, old-timer. See ye in Santy Fee. Giddap thar, Brown! *Heee-yahh!*"

A burst of cheerful, melodious whistling, fading in over the departing dustplops of the gelding's rhythmical trail gait, drifted back to the squinting Sam. The old trapper watched until the rider went out of sight and sound around the wooded bend of Indian Creek.

"Funny thing," he mused. "But it seems like hosses and women will sure make a man go to whistlin'. Grantin' he's still young enough to pucker I allow they sure will, anyways."

# 3

The first leg of the trail was the hundred and forty-five miles from Westport to Council Grove. Kirby pounded Old Brown every mile of the hundred and forty-five. He had himself a girl to catch and the trail between him and that green-eyed objective wasn't of much importance.

He made three sleeps: the first at Wakarusa Point, the dreaded "Narrows," where he spent half the night helping snake three swamped-down Conestogas through the two-mile quagmire that made this part of the Trail a nightmare to the overloaded freighters; the second at Hundred-And-Ten-Mile Creek, where he was visited by six Kaw bucks who sat to his fire all night, drinking his coffee and smoking his tobacco, and waiting for him to drop off to sleep so they could knock his head in and run off with his outfit; and the third at Big John Spring, where he struck a camp of Osages, employing the tedious hours of their company in fighting off the attentions of a toothless squaw who assured him with graphic gestures that she was by all odds the finest blanket companion on the entire South Road.

Of this first part of his projected trip to New Mexico, Kirby made resolute and dubious summation: Kansas Territory had the muddiest mud and the lousiest Indians there was. Further summation: the Kaws could have it.

But Council Grove was something else!

The morning he left Big John Spring came up as blue as a snow-water lake, and twice as clear. He had but a short two-mile trot to the Grove and when he topped the last rise and saw it, he had to pull Old Brown up and give himself a long look.

The Grove proper was better than a quarter-section in size and if ever a man saw more fine old hardwood trees he'd have a time remembering where. It for sure didn't take a wagon boss to figure why Council Grove was the main outfitting place for the traffic down the Trail. Why, in that stand of timber a good hand with an axe could cut himself all the spare tongues, axletrees, wheelspokes and oxbows he'd be apt to need for six trips to Santa Fe!

Inquiring at the first camp where he might find the Blunt and St. Clair outfit, he soon arrived at the information and, shortly afterward, at the destination described in it.

The Company wagons were spanned out in a neat square, tongues out, on the west fringe of the Grove. As the young trapper rode in, he made passing note of several things: the work stock was tight-bunched not far off, the wagons were loaded and lashed, a meeting of the train crew was in progress about the main campfire, *not a woman was in sight anywhere.*

As he came up to the group by the fire, the men, after the manner of old prairie hands on the approach of a stranger, held up their talk, waiting, hard-eyed, for him to make his play. Even before he spoke, his ranging eye picked out the hulking figure on the far side of the fire, and he knew he had met this man before he opened his mouth to ask for him.

"Howdy. I'm lookin' fer Tuss McLawry."

"Ye're lookin' *at* him, mister." There was no return of the "howdy," no invitation to "get down."

"I allow I am," nodded Kirby, making careful note of the human grizzly confronting him. "My name's Randolph. I'm aimin' to work fer ye, if ye'll have me."

"Thet'd be Kirby Randolph as worked fer Sublette?" The boss skinner squinted at Kirby with sudden thoughtfulness, his pig eyes glinting.

Kirby hadn't expected that. It hit him hard as the broad side of an axe. How in tarnal hell did McLawry know he had trapped for Sublette? Feigning indifference, he watched the big man closely. "The same." His soft Virginia drawl was easy. "How come ye to know?"

"Happen ye wasn't up the river long enough to know another mountain man when ye're lookin' at him —"

"Mebbe I was, mebbe I wasn't," Kirby sparred, the paws of his mind digging hard at the bone pile of the back years.

When the boss skinner spoke again his words were slow, his rumbling voice giving, as yet, no indication of the way his stick floated. It was obvious he, too, was sparring. "Happen ye wasn't at Big Hoss Hole the winter of 'thirty-three, Randolph?"

Kirby was on guard now, instincts singing-tight; 'thirty-three had been his first year up the river, Big Horse Hole, his first rendezvous. "Reckon ye've smelt out the wrong hound's butt, old hoss," he lied. "I didn't get up the river till 'thirty-five. Sold my first plews at Jackson's Hole, spring of 'thirty-six. I allow ye're mountain man enough but danged if I kin place ye. Ye say ye seen me upriver?" The young trapper's eyes were innocently wide.

"Mebbe so, mebbe no," grunted the other, his huge head wagging doubtfully. "Leastways, I've heered of ye."

"Whut'd ye hear?" Kirby smiled the question.

"Heered ye was pretty much of a salt-tail." The answer was returned without the smile. "Whut do ye want of Tuss McLawry?" The big boss skinner put uncommon emphasis on the name, watching Kirby as he said it.

"Want to work fer ye, Tuss. Heered ye was needin' a captain. Folks in Kansas City told me Mr. Armijo was thar lookin' fer one. And thet he didn't find him."

"Whut's thet got to do with ye? And make it quick. I bin made wagon boss of this outfit and we aim to roll in a hour."

"I'm allowin' I'll captain fer ye," responded Kirby, letting his voice harden as his eye ran around the circle of listening teamsters. "Unless thar's a better man fer the job."

If you could call a bear's grunt a laugh, Tuss McLawry laughed. "Hell's fire. Ye've got a gut like a Guv'ment mule. Ye couldn't captain fer me if all I had was two Dearborns and a buckboard to go four mile!"

"Happen I don't agree with ye," said Kirby evenly.

"Ye fer sure don't!" roared the wagon boss. "And even if I could stand ye, I wouldn't need ye. Mr. Armijo is goin' to captain this run hisse'f. Now haul yer freight, mister. We got —"

"Hold on, McLawry. What is the difficulty?"

None of the men had seen the speaker come up. Turning in his saddle, Kirby saw a tall, elegantly attired young Spaniard lounging gracefully against the nearest wagon wheel. He didn't need the wagon's boss's greeting to let him know this was Don Pedro Armijo.

"Oh, howdy Mr. Armijo. This h'yar jasper was allowin' he was goin' to do ye out'n captainin' the train. And I was allowin' he wasn't. Did ye find Jesse? We got to get rollin' if we're goin' to make Diamond Spring tonight."

"I found him," nodded the young Spaniard,

36

eyeing Kirby. "And we'll roll as soon as you are through electing your trail officers."

"All right, ye ignorant damn —" Tuss began addressing the teamsters, ignoring Kirby, but Armijo stepping toward Kirby, interrupting him.

"My name is Armijo." A dark flash of a smile broke across his face, quick as summer lightning. "Do I understand you are looking for a job?"

"Mine's Randolph. And I *was* lookin' fer a job. But Old Ephraim, thar," nodding toward the glowering Tuss, "leaves me to understand ye're goin' to captain the train yerse'f." Kirby threw a side glance at Tuss to see how he liked the reference to himself. "Old Ephraim" was the mountain men's name for the evil-tempered silvertip grizzly of the Upper Missouri. Considering the low reputation the grizzly held among the trappers, Kirby's use of its name on McLawry was no compliment. From what he made out in the one quick look, Tuss wasn't about to accept it as such, either.

"Why, ye god—" The growl sounded like it started down in the ground under the wagon boss's feet, but Armijo interrupted it before it got above waist-high.

"You are a mountain man, aren't you, Mr. Randolph?"

Kirby looked at the young don with new interest. "Somewhat. Why?"

"Have you ever been down the Trail?"

For a Spaniard, Kirby thought, this young cock spoke tolerable smart English. As far as he knew, Armijo had not come up soon enough to hear him and McLawry making the mountain talk. It followed he must have made his own deductions about Kirby's calling, and it ought to take a fair sharp one to see a mountain man under the new clothes he was wearing. He looked at a man straight, too. It might do to hear what he had to say. He made his answer short. "Nope. Way I see them a trail's a trail. I kin foller one if the light's jest so."

"Well, we don't need a captain, Mr. Randolph, it's true. But we can use a guide."

"A guide!?" Tuss's interruption was half challenge, half question.

"Why, yes, Mr. McLawry, a guide." The young don's gaze was as pleasant as his voice. "Any objections?"

"Whut the hell's the matter with Jesse Colley? Ye jest said ye'd found him. He's a'ready signed on and he's the best wagon guide on the Trail."

Young Armijo nodded, his voice still soft and pleasant. "There is nothing wrong with Mr. Colley as a guide. It is his condition I object to."

"I don't get ye. Whut's wrong with his condition? I allow Jesse got a shade stiff last night, but a leetle whuskey don't —"

"He is considerably stiffer this morning." The Spaniard's voice lost a little softness. "About

38

as stiff as a man can become, I imagine."

"Whar's Jesse? Whut's the matter with him?"

"The matter with him, Mr. McLawry, is *rigor mortis.*"

Kirby, enjoying himself right smartly, watched Tuss to see how he'd get rid of the apparent hook Armijo had just slung into him. When it came, the big wagon boss's question evidenced all the irritation of the rough finish which feels itself getting glossed over by the smooth. "Wal, whut'n hell's rigger mortiss? I ain't no perfesser, ye know."

"A permanent condition of the body muscles," nodded the young Spaniard, "commonly setting in after drunken knife fights."

"Holy cripes! Are ye sayin' Jesse got hisse'f kilt? Ye mean he's daid?"

"To borrow your own quaint term," Don Pedro bowed mockingly in appreciation of his wagon boss's astuteness, "he couldn't be 'daider.'"

The big man flushed, controlling himself in a way that let Kirby know he was just as dangerous as he had figured him. Tuss McLawry might look outsize and he might talk slow, but he was about as far from stupid as he could get.

"Wal, Mr. Armijo, whar does thet leave us?"

"With a new guide!" The Spaniard straightened, chopping his instructions like a man who had given plenty of them. "Sign Mr. Randolph on and count him in on the election. See that you hurry. I want to see wagon dust by eight!"

★ ★ ★

In Armijo's half-hour (it had been seven-thirty when the don handed Tuss his marching orders) Kirby got his head full of the way hard men ran a hard business. He had heard in Kansas City that most trains doubled up with other outfits on reaching Council Grove that they might find "strength in union" for the coming trek through Kiowa and Comancheland. It was not until McLawry started growling out his orders that he understood this was not to be the case with the Blunt and St. Clair outfit.

"This h'yar's a Company train, twenty wagons, all mule-hooked," Tuss began, his slow voice loud in the silence that fell as he spoke. "I aim to roll it thetaway. Most of ye," here his pig eyes swung over the hardfaced ranks of his listeners, "have driv fer me before, and them as hasn't kin speak out now if they allow they don't cotton to jumpin' off without doublin' up." He paused, meaningfully, was greeted by a chorus of head-nodded assents, and went ahead ponderously.

"We ain't holdin' any elections —" He left the statement up in the air, waiting the challenge which came quickly enough. A grizzled mule skinner eased up off his haunches.

"How come, Tuss? I ain't never drove the Trail without electin' officers at Council Grove. Whut's the idee?"

"Idee is, we ain't got time."

40

"Armijo said to go ahead and elect." This from another hardcase driver, coming to his feet to stand alongside the first. It took an extra look for Kirby to see that the second teamster was just a boy, no more than eighteen.

"Armijo ain't bossin' this train, he's captainin' it. I allow ye know the difference, Cooper." He blinked at the second teamster. "And you, too, Springer," he added, scowling at the old man. "Once we get shet of Council Grove, they ain't a man jack of ye takes a leak without he consults Tuss McLawry. Happen ye got thet in yer damn thick skulls, now?"

Kirby noted that most of the men didn't bat an eye. A man needn't have been on the frontier near as long as Kirby to know that these men were all hard lots. It was worth remembering how they were soaking up Tuss's bluff without so much as raising a hand to be excused. Old Thorpe Springer, though, was a different breed of cat. And so was the boy, Clint Cooper. They still stood.

"Wal?" Tuss eyed them. "Whut's eatin' you?"

"I allow we aim to know who ye got in mind fer guard commander, if ye ain't holdin' elections."

"Me," grunted Tuss. "Any objections?"

"Depends," answered the oldster.

"On whut?" Tuss's little eyes narrowed to slits.

"On whut we heered."

"Whut'd ye hear?"

"Thet we're towin' a mule train along. Outfit thet come in from Westport middle of last night. Forty mules, double slung."

"Ye heered right."

"Whut's the idee of them mules?" This from young Cooper.

"None of yer damn business. Them's Company mules and they're goin' along. Anythin' else?"

"Yeah. What're they totin'?"

Kirby could sense more than a simple question in old Thorpe Springer's quick interjection, and waited sharp-eared for Tuss's answer.

"Goods," said the wagon boss, shortly.

"We heered they was bad goods."

"Wal?"

"Wal, if them mules is packin' whut we heered they was, we should ought to have a regular guard commander. When the Kioways and Comanches get the wind of whut's laced onto them longears, ye'll have yer hands full jest bossin', without yer tryin' to run the camp guard, too."

"Whut's on them mules is Company business, I don't know nothin' about it. But I'm handlin' the guard and if ye don't like it, ye'd best haul out right now."

The old man hesitated, looked around at the others, found no support, nodded to the boy, sat down. After an awkward second, Clint followed suit. "All right," Tuss concluded. "Pay is thirty-five dollars a month and found, fer drivers. Packers and stock handlers twenty-five dollars. Found is fifty pounds of flour, fifty bacon, ten coffee, twenty sugar. Any more complaints?"

A wiry little Mexican, who Kirby subsequently learned was the loose-stock wrangler, smiled deprecatingly, his soft voice barely audible. "*Pues, señor,* we are told Don Pedro has along the Señorita St. Clair. A woman like that on the trail, señor —" The little wrangler ended the statement with an eloquent flourish of upraised palms.

Kirby straightened his back along with his hearing, all at once finding himself listening with his heart as well as his ears. Aurélie! Be God, he'd nigh forgotten her.

"Thet's right, Popo. Señorita St. Clair." The wagon boss's voice dumped some of its usual gravel. Apparently even Tuss liked the smiling little Latin. "Whut ye got in mind?"

"*Pues,* who am I to say?" Popo shrugged apologetically. "But if the Indians come to hear of it! *Madre!* What a ransom, señor."

"The hell with the Injuns!" The wagon boss appeared unduly stirred up and Kirby wondered what there was in the little Mexican's remark that could have nettled him so. "Who the hell put ye in mind that the red buzzards would try for the gal?" Nobody met his belligerent eye and Tuss finished off abruptly. "Now, ketch up. And jump it. We're rollin' in fifteen minutes. Yonder comes Armijo and our mule train!"

Turning with the boss's backhanded thumb wave, Kirby didn't see the forty loaded mules, nor the half a hundred loose head following them. He didn't see the picturesque, coffee-hued *arrieros* urging the long-eared pack animals along. Nor did he see the odd, angular bulkiness of the animals' burdens. He didn't even see Don Pedro Armijo jauntily cantering his sleek black stud. Nor the towering form of the Sioux giantess, Ptewaquin, stick-straight on her plodding mule. All he could see was what was sitting the flashy bay and white pinto filly at the black's side.

And what was sitting that filly, red-gold hair flying free in the morning sunshine, green eyes and white teeth flashing brilliantly in the dusky face, hard young figure tight in a near-white set of fringed Cheyenne buckskins, was Aurélie St. Clair!

# 4

Tuss sent Kirby on ahead as soon as the train was rolling. "Ye kin ride on to Diamond Spring. No need fer scoutin' as yet but ye might as well get used to the feel of havin' a train of Conestogies behind ye."

Kirby had been glad of the order. In helping catch up the teams he'd been able to keep away from Aurélie. No use risking discovery before they got started. One time she had passed close to him and given him a good look. But there wasn't anything in it but what any girl her age and looks would give six-foot-three of curly-headed plainsman. The Indian, though, that cow-sized Ptewaquin, had given him a plenty-long stare. She had stopped her mule and watched him for ten seconds.

After an easy four-hour ride over the level Kansas grasslands, Kirby spied a big hollow in the prairie ahead. From Tuss's description he knew this would be Diamond Spring. Riding into the hollow, he found a six-foot gush of water spilling right out of the naked ground. It was clear as mountain water and, strange enough, nearly as cold.

When he and Old Brown had watered, Kirby scouted around. Two miles east of the spring he found a wide gully whose stark contents put his Indian's nerves on edge for the first time. For two hundred yards the prairie was littered with the charred remains of wagon irons, trace chains, L-braces, rims, nuts and tongue-irons. There was no end to the trash. Must have been a hundred wagons burned there sometime or other. There were lots of bones in this gully, too, though by the size and shape of them they weren't all *stock bones*. Cripes. It made a man a shade uneasy running into sign like this right off the bat. Even if it was *old* sign.

The scout drifted back to the spring and on up the trail to ride in with the wagons. Camp was made without any fuss, the mess fires going bright and cheery with early dusk.

Once the fires were going and the smell of sizzling sidemeat and fried corn tortillas crawling around on the night air, Kirby allowed twelve hours was long enough for any man to go without food. As he unsaddled Old Brown and started rummaging around in the parfleches for some grub, young Clint Cooper lounged up.

"Howdy," the tall youth nodded. "Uncle Thorpe says if ye want ye're welcome to set to our meat."

"Wal, thanks," smiled Kirby. "I reckon I oughtn't to crowd in on ye."

"It won't be crowdin' us none." His visitor

grinned shyly. "Uncle Thorpe and me is eatin' alone, apparently."

"Whut ye mean, 'apparently'?" Kirby was curious.

"Wal, seems the rest of the boys is a leetle consarned about us standin' up to Tuss. When they paired off fer the messes, we was froze out."

"The hell ye say!" Kirby put out his hand. "I'd be right proud to jine ye. Name's Kirby Randolph."

"Mine's Clint Cooper." The other hesitantly shook hands. "Come on along, Mr. Randolph."

Half an hour later, with his lean belly full of fatback and corn cakes, Kirby leaned back against his saddle. "I allow ye kin really fry thet slab pork and corn sheets, Uncle Thorpe," he nodded, sucking hard to light his short stone pipe. "I ain't et so much since the last feed of humpmeat I tooken on."

"Man cain't keep his dobber up without he eats," said the older man, then, pausing while he eyed Kirby thoughtfully, he added, "Whut do ye make of Tuss McLawry, Mr. Randolph?"

"Front name's Kirby," the young mountain man answered quietly. "And I reckon Tuss ain't the only bear in this train with hair on his belly. Though I allow it'll do to give him all the room he wants, happen he goes to askin' fer it."

"Ye allow right," nodded the oldster. "Tuss is big and he's mean and fast. And I'll tell ye somethin' else. He's a plumb bad un. I think he kilt thet original wagon captain deliberate, so's he could take the train over and bring in them pack mules without any fuss. Him and Armijo, thet is."

"Whut ye mean?" Kirby's question mirrored the uptake in his interest.

"Wal, I bin with Blunt and St. Clair so long they've got into the habit of lettin' me check the bill of loadin' fer the train at Council Grove, instead of the captain doin' it."

"Wal?"

"Wal, when I asked Armijo fer the bill this morin' he told me to mind my damn mules."

"Whut ye make of thet?"

"We figger, Clint and me, thet them forty pack mules wasn't writ in the bill of loadin' at all."

"So?"

"So, we allow Tuss and Armijo is runnin' them mules on their own hooks. Thet's why they snuck them into the Grove last night. If they was in the original bill they'd of started with us from Westport."

"Whut ye figger they're runnin'?"

"Don't figger at all. I know."

"Guns, is thet it?"

"Sure. And Dupont powder and galena pills. You figger it. Them mules will pack close to three hundred pounds apiece. A gun will weigh near to ten. Them big jacks could be packin' ten rifles and a couple hundred pounds of powder and shot, each one. Ye foller me?"

Kirby frowned. "Whar ye aim they're runnin' it to? Injuns?"

"Nope, they ain't thet crazy. Mexico."

"Mexico? The hell ye say. Thar still a war on down thar?"

"Thar's allus a war on down thar. If thar ain't one goin' this minute, thar will be by the time we hit Santy Fee."

"Wal, I cain't see no great harm in runnin' a few guns to the Mexes, but I allow thar'd sure be hell to pay and with the devil holdin' the chips if the Injuns get wind of us packin's Holy Irons, though, eh?"

"Thet's exactly whut me and Clint figger."

"Ye figger they *will* wind them?"

"You tell me how they kin miss them. Ye seen them packs. A blind squaw could spot them five miles off."

"I seen them," smiled Kirby. "But I was lookin' at somethin' else."

"Happen I know whut ye mean." Young Clint's slow grin joined Kirby's. "I never see'd sech a purty female."

"Thet's the trouble with ye young salt-tails," grumped the older man. "With a flossy gal along, ye couldn't see a redskin fer sour owl droppin's."

Kirby grinned his acceptance of Uncle Thorpe's sentiments, before continuing soberly. "Wal, I kin see Tuss fittin' a deal like this but whar does Armijo figger in? Ye got any hunch the Mex's got somethin' more than guns in mind?"

"Wal, I dunno. Might be. Dogged if I kin tell ye whut, though."

"I keep thinkin' about whut Popo said." Clint broke his silence. "About the gal bein' top Injun bait, I mean. Them god-dam Kioways and Comanches is pure hell fer grabbin' white folks and holdin' them fer ransom. Big Foot and Satank has made theirse'fs rich doin' it."

"I've heered of Big Foot, but who's Satank?" asked Kirby, getting his answer from Uncle Thorpe.

"Young hot-tail buck. Hereditary chief of the Arkansaw Valley Kioways. And a white-hatin' son of a gun."

"Ye sure ain't figgerin' Armijo would let them get the gal!" Kirby's voice showed more than ordinary racial interest in the fate of a white Indian captive.

"I dunno. The whole thing stinks. Onliest thing I kin tell ye is thet we're headin' fer Santy Fee and thet some of us ain't goin' to get thar."

"I'm turnin' in," said Kirby suddenly. "I got me some tall thinkin' to do. I got to remember whar I seen Tuss before. Happen ye noticed him workin' me over about them beaver rendezvous. And happen ye remember me tellin' him I wasn't at Big Hoss Hole in 'thirty-three?"

"I heered ye."

"Wal, I was thar."

"And ye don't recollect nothin' about Tuss bein' thar?"

"Nope. Cain't remember him to save me.

Never even heard tell the name of Tuss McLawry till I hit Westport."

"Names is easy to change." Clint's offering came out of the darkness.

"So's a face and figger," added Uncle Thorpe, thoughtfully. "Thet's bin six year ago. Tuss started workin' fer Blunt and St. Clair jest thet long ago. He's changed considerably since I fust see'd him. Used to be a lot leaner and wore his hair long. Had a beard, too. Long, bushy one. Seems a man would remember a beard like thet, though. Red as a Three Point blanket."

The old man's last words jumped Kirby's head off the saddle. "Goddam!" The mountain man's curse, popping like a pistol shot in the stillness, was followed by a softly exhaled two words. "Red MacKenzie!"

"Whut did ye say?" Old Thorpe's query was sharp.

"He said 'Red MacKenzie,'" Clint offered abruptly, his announcement suspended in obvious expectation of Kirby's confirmation.

"I said nothin';" their new friend's voice was dry and brittle as rim ice. "Yer ears must need cleanin'."

"Mine are dirtier than a Comanche's blanket." Old Thorpe's agreement wasn't so quick that it hid the slight uneasiness in it.

"Mine, too," young Clint Cooper's concurrence came only after three coals had popped.

51

# 5

It seemed to Kirby his head had no more than hit the saddle than Tuss's bull-bellow was roaring through the darkness.

"Turn out! Turn out!"

The young mountain man rolled over and up to his feet, the long Hawkens swinging in a ready arc, muzzle searching the dark beyond the ghost-daubs of the Conestogas. "Save yer lead, boy," Uncle Thorpe's advice came through the gloom. "We ain't attacked. 'Turn out's' jest the first call any mornin' betwee h'yar and Santy Fee. Before ye kin get yer leggins laced Tuss will be singin' out 'Ketch up!' "

The old man's words were echoed by a lusty shout from the wagon boss. "Ketch up! Ketch up!" This was the command for the teamsters to get their mules rounded up, and all over camp now, Kirby could see the skinners rolling out of their blankets, the *arrieros* tumbling like sowbugs out from under their ponchos and serapes.

Five minutes after Tuss's first shout and while Kirby was still getting the saddle on Old

Brown, half the teams had been caught up. Another ten minutes and shouts of "All set! All set!" were booming out of the dawnlight as first one then another of the teamsters got his mules spanned in and ready to travel. When the last man sang out, Tuss's bellow gave the final order. "Stretch out! Stretch out!"

The cry came rolling across camp on a combing breaker of cracking skinning whips, whitecapped by some of the fanciest cussing Kirby had ever heard.

The puréed Spanish, Missouri and Texas invective continued to roll unceasingly as Kirby watched the lumbering freighters creaking into line. In fifteen minutes the entire outfit was strung out and rolling, with not yet enough light for a man to see where his horse was putting his front feet. As the loose herd came piling along the trail on the heels of the last pack mule, some unidentified skinner ruptured the Kansas dawn with a raucous "Hooray fer Santy Fee!" and Kirby's caravan was officially New Mexico bound.

Riding up the line of rumbling vehicles, the new scout sought out the wagon boss. "Whar the hell ye bin?" Tuss greeted him. "Ye're supposed to be leadin' this train, not pushin' it."

"Thet's whut I'm aimin' to ask ye," answered Kirby. "Jest whut aim I supposed to be doin? This trail's as broad as a buffler's butt and jest as easy to see. A blind man could foller it with his eyes shet."

"All right, now listen." The boss's voice went flat. "Scoutin' this trail don't mean a thing till we hit along about Turkey Crick. Thet's four days on. In between, we camp at Lost Spring, Cottonwood Crick, Pignut Draw. Trail fer them days is a son of a bitch fer the wagons but a gut-cinch fer the scout. Once we hit Turkey Crick, though, we pick up Pawnees. Fact is ye kin start earnin' yer pay as from Cottonwood Crick. I've knowed them to strike thet close in."

"These h'yar Pawnees bad Injuns?" Kirby spoke to the wagon boss as mountain man to mountain man.

"Bad as they come. Not like any ye knowed up on the Yellerstone. A Sioux or a Cheyenne will let ye know whar he stands. They're 'warriors,' happen ye know whut I mean."

"I allow I do," said Kirby.

"Wal, these Pawnees is squaws. Come crawlin' around on their bellies whinin' how much they love the white man and all thet brand of bull. Then turn yer back on them and yer whole outfit's gone. They ain't rightly killers like the Cut Arms or Pied Noirs, mind ye. But they'll kill ye quick enough if they figger they need to to get whut they're after. And whut they're allus after is yer hosses and mules."

"Their range begin along about this h'yar Cottonwood Crick, is thet it?"

"Thet's it. Cottonwood's a small stream but

54

the muddiest leetle buzzard thar is. No bottom to the son of a gun and goin' in and comin' out is tighter than a spotted tick. We allus get bogged in thar and them goddam Pawnees knows it. Most trains figger they're safe up to Turkey Crick. Ye'll see the rustin' wagon iron of three, four of them thet thought thetaway as ye ride up today."

"Happen thar might be trouble at Cottonwood Crossin', then?"

"I allus figger so."

"Whut ye want me to do?"

"Ride ahead. Scout out the track between Cottonwood and Turkey. Range out on either side. If ye spot any sign, drift on back pronto. Ye got thet?"

"I got it," Kirby acknowledged, again glad to be going on, keeping clear of Aurélie and Ptewaquin. "Reckon I'll drift."

"Hold up," growled his companion. "Let me tell ye somethin'."

"Sech as?" Kirby's stare was cool, his tender Southern temper not liking the foreshadow of threat in the boss's tones.

"Sech as this." Tuss stared him back. "And ye get it in yer damn head and ye keep it thar. We got forty mules taggin' along behind this train thet any chief in his right mind would give his left arm to lift. Happen ye let the Pawnees get in on us and run them mules off, I'll fix yer stick." The wagon boss paused, scowling. "Happen we lose them mules, Randolph, I'll kill ye." The following hesitation was almost imperceptible, Tuss setting his words down on top of it as carefully as a cat's feet. "Sure as my name's Tuss McLawry, I'll do it."

Turning Old Brown away, downtrail, Kirby let the redheaded giant have it. "Happen ye might, mister," his words were as slow and careful as Tuss's, his face as expressionless as a Sioux's, "jest as sure as yer name's Tuss McLawry."

Behind him, as Old Brown shuffled off, Kirby heard the big man's silent, indrawn curse, knew that from then on there would be more than Pawnees after the scalp of Blunt and St. Clair's new wagon scout.

That morning Kirby rode through a country as desolate as the far side of the moon. Not a tree big enough for a short dog to bother hoisting on lay between him and the endless sweep of the western horizon. About 10.00 A.M., having seen no Indian sign, he watered his horse at a narrow mud ribbon which he supposed went by the name of a creek in Kansas. The place was lonelier than a curlew talking the sun down back of the Big Horns, making even Old Brown nervous.

Lost Spring, hit about two hours later, was no better and Kirby, after carefully searching its marshy rim for fresh Indian sign, rode on. At Cottonwood Creek, which crawled in out of the prairie to snake across the trail about 2.00 P.M., things looked better. The creek was not in flood and was fairly clear and clean. A few ash, burr oaks and sycamores struggled along its bank. Again no Indian sign fresher than ten days showed. Beginning to be disturbed by the continued quiet, Kirby rode on.

From Cottonwood Fork, the country began to change rapidly, to look, Kirby thought, more like God had had a hand in laying it out. The tall grass began to give out, the short curly nap of the buffalo browze with which he was familiar to replace it. By late afternoon he was beginning to spot an occasional pile of long-bleached buffalo bones and had seen six or eight antelope. Still no Indian sign.

The prairie was all buffalo grass now, no cover on it bigger than a pipestem. A man and a horse stuck out on it worse than a tumblebug crossing a cowpie.

Kirby kept behind what slight ridges he could find that parelleled the trail, continually sweeping the plains westward for signs of movement. The instincts whittled war-ax sharp by seven years of keeping his hair on straight among the Hunkpapa and Oglala Sioux were beginning to tighten his spine. He put Old Brown off the trail about a quarter of a mile, threw him into a high lope, held him there. Forty-five minutes later he raised the meandering thread of the north fork of the Turkey. As far as his eye could follow the stream, no stick of timber showed on its banks.

With the half-hour of sun remaining, Kirby searched both sides of the stream and found no new sign. Now he had his problem. Another man would have thrown down and slept. There was water and plenty of dry chips for a fire. In half a hundred miles of riding he had not been able to spot one unshod pony track. But Kirby's hair wasn't as thick and curly as it was for his having made a practice of doing what another man might.

What he did right then was to ride Old Brown away from the soft stream edge and onto hard, dry ground. Then he got down off of him, mighty careful to make small moccasin print, and went to climbing the thirty-foot ridgeback that flanked the trail crossing, south and west. Topping the ridge he belly-flopped from force of habit. When he poked his head over, peering squint-eyed into the setting sun, he had reason to be content that he had.

Two miles out, straight across the prairie, heading in toward Turkey Crossing, black as dominoes against the rust-red sun, came a single file of mounted warriors. The line of them stretched three hundred yards or better, making upwards of a hundred of them, Kirby figured. And they were coming at an easy shuffle-walk, not a squaw nor a travois in sight.

This was a war party.

Kirby was down off that ridge in two seconds, even in that time having done his thinking. He had maybe fifteen minutes before those bucks broke over the ridge top. If they hit the Fork with any light left, they'd see Old Brown's tracks. And if they saw hot horse sign without seeing the horse to go with it, Kirby's fat would be pretty well fried.

In two jumps he was alongside Old Brown, snaking the saddle and bridle off him, his practised hand telling him he'd had his first good break. The twenty minutes of slow working around the Fork, looking for sign, had pretty near cooled the old horse out. He was warm under the saddle but not wet. If there was a special god for mountain men in a tolerable tight, Kirby found himself hoping he was looking down when he swatted the old gelding across the rump with the Hawkens' barrel.

Old Brown grunted, jumped, ambled along the side of the ridge a way, stopped, looked back resentfully, dropped his head and began grazing toward the Fork. Hoisting the saddle and gear on his shoulder, Kirby ran for the head of the only cover available — a shallow dry-bed gully, running north and east. Into this he dived like a prairie dog, popping up again to go tight-legged and doubled up down its narrow track.

At the first patch of goldenrod he dumped saddle and gear into the middle of the thick yellow growth. Standing quickly back, he noted the flowers had been disturbed very little, nodded with satisfaction. That cache might hold up — if the light didn't.

59

He covered the twenty-five miles back to Cottonwood that night, using the next morning's first light to convince himself the Pawnees weren't crowding him. Satisfied, he took two hours sleep in a plum thicket, setting out, rested, to dog-trot the twelve miles back to Lost Spring. About halfway, he spotted the dust of the caravan, twenty minutes later loping up to Tuss McLawry riding its head.

Looking at the approaching dust-caked figure, the wagon boss flung up his hand, bellowing backward. "Hold up! Hold up!" The wagons rumbled to a halt as Kirby came up to him.

"Let's have it, Randolph," was the big man's brief greeting, and without waste of words Kirby "let him." As the scout talked, his eye-tail picked up Armijo riding up from the train, Ptewaquin and the girl tagging him.

"Didn't see any sign this side of Turkey Crick. Sundown at Turkey give me above a hundred Pawnees ridin' in from the southwest. I turned my hoss loose to match up with the tracks he'd been makin' around the crick, dumped my saddle in a weed patch and rabbit-footed it down a dry gully. Made Cottonwood during the night, grabbed two hours sleep, saw no sign early this mornin'. I come on down the trail to h'yar."

"What is the trouble, Mr. McLawry?" Don Pedro's interrupting voice was pleasant as usual.

"Nothin' at all, Mr. Armijo," the boss answered, scowling at Kirby meaningfully. "Randolph, h'yar, jest rid his hoss into a doghole. Snapped a foreleg and he had to drill him."

"Where is his outfit?" By the suspicion in his query, Kirby reckoned the young Spaniard was bred and born enough to horse country to know a rider would lug his saddle to the last gasp.

"Cached it up toward Turkey Crick. Too fur a piece to lug it." Tuss was quick with the answers, again.

"Well, let's get on, McLawry." The too-easy tones let the listening Kirby know Armijo had only bought Tuss's story, not paid for it. "Mr. Randolph, you may have one of my personal horses. Any one of them. Popo will show them to you. Let's go, McLawry."

Kirby, all at once conscious of the girl's eyes on him, pulled his black hat lower, mumbled a hasty "thanks" to Armijo and trotted away down the line of waiting wagons. Behind him, Tuss's booming "Stretch out!" echoed rollingly.

Looking over Don Pedro's personal cavyyard, Kirby had no trouble selecting his mount. Getting it proved another matter.

"How's fer thet dishface roan?" he drawled to Popo, indicating a short-backed, Arabian-headed mare of about fifteen hands. "Thet blue one, I mean. With the snip and the star and the

61

hindsocks. She looks big enough to reach out and go."

"*Pues, señor,* I could not say," puzzled Popo frowningly, at the same time noting to himself that this tall Americano could see a *caballo* when he was looking at one. "That is almost Don Pedro's favorite. Next to the *entero negro* which he himself rides, she is his favorite. I don't know —"

"Wal, let's leave him have the black stud," grinned Kirby. "I'll take thet mare."

"*Válgame Dios, señor!* The mare runs with the black devil. They are *compañeros inseparables.* I myself have trained this *yegua* from a baby. There is none like her. *Válgame!* I say it."

"*Ya lo creo,*" shrugged Kirby, smiling.

Popo brightened a little at the use of the phrase. "*Habla Usted Español, señor?*" The diminutive Mexican horse wrangler awaited Kirby's answer hopefully.

"*Un poco. A sus órdenes.*" A slight deferential nod of the curly head, plus a touch of the fingers to the black hat, went with the admission. Popo returned the gesture, inclining his own head gratefully.

"*Gracias, señor.* Take the mare. She is yours. *De nada. No hay de que.*"

"*A los pies de Usted,*" said Kirby, bowing gravely.

"*Gracias, mil gracias.*" Popo executed a bow of equal gravity, flattered beyond all pleasure that one of the scout's coarse breed understood the little graciousnesses so dear to the Latin heart.

Watching the little Mexican rope the mare out of the cavyyard, Kirby felt he now had three friends in the caravan. Nothing like a little stiff-backed courtesy to warm the insides of a Mex. Funny people. Kind of like Indians in a way. Savvy their lingo and throw it back at them, and a man was all of a color with them — red or brown. Happen you couldn't read their sign and rattle it back to them, made no difference if you were a two-dollar king riding a four-bit mule, you were still a white son of a so-and-so.

They got to Cottonwood Creek along about 3.00 P.M., giving them good time to get the wagons across before dusk. Beginning with this stretch of the trail, Kirby learned it became hard-and-fast orders to cross any stream before making camp. Otherwise a flash rain or a high crest of water rolling down from the plateau to the southwest could flood-up the creeks over-night, making a hundred-foot torrent out of a ten-foot trickle and holding the train up for possible days of costly delay.

Cottonwood Crossing was everything Tuss had told him it was. Kirby never spent two harder hours. Still, dark found the last wagon and head of stock across, the cookfires going, the wet, muddy men squatted to their fried pork and cornmeal. The soul-lifting smell of pot-boiled coffee was abroad in the night air and here and there a man or two was beginning to allow he might live.

By their fire, Clint, Uncle Thorpe and Kirby hunkered down, talking low and seriously. Tuss had warned the scout to keep his mouth shut about the Pawnees, not bothering to add why. It was this situation the three companions were going over. Uncle Thorpe had the lead, Kirby playing to it.

"I allow ye know Injuns when ye see them."

"Ye allow right."

"Ye wouldn't take twenty-five, thutty, fer a hunderd."

"Would you?"

"Hmmm. No squaws? No kids?" the old man asked, accepting the back question.

"No squaws, no kids —" Kirby thought a minute, his pipe going steadily, before he added, abruptly, "Boys, I reckon Tuss ain't in cahoots with this bunch of Panani. He allowed he'd kill me if I let any Pawnees get at them pack mules."

"Nope, he ain't —" Uncle Thorpe was thinking, too. "I allow Tuss jest didn't want to get the train jumpy. No doubt he figgers no hunderd Injuns is goin' to hop on forty old trail hands."

"It appears to me," Kirby muttered, "thet he's got the wagons boxed a mite tight fer a man thet don't expect no Injun trouble."

"Naw, them Pawnees won't try nothin'." Clint, entering the conversation for the first time, made his statement slow with sureness.

"Thet depends on yer idee of nothin'." Uncle Thorpe frowned. "Ye're thinkin' a leetle short, Clint."

"Whut ye mean?" Kirby broke in, sensing the old man's earnestness.

"Happen ye was a Pawnee and was layin' out thar in the dark figgerin' how to run off our stock without a shootin' scrape, how'd ye figger to do it?"

Kirby sucked his pipe, thinking of the lay of the camp and the country around it. "I'd figger thet the new grass was almighty short, and thet thet last winter's hay still standin' all around us h'yar was almighty tall and thick together."

"And dry," added Clint, quietly.

"And how would ye figger the breeze?" Old Thorpe eyed them carefully. These cubs were mighty knowing but they hadn't learned it all, yet.

"About right," opined Kirby. "She's a south wind, blowin' in on us, and tolerably fresh."

"And gettin' fresher," appended Clint, sniffing the uprising nightwind apprehensively.

"Ye bin past Cotton Crick yestiddy, Kirby." Uncle Thorpe knocked the dottle out of his pipe, sucked noisily to clear the stem. "Whut happens to the grass up ahead?"

"She goes plumb short five mile out. Two-inch buffler grass from thar on."

"All right. If ye was countin' on havin' yerse'f

a muleroast, whar'd ye strike yer flint?"

"About a mile down south, thar. Ye figger they'll try it, Uncle Thorpe?"

"Mebbe a leetle closer than a mile," said the old man, ignoring Kirby's closing question. "So's not to give us time to get anything back acrost the crick."

"Ye figger they will?" Kirby repeated the question, pinning the oldster down.

"Happen about two A.M. ye see them cloud bellies down south, thar, glowin' sore-red as a blistered heel," the old driver eased back in his blankets, yawning, "and ye wake up with yer nostrils snotted up with grass smoke, ye'll have yer answer."

After an hour, Kirby gave up trying to sleep. Getting out of his blankets, he eased out to the mule herd.

"*Quién es?*" the sibilant Spanish hissed at him out of the darkness.

"It's all right, hombre," Kirby called back softly. "It's me, Randolph."

"*Dispensame Usted, señor.*" Kirby recognized Popo's voice now. "One gets nervous. You will understand, *señor*. With the wind just so and the grass so tall —"

"Nervous is the word," grinned Kirby. "Tell me, *Anciano*, have ye heered anything?"

"No, señor, I have heard nothing. But I will tell you, señor. It is too quiet."

"Did Tuss leave a hole in the corral?"

"*Sí*. Two wagons are pulled out."

"*A dónde?*"

"On the other side, señor, I have thought to have moved the mules closer to it."

"Ye have thought right," Kirby told him shortly. "How kin we get them around thar without botherin' the camp?"

"*De nada*. I do but lead María and they will all follow."

"Thet the bell mare?"

"*Sí, señor.*"

"Wal, ease them around thar. *Sabe?*"

"*Sí.*"

"And, Popo, listen. First sign of a flicker off south, ye drive them damn jacks through thet hole and into the wagon corral. I don't give a hoot if ye tromple every driver into his cussed blankets. *Comprende?* Get them mules inside thet wagon corral!"

"*Sí. Hacerete.*"

"Good. Wake up yer men and have them on the alert. Ready to run them mules. I smell Injuns!"

"*Sí, señor, yo también.* I, too, can smell the Indians. *Hasta la vista.*"

"*Id con Dios,*" responded Kirby, hoping he had said the right thing again.

"*Mil gracias, Patrón,*" the soft answer floated back, letting him know that he had. Kirby chucked his head. Good. The little wrangler had accepted him.

For hours then, not a sound came in off the

prairie, save those that should. Kirby lay atop a low hummock a hundred yards out from camp, his eyes and ears straining the blackness. Midnight went. And 2.00 A.M. A quarter-hour crawled by. A half. Three quarters.

Then, with the slice-thin moon dipping back down under the earth to the west, it came. A mile out east a coyote yipped dolorously. Its mate caught up the lament well down to the south. Over westward, a rival joined the chorus. Too perfect, those cries. Too close. Too well timed. Kirby went for the wagons as tight as he could leg it.

"*Buscara! Buscara!* Put them in, Popo! Put them in!"

The mules were already moving behind him, frantically hazed by Popo's yelling herders, as he got into the wagon corral. "Roll out! Roll out! The buzzards have fired the grass! On yer feet!"

So far Kirby hadn't looked behind him to see if they had or not. He had learned to lean on his ability to "smell Indians" so strongly it never occurred to him he might miss a snap guess. In this case he hadn't. Even as the startled skinners came stumbling and cursing to their feet, the night clouds, south, east and west, had their bellies bouncing to the ugly glow of old Thorpe Springer's "sore-heel red."

The mules came into the center of the wagon corral so close on Kirby's warning shouts that some of the teamsters were run over in their blankets. In the confusion no one knew or cared if his fellow were hurt so long as he himself was up and running. Tuss was already ranging the square of prairie inside the boxed wagons, bellowing orders.

"Backfire, dammit! We got to backfire. Get out thar past the wagons and start her goin'. And fer Gawd's sake don't let her eat back on ye!" The men were running for the grass beyond the wagons, grabbing grain sacks and saddle blankets as they went. A few seized smoldering firewood brands from the banked campfires.

For twenty minutes every skinner in the train was on the fireline, those who bore them, plunging their flaming brands into the dry grass, their following companions beating with the sacks and blankets at any of the resulting fires that back-lashed toward the wagons. By necessity the work was carried forward in among the growing flames of the backfire. Hair, eyebrows, beards and mustaches were charred off to the raw skin. On exposed hands and faces the skin itself blistered and shriveled in a matter of seconds. But in ten minutes a three-quarter circle of fire was growing slowly outward from the wagons.

In less than fifteen, the rolling sheet of fire lit by the Pawnees flared across the mile of open prairie, its belching front roaring in flames twenty and even thirty feet high. Quick as Tuss's men had been, their backfire hit the windswept Indian conflagration a scant seventy feet from the wagon corral. As the hideous glare of the coming holocaust bore down on the backfire, Tuss shouted furiously.

"Scatter back! Get back and get down before she hits. On yer bellies and hold yer wind. Fer Gawd's sake don't breathe when she shoots in!"

One fire fighter off to Kirby's right hesitated, still flailing at a small backfire. "Get back, ye infernal idjut!" Kirby's roar matched Tuss's. "Get on back!" The fighter turned, confused, the rolling forewall of the coming flames' gut-black smoke engulfing him even as Kirby yelled his warning. Throwing his blanket over his head, the scout dove into the black cloud.

Almost immediately he tripped and fell over the body. Getting the still figure up on his shoulder, he stumbled and fell clear of the blind inferno with the last strength in him. Seconds after he had scooped up the unconscious form, the living flame of the Indian fire shot in over the spot where it had lain.

Clint had seen Kirby go diving into the smoke and now, as the mountain man fell sprawling out of it, was waiting for him. "I got Kirby!" he hollered at Uncle Thorpe, just legging it up from the wagons. "Get the other feller!" The old man shouldered the smaller figure, ran a dozen lurching steps toward the wagons, following Clint. "Get down! Hit the sod!" shouted the boy, dumping Kirby face-forward into the hot ash. "H'yar she comes!"

Old Thorpe went down in a heap, taking his burden with him, landing almost atop Clint and Kirby. The latter got his head up out of the ash in time to turn and see the two fires meet and boom skyward with a crashing growl. He had just time to throw part of the blanket still clutched in his hand over the nearest form to him, that of old Thorpe's burden, and to pull the other half over his own head. Then the sheet of naked flame thrown out by the collision of the firelines shot in over them.

It was over that quick, once the firelines met: a roar, a rush, a booming explosion. Then all quiet. Quiet save for the last cherry-glows of scattered heaps of buffalo chips ignited by the racing flame. Quiet save for where the soft groans of the burned teamsters vied with the last popping licks of stubborn flamelets dying in some pocket of grassroots overshot by the firesheet. Save for these fitful beacons, the prairie lay dark as the pit — dark as the pit and quiet as the poles.

The hour following the burning out of the Pawnee fire was spent coating the faces and limbs of the more seriously wounded with thick daubings of antelope tallow. Though this crude treatment eased the intensity of their agonies, the remainder of the night was filled with the crying and groaning of the seared skinners. It was enough to make a man's hide crawl. In the smoke and the darkness Kirby had missed

Clint and Uncle Thorpe, but allowed they had made out all right. They had been right with him, and he had done fine.

Toward morning he left off working on the bad ones, turning his skin of tallow over to the insistent Popo. Back at his bedroll he found Uncle Thorpe had build up a little chip fire and made coffee.

"How'd ye make out, old hoss?"

"Few blisters. Nothin' a leetle tally won't quieten down." His voice sounded queer to Kirby.

"Whut happened to the leetle cuss I drug out'n the smoke?"

"All right. Smoked up a mite. Purty gutty, though, I'd say," nodded old Thorpe, his manner still absent. "Right up thar in front, sack-swingin' with the best of them."

"Whut the hell," Kirby grunted coldly. "Appears to me any man would have bin doin' the same."

"Any man, mebbe," his companion's voice again hit Kirby as being taken up with other things, "but damn few women."

Kirby sat stunned, his mind refusing to grab the bait, right off. "Ye don't aim to tell me" — he began, slowly —

"Yep," muttered the other, "I do. It was the gal ye drug in."

Kirby's heart jumped with Uncle Thorpe's answer, his tongue not wanting to wag about anything but Aurélie. There was something in the continued dull flatness of the old man's tones, however, which told him to hold up. "Whut's eatin' ye, Uncle Thorpe?" Then, even as he asked, Kirby knew. Cuss it. Sometimes a man got blinder than a mine mule. "Whar's Clint?" he muttered softly, his cracked lips stiff not with blistering alone.

"Yonder thar, under the blanket. He got it bad. I got him tally-ed over, but it ain't his outside thet's hurtin' him."

"How ye feel, Clint?" Kirby stepped across the fire, leaning over the form under the greasy blanket.

"Not bad. I couldn't wrassle a bear." Kirby flinched at the sound of the boy's voice. He had heard them before that way — rough, bubbly, sounding high in the throat, and shallow.

"I reckon ye know I owe ye one fer draggin' me in, Clint."

"I reckon."

"I won't ferget it, Clint boy."

There was no answer from the youth, and the old man called softly from the fire, "Leave him be, Kirby. Happen he won't make it through the night." The scout showed no surprise, stepped back to the fire.

"Thet bad?" The query was low, that it might miss Clint's hearing.

"He's burnt awful. Inside."

"Inside? How'd he get it so bad? He was layin' right with us."

"Fire's funny thet way. I allow a flame hit

him when it shot over us. He didn't have no blanket over him like us and the gal did. I figger it got into his lungs. He likely breathed jest as the fire hit. It don't take more'n thet. He's bin gettin' up lots of blood."

"Reckon thar ain't nothin' we kin do fer him —" Kirby knew there wasn't.

"Nope," the old man's headshake was slow, "I reckon not."

"He'll be all right, old-timer." The lie didn't sound good, even to the liar. Kirby's lips stiffened as he said it.

"No." Old Thorpe's words dragged slow-footed across the shift of the firelight. "He ain't goin' to make it. I seen too many of them go. Clint's fixin' to die."

The coals in the fire bed did the only talking then for several seconds. Thorpe Springer sat hunched and silent, only his shoulders moving a little now and then. Kirby reached his long arm across the fire, the big hand coming to rest on the old man's knee soft and slow as a snowflake.

"I allow it ain't no shame to cry, Uncle Thorpe. Happen a man has had a boy like Clint to love, it ain't."

# 6

Minutes after the last flame of the Pawnee fire had flashed out, the wind had dropped to a sullen whisper. It was almost as though Tiwara, their Great Spirit, had loaned it to the Panani for the express purpose of burning out the wagon camp — then, in solemn duty to his red children, redeemed the loan in time to leave the smoke of its spending spread over the shallow valley of the Cottonwood.

Kirby awoke to a funereal dawn. Smoke, gray and greasy as an old blanket, lay in slow-drifting banks among the shrouded tops of the Conestogas. A fine fall of silver-white ash piled in shifting drifts against the wheels of the wagons, mounded the blanketed forms lying ground-scattered where injury or exhaustion had dropped them and hung in the air like thick, windless snow. Through palled smoke and suspended ash, the morning sun filtered sick and red as an abscess.

Kirby found Tuss with six or eight teamsters hunkered over a chip fire, chewing cold dried beef and drinking hot coffee. As he drifted up, the wagon boss looked at him and waved him to a seat. To the scout's surprise the big man poured and handed him a tin of coffee. "Thanks, Tuss," he acknowledged. "I allow it won't injure me none."

No one spoke in answer. All sat staring into the smoke, or their coffee, or the smolder of the chips. They were like men hit by more than they could handle, Kirby thought.

"We got to move," said Tuss, talking to his coffee cup.

"I reckon." Kirby answered him only when it was clear the others weren't going to. "How many able to drive?"

"Most. All but five. We kin fill in with Mexes. They didn't suffer none."

"How's the gal?"

"Dunno. Ain't asked."

Kirby let it go. "Ye figger the Pawnees have gone on?"

"Like as not. Uptrail. Lookin' fer a way to make up fer missin' us. Some leetle outfit'll ketch hell."

"Like as not." The scout paused, the hoarse bray of a suffering mule breaking into his words. "Ye aimin' to roll now?"

"Yeah. Ye're all right, ain't ye? Ye kin ride?"

"Sure. I was lucky."

"Wal, get ridin' then. Mebbe them buzzards *is* hangin' around. Wagons will be along in twenty minutes."

"All right, Tuss. Want me to help with the ketchin' up?"

"I said get ridin'."

Kirby rode. All that day and the next. The wagons following close up, in a double row of ten each, the pack mules plodding between the two lines, the loose herd stepping in the wheel-tracks of the last Conestoga. There was no sign and no Indians.

At sundown of the first day, they took Clint Cooper out of the bed of the cook wagon. Old Thorpe asked Kirby if he would read over the boy and the mountain man simply said, "Sure, Uncle Thorpe. I'll say the words."

Shallow the grave was, and lonely as Kansas. The teamsters stood head-hung and wordless, the Mexican *arrieros* restless and muttering, crossing themselves continually. Armijo stood by the gravehead, the girl and the giant squaw beside him. Across the darkening prairie the coyotes were beginning to yip, and somewhere off against the red ball of the sun, a loafer wolf howled dismally.

Tuss was coming from the cook wagon then, the blanket-wrapped figure slumped in his huge arms, the hulking wagon boss carrying the six-foot bundle as lightly and gently as he would a child. Beside him, Uncle Thorpe followed along, head down, his gnarled hand holding a torn corner of the old blanket.

Thinking how small and huddled a big man always looked once he was done and blanket-covered, Kirby stepped silently back and Tuss bent in front of him, easing the boy's body into the hole.

"The Lord is my shepherd," said Kirby. "I shall not want. He leads me into green pastures and he makes me lay down by still waters. The Lord he gives and the Lord he takes away. Clint was a man growed, and the Lord has saw fit and tooken him away. Clint was good. His soul don't need no prayin' fer. Amen."

"Come on, Thorpe." Tuss's deep voice, strangely kind, broke the stillness. "Lay off'n yer holt of the blanket. We got to cover him up."

Midafternoon of the second day the charred caravan reached Turkey Creek. The graze had been dry and thin at the camp where they'd buried Clint, and now it was coming on to rain. The grass, all buffalo now, was short and sparse. A good rain would have the trail a river of mud ruts within an hour. The mules were gaunted from sixty hours without food, at least without a decent piece of browse, and the men were still suffering from their burns. To top it, with a storm crawling in on them, they had to get across Turkey Creek before spanning out.

The rain began as they put the first wagon into the Fork. By the time the last mule was over it had built to a steady downpour and the creek was running bankfull. Men and mules had had enough. Tuss ordered the span-out and a rest camp set up. "We stay right h'yar," he announced, "till the stock is grazed back into shape and the goddam rain lets up."

Kirby had been in some wet camps but never a one to touch the slop of that one at Turkey Creek. There wasn't a stick of wood within twenty miles and what buffalo chips they were able to get in were so wet they had to be wrung out before they'd even make smoke. He and Thorpe had done what every skinner in the train had — sheeted in their wagon wheels, tight and fast, and crawled underneath the Conestoga-bed to weather the blow.

Withal, slop or no slop, a guard was run, Kirby standing the first quarter, getting back under Thorpe's wagon about 10.00 P.M. Thorpe had the second swing, from 10.00 until 2.00, going out on it as Kirby came in.

The younger man pinned the sheets after Thorpe crawled out, and skinned out of his wet clothes. He had no more than gotten a dry blanket around him than the old man was back, scratching for admission. "Hold on, Thorpe," Kirby laughed. "Keep yer damn shirt on, ye old saltbutt! Ye won't drownd!"

In a second he had the bone lacing needles pulled, and the canvas flap held back. The figure which squeezed in out of the storm was a shade smaller and rounder than old Thorpe. "It's some wet out, mister!" The white teeth flashed under the rain-drops coursing the dusky skin. "Thanks for asking me in."

"Gosh, ma'am," stammered Kirby. "I didn't

have no idea. I'm sorry I called out at ye so rough."

"It wasn't rough enough to worry about and besides" — the voice, a low, throaty one, struck Kirby as being powder-soft, and the long green eyes, he thought, would have looked smoky anywhere — "a man's got more than rough talk to be careful of in front of ladies."

Following her direct gaze, Kirby looked down at himself, gasped, clutched frantically at the gaping blanket, scrambled for his hat, jammed it over his ears. When he had gotten his breath, the girl, still on her knees by the entrance, spoke again. "Well, now that you're dressed" — the quick candlelight of the smile lit her face again as she gestured mockingly to the crammed-on hat — "don't you ever ask visitors to take off their things and sit down?"

"Uh, sure. Yes ma'am. I guess, anyways." Kirby's natural ease with females was swimming to the top of his first flood of embarrassment.

The girl nodded, pinned the flap behind her, took off her hat to reveal the bright hair piled high and loosely pinned beneath it, slipped the dripping poncho off over her head, crawled over by the lamp and sat down across from him. "Have you got another dry blanket, Mr. Randolph? My leggins are soaked through. And just in case you might have wondered, my name is Aurélie St. Clair. Pleased to meet you, Mr. Randolph. You must have been left outside the tipi when the manners were passed around."

"Uh, yes ma'am, I've got a blanket. And, uh, I'm pleased to meet ye, too."

" 'Uh' seems to be your favorite expression, Mr. Randolph."

Kirby looked at her, beginning to be needled by her talk. Apparently her tongue was as sharp as her mouth looked soft. "Yeah," he grunted, eyeing her narrowly, "it's the Injun in me."

"Well then, chief, how about the blanket? I'm still wet."

"Sure," said Kirby, reaching her one from the pile on Thorpe's war chest. "Anything else?"

"Turn your back and count ten," she told him, taking the blanket.

"I'll try," muttered Kirby, swinging his broad shoulders around. "But I won't guarantee nothin'. Dunno if I kin go thet high."

When he had made his count and turned to the girl again, his eyes widened. Not only the leggins, but the fringed Cheyenne skirt, were draped neatly over the Conestoga's rear axle. The blanket was wrapped carelessly around what the leggins and skirt had just come off of. One pink foot and slim ankle failed of finding cover under the loose wrapper.

"It's a foot," said the girl drily, noticing his appreciative gaze. "Five toes. Just like the other one." Here the slim member's mate slid out from under the blanket to prove her contention. "See?"

"Yes ma'am." Kirby found himself suddenly

wondering if the rest of it came up to the feet. "But I ain't never see'd two sech purty ones. I knowed a Arapahoe gal once thet had one tolerably handsome foot, but the other one had bin tromped on by a barefoot pony and —"

"I'm not interested in your clubfooted Indian lady friends." The dark rose of the cheeks dimpled in a curtsy to the curving smile beneath them. "I came over to thank you for saving my life in the fire."

"I didn't know it was you." Kirby spoke before he realized how it would sound.

"Thanks anyway." Her laugh was as pretty as the rest of her, Kirby decided. "I owe you one, regardless."

"I didn't mean thet, ma'am. I —"

"What's the difference? You saved me. That's what counts to me." The pause was just long enough to be called a pause. "I guess that's not all you saved, either. Popo tells me we'd have lost the mules but for you."

"Mebbe." Kirby shrugged, easing back away from the light of the tallow-candle lamp as he noticed the girl beginning to look at him with a curious frown. "In a tight like thet everybody works."

"Where have I seen you before?" the girl asked, ignoring his answer. "You know, the first time I saw you in Council Grove I thought I'd seen you somewhere. I haven't had a good look at you since. Now I *know* I've seen you before. Where was it?" She hesitated, then added, "I never forget a face. That's the Indian in *me*."

Kirby took note of the emphasis on the last word, but was too interested at the moment in covering his own identity to go to worrying afresh about her pedigree. "It's a funny thing." His grin was embarrassed, showing just the right amount of deference. "People will get thet kind of a idee in their heads. Me, now, I got the feelin' I've see'd ye somewhars before, too. And land knows I ain't."

"I've heard that voice before, too." Again she ignored him.

Kirby didn't get much relief out of her last remark. Best get the girl out of there right quick. Before she got to remembering other things beside his face and voice. "Ma'am, ye'd best go. This ain't no place fer ye to be."

"My place in this train is any place I am. My father and my uncle own these wagons."

"Wal, ma'am, Don Pedro then. He wouldn't —"

"Don Pedro is nobody to me but my cousin. He hasn't any more to say about me than you have. And that's nothing, mister."

Kirby was beginning to wonder if he had misjudged her. Damn if she wasn't a bitch cub. He felt his back getting up. A man didn't take to having his haunches spurred by any drip-nose kid of a girl. He must have been out of his mind to figure her a woman grown. His words ground hard into the gravel bar of his anger.

"Wal, the Injun Ox then, dammit! I don't

want to have to lambast her again. I —" He
snapped his teeth down on the statement, was
too late to more than cut the tail off of it. He
saw the girl's eyes widen, her curving lips part.
Her voice came at him flat and quiet.

"Take off your hat, mister." She was moving
around the lamp toward him, leaning so close
her clean breath touched him. "A gentleman always takes his hat off in front of a lady."

"I ain't no gentleman," growled Kirby, des-
perately pushing back and away from her.

"And I'm no lady!" The words came snapping with the hand that shot out and knocked
his hat off. The guttering light of the candle
lantern was not so bad but what the broad
white lock through the scout's dark curls stood
out clear as a streak of silver across a freshcut
mine face.

It had moved so fast neither of them was
ready for it. The girl recovered first, the rebel-
lion starting with a flash in the green eyes,
ending up in a snarl of the snowy teeth. "If I
had a gun I'd shoot you again! I'd — I'd —"

Kirby for all his recovery was slower, made a
better job of it. "Ma'am, I've got jest the thing
fer ye. Bin totin' it along fer jest sech a celebration." His gray eyes never left her face as the
long arm reached behind him to feel in the
parfleche of the saddle against which he leaned.
"H'yar — ketch!" The nickel plate of the little
Colt Paterson flashed dully as he tossed it toward her.

Her hands, moving automatically, caught the gun, then fumbling, dropped it into the deep pile of the buffalo robe beneath her. She snatched it up, holding it on the man across the lantern. "If I could just be positive it *was* you, she breathed. "If I could just be certain —" Watching her, Kirby's eyes narrowed, his breath surging.

In catching the gun, the blanket around the girl had been twisted and partly opened. A bare leg, slim and graceful as a doe's, curved from beneath the rough cover. "Whut would ye do, ma'am?" Kirby's voice came thick and slow as his shadow passed over the lantern. "Whut would ye do if ye *could be* sure?"

She recoiled before him, bending far back on the robe, the little gun still pointing. "I — I don't know —"

He was over her then, brown-muscled shoulder bared as his arm supported his crouching weight. "Ye shot me once when I kissed ye, ma'am." The arm came slowly around behind her neck, she seeming powerless to move to halt or escape it. "Let's see if ye'll do it again." The arm tightened, leaping and crushing inward like a sprung trap, the wide, hard mouth seeking and finding the soft, full one.

The slim body tightened beneath him, the smooth right arm driving the Colt barrel up into his lean belly, the slender finger closing on the trigger. As the barrel came against him, the mountain man moved his body in to meet it, throwing his belly forward into the girl's. He felt the fragrant heat of her as she came in to him, felt its racing flame spread like fire beneath him, felt the steel go out of her arching back, the bared arm sliding behind his dark head, tensing in sudden spasm to return the fury of his kiss.

He didn't see the gun fall from the nerveless fingers, nor the fireburst of the green eyes as she tore her lips from his, to bury her white teeth frantically in his cupping shoulder.

As he recoiled from the sharp pain in his shoulder, sudden anger overrose the floodgauge of physical passion mirrored in the mountain man's face. This in turn, and as swiftly, was replaced by the flicking grin which smoothed the quick-hardened edges of his craggy features. "Wal, anyhow, ma'am," his voice, harsh and deep as a muttering bear's, accompanied the rueful smile, "ye didn't shoot me this time. Happen we're makin' a leetle progress, Miss Aurélie."

The girl didn't answer, cowering, arm-braced where he had forced her back, her long fingers touching her bruised lips, her green eyes watching him wide-spread with wonder.

"Ye'd best go now, ma'am." Kirby's voice was his old soft one, the growl gone from it. "I'll turn my back fer ye to get your outfit on." Again there was no answer, and when he turned once more toward her, she was at the entrance flap.

The scout's eyes, running over the poised,

wild beauty of her, carried his mind to the almost identical memory of her half-defiant, half-worshipful regard of him that other time back in the St. Louis carriage barn, reminding him as they did so of his bitter words on that occasion. His low voice grew softer still under the clear caress of her return gaze.

"Before ye go, ma'am," he murmured, "I want ye to know thet I'm sorry I called ye whut I did, back thar in St. Louis. I hadn't no right to say thet, ma'am, and I reckon I know, now, thet ye ain't no halfbreed. Ye jest couldn't be, Miss Aurélie."

He saw, then, without understanding it, the quick stab of pain that narrowed her widened eyes. Heard, without realizing its cause, the sharp intake of breath which accompanied the stricken look.

*"Oh, Wasicun! Wasicun — !"* was all she said before the entrance flap and the driving rain closed behind her, but the broken sob beneath the fierce words drove into Kirby hard and deep as a war arrow. And deep as the sob had driven the shaft, the Sioux meaning behind the words drove it deeper still.

Long after she had gone, Kirby sat motionless under the candle's guttering glance, the dark litany of blood-admission in her passionate outcry reading itself over and over into his sinking thoughts.

*"Oh, Wasicun! Wasicun!* — Oh, White Man! White Man. . . ."

# 7

The rain held for three days. By the time it let up, every blanket in camp was crawling with blowfly maggots. The men hadn't had hot food or coffee for forty-eight hours, and the trail was a mire of mud stifle-deep to a tall mule. The fourth morning showed up as clear as only a prairie morning following a three-day rain can.

Tuss declared they would take the morning to dry out the wagon goods, hit the trail after noon dinner, drive all night to make the seventeen miles to the Little Arkansas in one hitch. A night drive was risky but the trail ahead was level and open and all hands knew there was time to make up. The enforced layover brought two surprises to Kirby, the first pleasant, the second harsh as the hair on an angry dog's back.

First, Don Pedro called him up to his tent, made a gracious Spanish acknowledgment of the train's debt to the scout's work at Cottonwood Crossing and presented him with the roan mare as a gift in token.

"Her name? *Dispensame, señor. Mil pardones. Jacinta-salvaje*, Bluebell. She will go all day and all night, takes only a breaking hackamore, sits soft as a cloud, travels easy as the wind. Her bad habits, señor? Absolutely none. She reins true or will go by the knees alone. She is afraid of nothing and always watches where she puts her feet. Her temper? Good! *Excellente!*"

Leading Bluebell back to the wagon, Kirby figured he had had quite a morning. A man didn't just pick up a top mare every day in the week. Made a body wonder if his luck wasn't stretching its seams a mite. Something was bound to happen.

And along about noon it did, a solitary figure showing up afoot on the backtrail.

To an eye as sharp as Kirby's, distress was spoken in every lurching motion of the staggering stranger. He wouldn't last to the creek, Kirby figured, and he didn't. Twelve yards short of the stream and even as Kirby was swinging up on Bluebell, he went sprawling, face-forward, into the trail muck.

Kirby was first man to the creek, putting the roan mare into the racing tide, hanging hard to her tail as she surged across. The flood carried them three hundred yards downstream before a landing was made. Spitting sand and water, Kirby got a leg up on Bluebell, kicking her into a full gallop. He recognized Sam's still figure as he hit the ground and ran to the old mountain man's side. "Sam! Sam! Ye old sun of a gun? Whut the hell hit ye?"

He got his answer only after he had gotten

the old man back across the creek and forced the best part of a tin cup of trade whiskey through his cracked lips.

"Howdy, young un." Sam's greeting tottered weakly. "We're out'n business. Damn buzzards hit us five days ago at Mud Crick. Must of bin a hunderd of them, mostly Panani." He used the Sioux name for the Pawnees, and Kirby nodded.

"They was Pony Stealers, all right, old-timer."

Sam nodded in turn, continuing his story. "I was trailin' with a leetle outfit of Texas folks. Bein' in a fever to ketch up with ye, I had throwed in with them at Council Grove. The Panani got us proper. Burned every wagon. Run off every mule. Thet war five days ago, and h'yar I am." The old man drew a labored breath, concluding, "I allow it ain't much use goin' back to try and help them Texas folks, now."

"We wouldn't go back nohow." Tuss's deep voice broke in flatly. "We're loadin' right now, rollin' in a hour." Turning to Kirby, he continued, hard-eyed. "Blanket the old goat down in the cook wagon whar we had Clint. Give him a feed. And by the way, Randolph," Tuss's pig-eyes clamped down on Kirby, "who is the old beaver, anyhow? Seems mighty familiar to me, somehow. Cain't place him, though."

Kirby winked at Sam, reached his long arm down, placed his great hand affectionately on the narrow shoulder. "Boys" — he announced, dramatically — "I want ye to meet my mother — Mr. Samuel Q. Beekman!"

"Beekman?"

"Sam Beekman?"

" 'Old Sam' hisse'f?"

"The riverman?"

The questions came from a succession of the older teamsters, men who had been on the frontier long enough to have heard "Beekman" mentioned in the same breath with names like "Bridger," "Colton," and "Beckwourth."

"The very same!" smiled Kirby, beaming proudly down on the old man who, by this time, was scowling furiously. "The old top-dog river hoss, hisse'f!"

"Whut's the 'Q' stand fer?" Tuss's demand for information came slow and heavy, the glint in his tiny eyes belying the innocence of the query.

"It stands fer 'Questions'," old Sam answered up for himself. "I don't ask them and I don't answer them." His own squinted gaze matched Tuss's.

The wagon boss glanced sideways, first at Kirby then back to the old man. His statement, when it came, stepped a little faster than usual. "I allow we'll get some askin' and answerin' done around h'yar before very long, you two. Ye kin mark thet."

The trail was fetlock-deep in slop for the best

91

part of the afternoon, but a steady south wind and rising country, between them, combined to make a reasonably good road by nightfall. They halted at dusk, built fires and cooked supper, rested for two hours to give the early moon and the first, fat stars time to build up a little light. By nine o'clock they were rolling again.

Tuss had every available hand working as outriders, even Aurélie and Ptewaquin saddled up and rode with Don Pedro. The whole night through, the mounted band flanked, headed and tailed the train. Sam, refusing to accept his consignment to the jolting hell of the cook wagon, caught up a mule and jogged along with Kirby, half a mile out front of the wagons. Tuss himself rode the trail a dozen yards ahead of the lead wagon driven by Uncle Thorpe. There was no trouble and no sign of trouble.

They halted at 6.00 A.M., spanned out, made coffee, rested two hours. Noon found them pulling down on the Little Arkansas.

All morning, as they rode, Kirby and Sam had noted the increasing buffalo sign, though so far not a single animal had been spotted. But the piles of chips and the white blemishes made by the bleaching skulls and jagged racks of ribs dotting the prairie were becoming heavy enough to let any old hand know that Uncle Pte was bound to show up soon — and in force.

"I allow this h'yar Leetle Arkansaw marks the beginnin' of the buffler country down in these parts," grunted Sam, scanning the growing sign uneasily.

"Yeah, Uncle Thorpe says they got into one hell of a herd down h'yar last spring. Took them a day and a half to drive through."

"I'd jest as lief not get into no sizable herd with a heavy bunch of loose mules like we got. Ye kin get yerse'f into six kinds of hell before breakfast thetaway."

"I suppose," nodded Kirby. "But it don't seem hardly likely."

"Oh, don't it now? Thet's because ye've done all yer associatin' with the ornery cusses from the back of a top buffler pony. These h'yar Trail freighters hates them. And ye kin bet yer ruby-red neck they got theirse'fs mighty good reasons fer so doin'. Specially a mule outfit like ourn."

"Why fer ye say thet?"

"Wal, ye take a ox train now, it ain't so bad. A ox has got a mort in common with the shaggy sons of guns. A ox ain't much but a yoke-broke buffler, nohow. But mules now, boy! Thar ye got somethin' else again. When ye get a trail herd of loose longears into real buffler country, happen ye've go yerse'f a right smart handful. And I ain't jest a'honkin', mister."

Kirby grinned. "Sam, I swear ye're gettin' jumpy as a bit-up old bull in flytime. Happen ye see a few piles of chips and two, three skulls, ye're figgerin' we already done lost the mules and are hoofin' it the rest of the way to Santy Fee."

"It ain't so much the buffler I'm thinkin' of," Sam frowned. "It's the cussed gnats."

"Gnats?" Kirby's question indicated he figured the oldster was slipping his head hobbles. "Ye mean plain, ordinary buffler gnats?"

"I don't mean no other variety. Ye see, it's like I done told ye so many times, young un. Comes to savvyin' all thar is to know about buffler, ye're a good plew hunter. Happen ye know whut I mean."

"Stream ahead — !" Kirby stood in his stirrups to make the interruption. "Thet'll be the Leetle Arkansaw, likely."

"Likely," nodded Sam, not bothering to dignify the laconic agreement with a corroborating look. "And as muddy a leetle slough as ever the Cottonwood."

The Little Arkansas proved just that, for all it was a scant six yards wide. Camp was finally made at 4.00 P.M., all hands pitching in to repair the wagons damaged in the crossing. With dark coming on, the heat, oppressive all day, seemed to grow. Clouds, thick as top cream and black as a bat's mouth, began to pile up southward on the prairie rim. Sitting to their fire with Sam and Uncle Thorpe, Kirby's eye roved the surrounding territory apprehensively.

As far as he could see, the lingering twilight lit up a scene of eerie loneliness. Disused buffalo wallows by the score, glinting full of rain water, ringed by golden coreopsis and brilliant scarlet mallow, puffballs, big and white as human skulls, dotting the shadowy clusters of purslane and lamb's-quarter, and everywhere the curly, blue-gray nap of the buffalo grass, combined to make a depressing ghost vista stained sick-yellow by the weird cloud light.

Turning to the others, he hunched a shoulder at the building clouds, muttered quietly, "Them's fair dirty clouds down thar, ain't they?"

"Tolerable." Sam cocked a professional eye horizonward. "But them clouds'll never hurt ye. Happen we might get some shortly thet will, though."

"I allow I foller ye." Uncle Thorpe entered the conversation. "I bin thinkin' we seen mighty heavy buffler sign today."

"I suppose ye two old mossybacks are still frettin' about yer infernal gnats."

The old men sucked their pipes, each apparently deferring to the other in the privilege of handing the cub his cuffing. Finally Uncle Thorpe looked around for a stone, found one, knocked cut the dottle of his pipe, blew through the stem to get the spittle clear and addressed his remarks to the open darkness beyond the fire.

"The buffler gnat," he began, speaking with the pained weariness of a schoolmaster fronted by a chronic dullard in the class, "is a leetle old midge of a thing, no bigger then a speck of dust in the tail of a man's eye. He'll bite ye, right out, on the hands and face to make ye feel like somebody was pitchin' porkyhog needles into ye by the pawfuls. Or, more likely, he'll crawl under yer duds and fasten hisse'f onto ye like a Texas tick. When he gits in thar he'll put his leetle drill in ye and hang on till he's blowed hisse'f plumb up suckin' at ye. And when he's got his gut full and goes to droppin' off, he'll leave ye a welt big as yer thumb and sore as a moccasin blister. Now thet's yer buffler gnat fer ye. And whut he kin do to a human critter, he does ten times over to any kind of stock he kin get his stinger into."

The old man paused long enough to spit into the fire, then concluded. "Tooken by hisse'f he don't mean a tarnal thing. But tooken in clouds and swarms and waves thick enough to choke a ox, he's apt to mean aplenty."

"Sech as whut, mebbe?" Kirby's question came more as an acknowledgment of the lecture than as an expression of interest in it.

"In this h'yar case," the old teamster stretched the statement significantly, "sech as mebbe a mule stampede."

The first cloud of gnats drifted in about ten o'clock. From then until midnight the men in their blankets, the saddlestock on their pickets, the mules in their loose herd, tail-slapped, bit, brayed, scratched, groaned or cursed, each in his own way fighting off the myriads of invisible insects.

At one, a second, vastly thicker horde of the pests lowered down out of the night skies to join their fellows. The sufferings of man and brute became swiftly more intense.

When, at one-thirty, Tuss ordered the skinners out of their blankets to join the *arrieros* in holding the frantic mule herd, Kirby's face was already a beefsteak of welts, his hands swollen and puffed until they could scarcely open and close. Yet when he rolled out to mount up and rode with the others, he found he had just begun to suffer.

Listening as he rode, to the fearful whining hum of the multi-billions of the invaders' tiny wings and the hoarse braying of the biting, wildly kicking mules, Kirby wondered how the four-legged brutes could stand up to the torment. It was all he could do to keep from screaming himself, and he was a human being with a brain in his head. And hands to scratch with, too. Those poor damn mules had nothing. They could kick and bray and bite, that was all. Otherwise they just milled and jumped around snapping and tail-slapping at themselves, and taking it.

One thing a man knew. If the swarm didn't let up soon, there would be no holding them.

God! If it would just come on to rain good and hard. That would fix the little devils. And quieten and soothe the mules, too. Cripes, what the hell was that? A man could get off-centered getting bit and stung so heavy, and with his head spinning from the vibration of those damn wings. But, listen. No, by damn, he *wasn't* crazy! The hum *was* building!

The third swarm hit about two o'clock, the mule herd breaking before it to go plunging and braying off into the blackness, the hammering drumfire of their panicky hoofs rising briefly above the ear-ringing hum of the insect horde and the screaming, helpless curses of their human pursuers.

Then there was nothing but the continued whine of the whirling black host muffling the bitter, weeping profanity of the weary, nerve-worn men.

The mules were gone.

# 8

The morning following the gnat stampede was spent in riding ten miles of prairie draws and gullies, rounding up what was to be found of the five hundred mules which had composed the company herd. The final count, made after noon dinner, showed thirty head short. Another ten head were so miserably bitten as to be totally blinded, or so swollen by their hundreds of venomous welts as to be useless in harness. These were humanely shot.

The white mule skinners and Mexican *arrieros* were hideous with puffed, inflamed faces, splitting lips, bleeding ears and noses. Some of them, too, were actually blind, their eyes swollen to sightless slits.

The wagons rolled at dawn next day, reaching Cow Creek in a hard twenty-mile drive. The next day and another sixteen miles brought them rolling into the Valley of the Arkansas River, the "Grand Arkansaw."

The Arkansas was always a great sight for the Trail traveler and in Kirby's case its impact proved no exception. Its broad valley was everywhere covered, thick as bristled fur, with the tough, wiry little grama grass. Stunted sun-flowers, ill-formed, sapless cottonwoods and occasional willows dotted the unending carpet, while rearing bluffs of red clay and yellow sandstone ruptured its smooth expanse in slashes of raw color. The river itself where Kirby, ten miles out in front of the train, first rode in sight of it was about three quarters of a mile wide, no deeper than four feet, swirling and snaking along with a five-mile current.

When he got up to it he found the waters to be chalky white with alkali. This peculiar opacity was so marked as to nearly resemble milk, and Kirby, bellyflopping to drink up-stream of the busily sucking Bluebell, allowed the stuff tasted near as good.

It was now about 2.00 P.M., and the weary scout, satisfied by his morning's ride that the valley was clear of Indians and that therefore no need existed to hurry his return to the wagons, loosened the cinch and dropped the reins on Bluebell, putting her to graze in a lush swale alongside the main channel.

It took him all of ten seconds to shuck out of his buckskins. And very presently the milky wa-ters of the Arkansas were being splashed and splattered by a commotion giving no odds, for sheer power and noisy enjoyment, to the plea-sures of a bull buffalo in an eight-foot prairie wallow. After a few turns and explosive por-poise-snorts, Kirby was seized with a well-nigh disastrous burst of humane inspiration. Blue-

bell looked dusty and lathered from her six-
teen-mile jaunt from Cow Creek. Grazing
busily along the bank, hock-deep in heavy
grass, the mare had never in her life been less
in need of a bath.

But give the average boy, be he sixteen or
sixty, a fine wide river, gentle current, clean
sand bottom and a hot afternoon, well, you've
got yourself a swimming party.

Kirby caught the mare up, slipped her girth,
left the saddle lying on the grass of the bank.
To mark the spot there was an old snaggle of a
cottonwood thrusting its stumpy fang up
through the hard-packed sand of the shelving
bank. Inspired by a belated sense of order,
Kirby retrieved his Hawkens from the grass
where he had carelessly flung it and neatly
crotched it in the old tree. Then, with nothing
between him and Bluebell but a loose-braided
Mexican hackamore, he plunged the mare into
the current.

After a balky start Bluebell got into the sui-
cidal spirit of the thing. She galloped, snorting
and splashing, over the sandbar shallows,
plunged and buck-jumped through the deeper
channels, wound up tail-towing Kirby around
in a sufficiently deep pool of quiet water
stretching perhaps fifty feet along the eight-foot
bank that bore the snaggle-toothed cottonwood.

In a few minutes Bluebell had had enough. A
broad sandpit paralleled the bank about twenty

yards out from the tree, and toward this the mare shortly swam her way, towing Kirby with her. Clambering out on the spit, she shook herself like a giant dog. Kirby had just started to follow her up on the bar when he saw her stiffen, swinging her head bankward, ears pricked, nostrils belled.

Instantly every nerve in his body went catgut-tight.

Forcing a loud laugh and affecting much playful splashing, Kirby waded up on the sand to join her, keeping his broad back squarely turned on the bank behind him. Alongside the mare he made a great show of rubbing and slapping her, calling out a string of nonsense and pet names. At no time did he present anything but his back to the bank.

As he laughed and loud-talked her he worked up along her wither, pressing his body in close, laying his head affectionately along her neck — so affectionately he was able, shortly, to grab one fleeting glance shoreward from behind the cover of her curving neck. It was only a little flash of an eye-corner glance, but the picture it mirrored hung in Kirby's mind far longer than most good straight looks he had ever taken.

The cottonwood tree was no longer lonely. It had company.

Sitting their shaggy ponies, utterly motionless, gravely studying the antics of the naked white idiot on the sandbar, were thirteen Kiowa braves.

Still loud-talking the mare, Kirby asked his

eye-memory for details: got enough of them to lift each individual hair along the nape of his neck straight on end. Those red sons were no friendlies. Their gargoyle faces were smeared black with charcoal grease paste. Blazing bands of ocher and vermilion slashed across their broad cheekbones, zebra-striped their low foreheads, cornered their wide mouths. They were in full headdress, their lances, bows, bridles and persons hung and decked in war feathers.

A hunting party would be plain-shirted, unfeathered. These birds had on more plumage than a cock grouse in drumming time.

And there wasn't a boy or even a young apprentice warrior among them. There wasn't a one of them wore less than eight headfeathers, and if the Kiowa counted them like the Sioux, a feather for each major coup, he had himself a real salty bunch over there on the bank.

Of the first twelve warriors there was not the slightest doubt in this respect, of the thirteenth, less than that. He was a short, squat man, black almost as a plantation slave, great flat-boned face, mongoloid as a Hun's, a tremendous jutting nose and ear-to-ear knife slash of a mouth, the whole adding up to making him the ugliest redskin Kirby had ever seen.

And this beauty was no subchief or neighborhood nabob. The snowflash of feathers cascading down his back and foaming across his pony's flank trailed to the ground — seven feet of them, a hundred *coup*-claims at least, maybe more.

This one was a *chief.*

For one detail and one alone, Kirby thanked his faithful eye, praying even as he knotted his fist in Bluebell's mane that the eye had gotten it straight. They were lance- and warbow-armed. There wasn't a gun visible among the lot of them.

The white scout now paid silent respect to the fact that in the few days he'd had her, he had already fooled around with Bluebell, getting her to stand for a rightside mount. A white man will mount from the left. An Indian from the right, always. Watching him now, standing back to them as he was, on the mare's right, those red sons wouldn't be looking for a swing-up — maybe.

Well, they weren't.

Kirby, knotted right fist tightening in the long mane, went aboard Bluebell like a cougar crawling an orphan colt. His snaking left hand jerked the hackamore rope so hard he nearly broke her neck getting her spun left-around. At the same instant his heels pistoned into her ribs and the panther scream of the Oglala Sioux war cry exploded in her pinned-back ears.

*"Hiii-eeee-Yahhh!"*

The Spanish mare went flying off that sandbar and buck-jumping across the shallow Arkansas quicker than a broom-swatted cat. Behind her the yells of the Kiowas blended with Kirby's Sioux shout, and the splashing and snorting of their eager ponies echoed the watery noises of her own flight.

The scout's escape depended on two things: whether he could get off the sandbar before catching a fatal dose of arrows and, once off, whether he could hit enough shallow water between him and the far bank to let the mare keep moving at a top clip.

The first, he made, getting away from the bar, clean. Half a dozen shafts grazing him and one grooving Bluebell's rump served but to encourage man and mount to nobler effort. Now, clear of the bar, his previous half-hour's play in the river channels paid off. Had he hit a deep hole or even a considerable stretch of three- and four-foot water, he'd have been slowed enough for the pursuing Kiowas to plumage him up with arrows thicker than a snow goose in winter feather. But by kneeing the lunging mare hither and yon as he remembered the shallows he made it to the far bank without collecting a single shaft, even opening up the distance between him and his howling rearguard while dodging their arrow shower.

Plunging out the far side, a back-flung glance showed him that half the Indians had jumped their ponies into the river, that the other half, including the squat chief, exercising cooler tactics, had raced their ponies down the bank to cut him off from re-crossing to the Trail.

Giving Bluebell a little head he let her gallop

down the bank on his side. Behind him the first bunch of braves were just coming out of the river, flailing their scrubby ponies along the bank after him. Across the stream the other bunch was paralleling him. Keeping the long-legged roan mare to a hand-gallop, Kirby set himself to a little late-in-the-afternoon thinking.

Between them the two groups of Kiowas had him in a hell of a fine spot — for them. If he lagged, the bunch on his side would nail him. If he tried crossing over, the second bunch would trap him coming out. Looking back he saw that the bunch on his side had pulled up on him a little, the bunch on the far bank gotten out ahead a mite. At the same time he saw two other things: a moving dust cloud full of small black dots rolling up the valley from the southwest, a narrow bend in the river looming ahead. The first could be nothing but plenty more Kiowas, the second nothing but his last chance to keep his curly top-piece.

As he put his heels into Bluebell he prayed she was as fast as she looked, the downriver bend shallower than it seemed. The Lord split 50-50 with him. Bluebell was faster than chain lightning with a link snapped — the far bend deep enough to wash a high horse's withers.

He had gained a quarter-mile on the group pacing him on the far bank, could have made the narrow crossing nicely had it proved less deep. Now he wondered how it was going to feel when his hair came off. Even as he wondered, salvation loomed ahead. Beyond the deep-running narrows the river sprawled out in two channels, each coursing straight and shallow, the sandbar between them running level and hard for nearly a mile. If he could slant the mare across the first water, then make up enough ground racing down the center strip before trying the second, he might just keep his skull-piece. One easy thing about the whole matter — he had no choice in it at all.

It is the natural fortune of the trail for those hardy souls assigned to ride the head of a line of Santa Fe freighting wagons, in this case leathery old Sam Beekman and the scowling giant, Tuss McLawry, to ride up on many a strange sight.

"Fer Gawd's sake!" bellowed Tuss, reining his horse in and waving the wagons to a halt.

"My sentiments perzackly," nodded Sam, likewise checking his mount to admire the approaching rider. "A feller would think a man would have more respect fer the ladies."

"The son of a gun must have go'd crazy," growled Tuss. "Either thet or I ain't seein' whut I'm seein'."

"Ye're seein' it, all right," Sam reassured him. "And I allow it's somethin' to look at, too!"

Sam allowed right. Six-feet-three of heel-hammering white scout and eleven hundred pounds of blue Spanish mare, belly-stretched in a flat gallop with nothing between them and the late afternoon sunshine but a thin Mexican hackamore, was indeed "something to look at."

"Now whut the hell?" shouted Tuss, as Kirby slid the mare to her haunches in front of them.

"Gimme yer shirt, Sam. Fer Cripes sake, gimme it!" The scout's voice was desperate, his eyes anxiously roving the halted train.

"Whut's yer hurry, young un?" The old man made no move to divest himself of the requested garment. His answer was a groan from Kirby.

"Oh, dammit, h'yar she comes! Gimme thet shirt before I tear it off'n ye!"

Sam looked back to see Aurélie and Armijo riding out from the train. "Whut of it, boy? Ain't ye the jack mule whut's allus brayin' about God givin' him more'n his share? Sit up thar, boy. Quit hunkerin' over like a gut-sick squaw!"

Kirby's answer was to drive Bluebell into the old man's mule, ram one frantic paw into the back of the neck of Sam's fringed shirt, rip the buckskin off him in a desperate wrenching twist which spun the oldster off his mule and deposited him butt-first, blue-cussing and waist-naked, in the dust of the trail. Whipping the shredded shirt hastily around his own nakedness, the young scout whirled on Tuss.

"I got jumped by a scout party of Kioways up by the Big Bend. I was in swimmin' when they rode up on me. Lucky fer me I had the hoss in with me and the hackamore on her. I got a leg up on her and made big tracks away from thar."

Sam, dusting off his bottom and grabbing for his mule's rope, vented himself of a scathing summation of the whole affair. "When a man sets out, deliberate a'purpose, to make a complete hoss's neck out'n hisse'f, it's a tarnal shame to have a leetle thing like a six-bit Mexican hackamore spoiling a otherwise perfect attempt."

By the time Sam had concluded his observation, Armijo and the girl had ridden up, joined by the Sioux giantess and Uncle Thorpe. "How many of them was thar?" Tuss ignored the new comers, demanding his answer of Kirby as the latter shifted uncomfortably under the eyes of Aurélie St. Clair.

"Twelve braves and a chief."

"Whut'd the chief look like?" Tuss again, his scowl growing rockier by the second.

"Leetle squat-leg runt. Broad, bony face, biggest nose I ever see'd. Dark color, black almost like a darkie. White heron feather bonnet trailin' the damn dirt. *Woyuonihan.* He was a real chief. *Wagh!*"

"Never heard of him," said Tuss shortly, but Kirby, watching him as he said it, saw the quick shift of the eyes, saw, too, the expression that clouded Uncle Thorpe's face at the wagon boss's denial. "How ye figger to be so damn certain they was a scout party?" The big man's voice struck Kirby as more-than-called-for belligerent.

"As I come out'n the valley, I seen a cloud of riders headin' in toward the Bend from down southwest. Thar was a passel of them. I figger they was the main bunch. I'd say two hundred of them. Anyways, enough so's we'll have to corral right h'yar."

"Ye mean without goin' on to water?" Tuss was incredulous. Maybe a little too much so, thought Kirby. He wasn't acting just like a boss ought who had just been told he had two hundred Kiowa hostiles out in front of him.

"I mean jest thet. Ye've got two hour's hard drive to make the river. It's near six, now. Thet'd mean it would start to darken on us before we got camped and corralled."

"Wal, whut of it? Ye ain't afeered of Kioways, are ye?"

"Ye bet. Ye roll this train on up this evenin' and ye're rollin' it agin my report."

"Wal, get out'n the way then, mister, because we're rollin' her." Tuss's whole face seemed to stiffen like scum ice setting up under a freezing wind.

"Just a moment." Don Pedro's soft voice halted the forward thrust of Tuss's horse. "Randolph's right, of course. We can't travel in twilight and make camp in the dark with several hundred savages around. What are you thinking of, Mr. McLawry?"

"I'm thinkin' we ain't got no wood and no

water, and thet the grass ain't good right
h'yar."

*"Anything else?"*

"Sure. Them Kioways ain't goin' to bother us
none."

Kirby, watching the two men, saw the Spaniard's eyes narrow. "How do you *know* they
won't, Mr. McLawry?" The young don's question was soft in sound only. The tones under it
were hard as Toledo steel. Kirby once more
made mental note that the Governor's nephew
was a man to keep in mind if things got to a
tangle.

"I don't *know* they won't." Tuss reddened,
clearly upset. "I'm jest sayin' they won't. Thet's
my opinion."

"It ain't mine," said Kirby flatly, being paid
for the remark by a pig-eyed promissory note of
deferred settlement flashed at him by Tuss.

Ignoring the wagon boss, Don Pedro smiled
graciously at Kirby. "What do you propose, Mr.
Randolph?"

"Thar's a rise half a mile ahead. High
ground, good graze, no gullies to cover an approach. I'd span out thar and corral, tight. Pull
all the stock ye can inside the wagon square,
picket or wagon-tie the rest. Every damn head.
Ye kin graze them an hour while it's still light.
We eat cold, no fires. Pickets out a hundred
yards on all sides."

"Is that all?"

"Yeah. Savin' fer me. I aim to scout them

Kioways, come dark." He saw Tuss look at him as he said it, suspected the shot had hit home.

"Sounds logical, Mr. Randolph," nodded the Spaniard. "Let's roll, Mr. McLawry. We'll span out and corral as Randolph says."

Tuss's only answer was a grunted "Yes sir," and the slow stare he turned on Kirby as the latter rode past him on his way to the wagons.

The camp was quiet. All stock was in or tied. The cold, dry supper was down, the first-shift pickets out. Kirby, ready to leave on his night scout, was talking to Sam and Uncle Thorpe.

"So thet was Satank I run into today, eh, Uncle Thorpe?"

"Couldn't be no other Injun fit thet description. It jest so happens, I *know* the scut, personal."

"Ye'r sure, now?"

"Certain sure. And Tuss knowed it was him, too. Thet's whut bothered me. I cain't figger him playin' innycent thetaway."

"Somethin's wrong, som'ers," allowed Sam quietly.

"Yep. Did ye ketch the way Armijo called him on it?"

"Yeah. Why?"

"Wal, ye recollect me tellin' ye I figgered Tuss and Armijo was in cahoots on runnin' them guns to the Mexicans?"

"Yeah."

"Wal, why do ye suppose Tuss lied about Satank, then?"

"Dogged if I know. Got any idees?"

"No, but it don't figger, him lyin' thetaway, if they *was* in cahoots."

Sam took his pipe out from between his teeth to enter the discussion. "Ever hear of a double-cross?"

"Whut ye mean?"

"I dunno. Mebbe Tuss is thinkin' of a one-way split."

"Sech as?" Kirby prompted softly.

"Sech as makin' a independent deal with Satank to run them mules off, guns and all. And to hell with Don Pedro."

"Naw!" Uncle Thorpe was positive. "Tuss is a hard-case but he ain't thet bad. He wouldn't let them red devils in on us. Pullin' a delivery to a bunch of Mexes is one thing. Messin' around with Satank and two hundred Kioways is somethin' else. Even Tuss ain't up to no trick like thet."

"I allow he is." Kirby's contradiction was flat. "He'd murder his best friend fer a carrot of smokin' terbaccy. Or mebbe a bundle of sable peltries."

Sam challenged his young companion. "Ye sound like ye meant thet, young un. Whut ye got in mind?"

Hard-eyed and mouth-tight, Kirby brought the old man up to date on Tuss's identity. The young scout could hear Sam's breath catch, the exhaling of it come short-out, sharp as an arrow's hiss.

"Red MacKenzie! I should have knowed him, dammit. Whuskers or no whuskers."

"Wal, now ye do," grunted Kirby.

"Whut's our move?" The question came from Uncle Thorpe. "If Tuss aims to do business with Satank he'll have to get in touch with him." Kirby scowled. "And thet means one of two things. Either a Injun will ride into the train to make talk with Tuss, or Tuss will ride out'n the train to make talk with the Injuns."

"Then we got to wait fer Tuss to make his move." Uncle Thorpe's voice was uneasy. The other two merely grunted, saying nothing. After a minute, Kirby stood up.

"Reckon I'll drift. Don't want to keep Satank waitin'."

"Wal, step easy," admonished Sam.

"I allow I will," muttered Kirby, and faded away in the gloom.

Seconds after Kirby had gone, another figure shadowed up toward Thorpe's wagon. It proved to be Popo, bearing an order from Tuss for Kirby to stay with the wagons, taking on Tuss's spot at guard command, while the wagon boss himself went Kiowa-hunting. It was Don Pedro's order, Tuss had said.

Sam had his head thrown back in his and Kirby's "stud-horse signal" almost before the little Mexican had finished speaking.

"*Nombre Dios, señor!* Never have I heard a thing so beautiful. *Caray!* It was more real than real!" Too much the bone-bred horseman, Popo Dominguez, not to recognize sheer genius when he heard it.

"Shet up!" snapped Sam. "Yonder comes Kirby."

The gray-eyed scout listened without interruption to Sam's report, his orders following dry and hard on the old man's conclusion.

Sam, who had struck up a trail acquaintance with the giant Sioux, was to scout out Ptewaquin to see if she knew anything about Tuss and Don Pedro. Thorpe was to take Kirby's spot at guard command.

The two old men departed at once and without words, leaving Kirby alone with Popo. The young mountain man turned on the little Mexican wrangler, his words rapping quickly.

"Now ye listen, Popo. Which way did Tuss go? And how long ago?"

"To the south, señor, along the Trail itself. Three, perhaps five minutes ago. No more."

"Walkin' or ridin', *compadre?*"

"With the horse, señor."

Kirby still didn't trust the little man; knew he had to all the same.

"Listen, Popo. Ye savvy thet we're all in big danger? *Peligro mas grande? Sabe?*"

"*Sí señor. Muy peligro.*"

"All right. I don't know whut's goin' on in

115

this train but I aim to foller Tuss and find out. I don't mean to let nothin' happen to Señorita St. Clair." He referred to Aurélie deliberately, hoping to buy the wrangler's loyalty. It was a wild shot, but not wide.

"I, too, señor," the little Mexican's statement was quiet with the keen dignity of his race, "intend that no harm shall come to *la hija.*"

"I am yer friend, Popo." Kirby returned the gift of dignity, carefully. "And I have trusted ye. Remember thet."

"*Gracias.* I shall remember it, señor."

"Good. *Hasta luego.*"

"*De nada. Hasta la vista, señor.*"

Kirby's guess was that on a moon-dark night and on business that was best kept quiet, a man would make vastly better time on foot than a horse. It was the kind of guess a man in his business was likely to have to make every day in the week and twice on Sundays.

In this case he made it right, the shrewdness of the surmise being swiftly borne out. After only ten minutes of powder-footed loping along the murky trail his waiting ears picked up the muffled plop-plop of a shod horse going in deep dust. He swung off the trail, paralleling it a hundred feet out. In seconds he was abreast of the shuffle-walking horse.

For another fifteen minutes the sounds continued, then stopped. Kirby waited a dozen slow breaths, then slunk in toward the trail. Ten yards out, he found a proper gully, slid into it, paused, listening. Tuss had been places where it took more than a boy to keep his hair on straight. Kirby knew that. He wasn't the one you went tromping up on in the dark — without you tromped mighty soft.

The scout waited. Presently he heard the restless jingle of a spade bit, the blowing snuffle of a nervous horse, the low, answering grunt of its rider, soothing it.

Another wait while he counted his breathing again. Now! Kirby poked his eyes over the lip of the gully.

Beyond there, in the trail, easily seen in the starlight at such blank range, Tuss sat his horse. Just past him a stunted cottonwood loomed black against the night sky, marking, Kirby figured, the agreed meeting place — if indeed there was to be a meeting.

There was.

Presently a poorwill whipped sleepily out on the prairie. Tuss whistled back, the first poorwill whipping twice in reply. Ear to the ground, Kirby picked up the walking approach of several barefoot ponies. In another ten seconds their shadows bulked up out of the gloom, halting some yards from the waiting Tuss.

A single shadow detached itself from the group, drifted up to Tuss. Even in the uncertain starlight Kirby recognized the rider. *"Hau,"* called Satank, softly, his voice as deep and guttural as a grizzly's. And *"Hau,"* answered Tuss, his own tones giving nothing to the Indian's for depth and vibrancy.

"We meet again," said the chief, to Kirby's vast relief addressing his white accomplice in good English. Kiowa was not one of the red tongues Kirby savvied, and sign language was out in such a darkness.

"Yeah. I take it ye got my message from Council Grove? And thet ye took care of the Pawnee whut brung it?"

"*Hau.* The Panani found us camped a day beyond where we now talk. We killed him when he had spoken."

"Whut did he tell ye?"

"That you had many guns and would make a treaty with Satank."

"Thet's right."

"How many?"

"A hunderd, fer *you.*"

"How many all guns?"

Kirby could sense Tuss's hesitation, thought the renegade might well hesitate. Dealing guns to an Indian was about as risky as a man could get.

"Four hunderd," said Tuss at last, flat defiance in his growl. This time Satank hesitated, but then only asked softly, "What is to be done?"

"Ye know the Point of Rocks?"

"*Hau.* Across the desert. Across the water you call the Cimmaron."

"Right. Past the Jornada, across the Cim-

118

maron. Ye'll bring the guns to me thar, at Point of Rocks."

"You are a fool. I will keep the guns. I will keep them all."

In his gully, Kirby smiled. The damn red sons were all alike. Right to the point. No tricks. Happen they figured they had you by the short hair, you were in for a sore scalp.

"Yeah, I thought thet all out —" Tuss's voice suspended the sentence, passing the move to the Kiowa.

"What have you thought?"

"Thet Satank is well known. A great chief. Thet the Grandfather in Washington would know right whar to find Satank if he should hear thet Satank got those guns. Thet the Pony Soldiers would get Satank because they would know thet he had done this bloody thing."

"Where do you see the blood? You did not say there would be a fight."

"Of course thar'll be a fight, ye red idjut. And the way I got it figgered, at least three whites will get kilt. By the *Injuns*, Satank. And thet's *murder*. The Grandfather will call it *murder*, and he hangs his children fer thet. Ye know thet as well as I do."

"But I shall stay out of sight. None shall know that Satank did this thing. None but the wagon chief. And that is you, and we shall kill you, too. What then?"

"Now look h'yar, Satank. This ain't the first time me and ye've worked out a business deal.

119

Is my tongue straight?"

"Your tongue is straight. We have dealt before."

"All right. I know ye. And I know ye'd sculp me in a minute fer *one* gun, let alone four hunderd. Is thet right?"

"It is a true thing."

"Wal, listen to this, then. I have made signs on a paper. This paper is with the great chief, Blunt, in Taos. If I am nor thar in three weeks to get this paper back, Blunt Chief will open it. Ye savvy who Blunt Chief is?"

"I have heard of him."

"All right. Inside thet paper are more signs. Heavy medicine. To pertect me. Telling about how Satank took the guns. Ye savvy?"

"What do you think Blunt Chief will do when he reads your medicine signs about Satank and the guns?"

"Best way fer ye to find thet out, chief, is *not to* deliver them guns whar and when I tell ye."

Kirby whistled silently to himself. There might be a lot of things Tuss didn't have. But guts wasn't one of them.

The mountain man had never heard a colder bluff, thought sure Satank would call the white traitor on it. To his surprise the chief folded. Tuss had figured mortal close, and dead right. Forty mules full of Holy Irons against the southern Plains Indians' universal respect for William Blunt, and the fact that the red sons were beginning to get it through their copper-coated skulls that if the white man could prove a particular Indian did a particular scalping, he would hang him for it. Two thin deuces against four hundred muzzle-loading aces — and the pig-eyed wagon boss had stolen the pot!

"You are not a fool," grunted the Kiowa. "The guns will be at Point of Rocks. Satank sought but to test your heart."

"The hell!" snorted Tuss. "Ye don't trust me and I don't trust you. Ye'd sculp me and steal them guns if ye could. Seem's they'd hang ye fer it, ye won't do it! That's all."

"*Hau*," nodded Satank, a trifle too fast and easy to Kirby's thinking. "Where do we seize the guns?"

"Happen ye know Walnut Crick?"

"*Hau.*"

"All right. The guns will be in the first three wagons. Ye got thet? The first three goddams will have the guns in them." Kirby smiled at the use of the word, knowing the Kiowas and Comanches called the Santa Fe freight wagons "goddams" from the association of them with the constant strings of the word in question from the rageful lips of the mule skinners who drove them. "Now then," Tuss was continuing, "we'll camp this side of Walnut Crick. Thet'll be tomorry night. Next mornin' I'll put the three goddams with the guns in them acrost the crick, first. I'll be drivin' the fourth goddam and I'll mire it in the crick. When ye see me stuck, ye jump the three wagons that are al-

121

ready acrost, and run them off. Ye'll have to kill the drivers."

Satank grunted, very pleasantly, Kirby thought.

"Have ye got three bucks whut kin skin a mule team?" Again Satank grunted assent, and Tuss concluded. "Good. When ye've shot the skinners, drive the goddams out of sight along the trail. I'll see nobody follers ye. Then unload the guns onto ponies and make tracks fer Point of Rocks. I'll meet ye thar in seven suns. Ye got all thet?"

"*Hau.*"

"Ye got it straight about the sign-paper in Taos? With Chief Blunt?" Another grunted nod from the Kiowa.

"Fine. Now get goin' and keep out'n sight of the train. I don't want my scout seein' no Kioways tomorry. Ye savvy thet scout, Satank?"

"The Big One? The crazy one who rides in his white skin only?" Kirby felt complimented by the obvious interest in Satank's questions.

"Thet's the one. He's a sharp-eyed devil. Ye don't fool him none."

"I believe this," grunted the Kiowa, admiringly. "He is a chief."

"I got to go," said Tuss, ignoring Satank's statement. "Think about thet sign-paper in Taos."

"Satank is thinking of it."

Kirby waited five long minutes after the last shadow had melted off the trail, then swinging wide, ran for the wagons. His long legs ate up the darkness, but swift as they were, his mind outran them. So far, so good. But if Tuss beat him back to camp, to come looking for him and find him gone — !

Things moved fast back at the wagons. Kirby found Sam waiting for him with the news that Don Pedro wanted to see him at once. As the young scout started off, Sam warned him, acidly. "And be damn keerful whut ye say to Armijo. Popo has mebbe told him about ye follerin' Tuss, but play it dumb. Remember, we don't yet know fer certain whar Armijo stands."

"Ye're fer right, we don't," nodded Kirby, grimly. "I'll play it as dumb as I know how."

"Wal, don't strain yer milk tryin'. Ye kin be a'plenty ignorant without strugglin' to make a job of it, 'Hackamore Boy'!"

Sometimes a man wished he didn't walk like a cat — and see like one, too. Sometimes a man could do better making a little noise when he walked up on people. And sometimes he'd be happier if he didn't see so good.

The two figures stood close-bound as pages in a book. As Kirby came up, Don Pedro muttered a Spanish oath, stepping quickly back. Aurélie swung around, startled, lips still half parted with the passion of the interrupted kiss.

"Beg pardon, ma'am." The young mountain man's words were as hushed as had been his

123

approaching footfalls. "I didn't see ye all."

"I, I was just —" The girl's voice faltered in mid-sentence, letting Kirby imagine the quick bite of the white teeth on the full lower lip. He was glad, all the same, that she'd stopped herself short of lying to him.

"Miss St. Clair was just going." Don Pedro finished the sentence for her, his way as easy as though he and old Ceran's girl had been sharing a tin of coffee instead of each other's lips. Kirby, turning his shoulder on the girl's shadow, heard her quick-caught breath behind him, then the running footsteps dying away. "Now then, Randolph" — the scout didn't miss the omission of the usual "Mister" as the don's velvety voice stiffened — "I'd appreciate straight talk. We're in some sort of trouble here. I don't know what it is but I intend finding out if you're involved in it. Where did Mr. McLawry go tonight?"

Kirby laughed right out. "Hell! I'm not his wet nurse. He went to take a walk fer all I know."

"You know what I mean, please."

"I don't know a damn thing. Popo told me Tuss wanted me to stay at the wagons and run the guard command, while *he* scouted the Kioway, personal. And by yer orders, by God. Wal, I stayed."

"Indeed, Mr. Randolph? Now really, sir, don't you think you should have come to me and inquired what was going on when the wagon boss gave such an odd order in my name? Surely you must have thought it peculiar?"

"Naturally. I ain't no damn fool, Mr. Armijo. For all I may look it."

"I assure you, you don't look it. You stayed at the wagons and slept, then. Is that it?"

"Thet's it."

"I see —" Armijo paused and Kirby could almost see him pressing his fingertips together, arching his fine black brow. "Mr. Randolph, what was your old friend doing sneaking around my tent tonight?"

Damn! He hadn't been ready for that. Sam hadn't said anything about being seen. Kirby scowled, playing dumb and honest. "I dunno. Like I told ye, I bin sleepin'."

"Well, Mr. Randolph," Kirby sensed the sardonic smile in the words, relaxed a little, "please tell him that next time he feels called upon to rendezvous with that ox woman of Miss St. Clair's, I suggest some more remote bower than just outside the back wall of my tent. A creature that size moves the very earth with her ecstasies. It was as though one were sharing one's canvas with an amorous and eminently successful bison-coupling."

"I'll tell him," said Kirby, inwardly cursing the old trapper. No wonder the old goat hadn't gotten any information out of Ptewaquin. There was just one thing a woman would rather do than jabber. Trust old Sam to

125

get her to doing it, too.

"There's an old Spanish saying," mused Don Pedro presently. " 'Be slow to close your eyes when your friends travel at night.' "

"So?"

"Mr. McLawry has been night-traveling."

"Wal, he's yer friend, he ain't mine. Whut do ye want of me anyhow, Don Pedro?"

The Spaniard's answer came only after a slow second had wandered off into the darkness. "You were night-traveling, too, Mr. Randolph."

Kirby felt the anger coming up in him, haltered it, short-up. "Thet shouldn't bother ye and yer old Spanish sayin' none. I ain't yer friend."

"Nor are you my enemy," replied Armijo smoothly, "until you declare it."

"Whut makes ye think I'd go to makin' any declarations about it?" Kirby was forgetting old Sam's injunction, his own intent to play dumb.

"Your kind always does, Mr. Randolph — fortunately."

"How come 'fortunately'?"

"Because it allows lesser men to beat you. It's your Achilles heel, Mr. Randolph. It's some sort of quirk in the gringo mind, some Anglo-Saxon vanity. You Americans enjoy a good killing as much as does any son of old Castilla. Yet you must forever be crying the intent before the deed. As though death were something to be hawked abroad before being handed out. Have you any English blood?"

"Whut ain't American. Why fer?"

"I thought so. You're quite chivalric. Always the fair warning, is that it, Mr. Randolph?"

Kirby had been trailing the young don's rambling remarks pretty well but now he was beginning to run a circle on them. "I don't foller ye. I ain't bin tryin' to warn ye. Are ye tryin' to spur me, Mr. Armijo?"

"No, I'm not. And yes, you did." The mountain man sensed the thin smile back in the voice. "A moment ago you most certainly warned me. Exactly, I think you said, 'I ain't yer friend.' That was your English blood. Always the *'en garde'* before the *'coup qui porte.'* It's a bad habit, Mr. Randolph. I suspect it will kill you one day."

Kirby, squatting in the darkness, knew that his original and subsequent hunches that this tall young caballero was a plenty-dangerous hombre had been as right as calf-bait in a wolf trap. "I got a notion ye're crazy as hell," he said, suddenly. "Ever hear of Don Quixote?"

"*Caray!* But of course."

"Wal, if he didn't invent this chivalry business, he fer sure put the finishin' touches to it. And blamed if he wasn't a Spaniard."

"Yes?"

"So I reckon ye've bin warnin' me, too, Mr. Armijo."

The don laughed delightedly. It was a boyish sort of laugh, sounding genuine to Kirby, and Kirby was a man who had always found it tough to hate a fellow who could laugh right out and mean it. "Why, goddamit, Randolph! *Touché! Touché!* You've got the makings of a gentleman. But look now. Don't blame poor old Cervantes. My great-grandmother was *Inglés.* A duchess, I believe."

"Wal, I'll go along, Mr. Armijo." Kirby grunted the statement with intentional ignorance of the momentary friendliness in the other's tones. "We're in fer trouble tomorry, I'm thinkin', and a leetle sleep won't bother none of us."

"You still insist on shielding McLawry?" If a smile had been in the voice a moment gone, it was patently absent now. Kirby caught the change in tone, used it in his answer.

"By God, I ain't shieldin' the buzzard. Whut would I know about whar he went tonight? I didn't foller him."

"I think you did." The Spaniard's words slammed onto the end of the mountain man's angry denial like a banged-shut door. But when they continued they had gone soft and persuasive again. "I think you did and I think you know exactly where he went, and what he did there. If I'm right, I'll ask you to remember there are other lives than our own involved in harm to this train."

For a moment, thinking of the very real truth in the don's shrewd guess, and of the danger that truth presented to Aurélie, Kirby was on the verge of blurting out about Tuss and

Satank. Then the natural caution of the trained hunter reached up and grabbed his tongue, as the thought of the girl in Don Pedro's arms made it hesitate. "Ye're thinkin' crazy," he finally lied. "I never left old Thorpe's wagon. If ye think I did ye'd best start callin' me a liar. And if ye start callin' me, ye'd best mean it."

"We'll call no names, Mr. Randolph. Morning will come and with it, light. You will see how a Latin differs from an Anglo Saxon. *Buenas noches, señor.*"

Kirby started to leave without answering. Don Pedro called softly after him. "You've had *your* warning, Randolph. You won't get another."

Kirby stood a moment, looking back through the darkness. "Thanks," he grunted. "Now, I'll give ye a tip. Don't expect no Anglo-Saxon vanities from neither me nor Tuss. Ye've got a leetle to learn about mountain men, Mr. Armijo."

The Spaniard's answer came quickly. "As for you!" there was that laugh again, "I expect much. As for McLawry, *mierda!* Vanities are human frailties, Mr. Randolph. One doesn't look for them in animals. *Hasta la vista!*"

"Go to hell," growled Kirby.

# 9

Because of the presence of the Kiowa war party, or so he said, Don Pedro ordered the wagons to wait for clear daylight before breaking the square and catching up. At seven he called the entire company into the square. He had, he said, an announcement of some importance to make.

As the men gathered, the usual ribald humor and raucous profanity were strangely absent. An uneasy quiet set in and grew. Kirby and Sam were the last ones to appear. Sam had been given the whole story of Kirby's tracking of Tuss and its sequel of the interview by Don Pedro. Both he and Kirby felt their suspicions that the don was in league with Tuss and merely trying to stampede a confession of knowledge of the fact out of Kirby were well founded. Consequently, when they heard of the Spaniard's order for a general assembly at his tent, they had a fair idea that whatever trouble was building would find them, or at least Kirby, in its middle. Accordingly, and at Uncle Thorpe's insistence, Kirby had accepted the dead Clint's pistol, a nearly new Johnson Flintlock altered to percussion, and had strapped its worn-holstered weight low to his right side.

Don Pedro was sitting on a pile of duffle before his tent, apparently absorbed in cleaning and oiling a beautifully worked, double-barreled Spanish pistol. As the two friends approached, he glanced up, nodding.

"Good morning, gentlemen. Are we all here?" He made no motion to rise or to continue speaking and after a moment Tuss spoke for the group.

"All h'yar, Mr. Armijo. Whut's the idee?"

Still fondling the slim pistol, Don Pedro looked pleasantly around the ring of men, shrugged, arched his delicate brows, sighed with regret. "The 'idee,' Mr. McLawry, is that we have a traitor in camp."

Kirby saw Tuss start, but that was because he had been watching him. The others missed the boss's flinch for the good reason that most of them had shifted their eyes to Kirby as the don spoke. The slender Spaniard went on, his gaze, too, now shifting to the scout.

"Someone went out of this camp last night, presumably on an honest Indian scout."

Tuss had it in him now, and he had to get it out. He was sly, Tuss was, in the way a loafer wolf is sly. Far too cagey, now, to play dumb to the don's implication. "Are ye talkin' about me, Mr. Armijo?" His heavy voice expressed disbelief. "I went on a scout last night." At once all eyes flicked from Kirby to the wagon boss.

131

"Yes, I know, Mr. McLawry. But you weren't the only one who went scouting last night. Mr. Randolph felt called upon to leave camp, also."

Watching Tuss, Kirby could see this was news to the wagon boss. The big man was quick to sense the sudden shift of the conversation. It was clear now that Don Pedro suspected the new scout. For a bad moment Tuss had looked like he was thinking it was himself the young don was after. Greedily, he took Don Pedro's carefully thrown bait. "I told the lousy son to stay in camp," he grumbled. "I don't trust him."

"Neither do I, Mr. McLawry. But may I ask why you had him stay in camp while you yourself went scouting?"

"Sure. Like I said. I don't trust him. He's smart. Savvies them Injuns. And him and his partner lost their whole stake to the Pawnees. I figgered he wouldn't be above strikin' a deal with these Kioways to run off the mules. When a man needs money he'll do most anything. Even traitor on his own blood."

"Excellent!" Don Pedro bobbed his head in appreciation of Tuss's loyalty. "And did you see any Indians, Mr. McLawry?"

"Nary a one."

"You, Mr. Randolph?"

"I didn't go out."

"Oh, come now, Mr. Randolph. I know you did. Popo's first loyalty is mine, you know. You went out, Mr. Randolph, and after Popo had

132

told you it was my orders that you were to stay in camp. That's what you told Popo to tell Randolph, isn't it, Mr. McLawry?"

"Yes sir!" barked Tuss. "I fer sure did, Mr. Armijo. Figgered ye'd want it thet way."

"Fine, fine. Now, gentlemen —" Don Pedro eased gracefully to his feet, holstering the pistol with a flexing speed that Kirby made sudden note of. "One of you is lying. I'm satisfied you were both out last night. I'm also satisfied that one of you had no business being out last night. I'm satisfied, too, that I know which one it was. It is getting on in the morning and we've a long trail today. Let us find out if I have picked the right man."

He paused, making a slow nod in the direction of first Kirby, then Tuss. "You are both armed with pistols. I am going to count slowly to three. At some time during that count, choose your own time, please, the one of you who feels he is the subject of my little talk had better us his pistol — on me. For at the conclusion of the count of three, I am going to gut-shoot my man. I present this little warning out of a mutual respect Mr. Randolph and I enjoy for the Anglo-Saxon vanities. Right, Mr. Randolph?"

Kirby stepped back, one pace, quick and quiet as a cat. As he went, his hand hung motionless and fingerspread a foot from the protruding butt of Clint's pistol. "Ye kin start countin', Mr. Armijo. Ye was never righter."

133

Tuss, until this moment, tense with the lingering traces of uncertainty as to Don Pedro's target, relaxed into a rare phenomenon for him. A smile.

Don Pedro, never taking his eyes off Kirby, spoke quietly. "Ready gentlemen —"

Kirby felt his stomach balling up, felt the small of his back draw in like a clenching fist.

"One —"

Neither Kirby nor Tuss flicked an eyelid, the former, mask-faced, the latter still grinning.

"Two —"

Kirby's mouth corners twitched, drew down. Tuss let his grin loosen a notch. Don Pedro stood relaxed, graceful, looking at neither man, seeing both.

"Three — !"

Kirby had a crazy flash to drive for his gun, fought it down, held his hand precisely motionless. Don Pedro still had made no gesture toward his own pistol.

"Gentlemen, I'm disappointed. The guilty one is not alone a traitor, but a coward. So much for chivalry you see, Mr. Randolph. Now I am forced to shoot a man down in deliberation. And all because," here a helpless gesture of the long hands, heavenward, "lacking the finer instincts of a gentleman, he fails to comprehend 'en garde' when he hears it."

"Go ahead, give it to him." Tuss's rumble was hoarse, the brute smile still spreading the thick lips. "The damn Siwash sure has it comin'."

It was ironic that one who had lived without smiles should die with a fat one on his face. "Indeed he has, Mr. McLawry." Don Pedro let his gaze leave Kirby for the first time, turned his body slowly with it to face the wagon boss. "Indeed he has!" Tuss's tiny eyes had time to widen but the grin was too slow in leaving. It was still smeared, sick-white, across his face when the two slugs from the Spanish pistol smashed into it.

Don Pedro, the smoking weapon held carelessly, stood gazing thoughtfully down on the mountainous mortal remains of Tuss McLawry. "I shouldn't have done it," he shrugged deprecatingly to Kirby, who had come up to stand across the body from him.

"Leetle late fer them sentiments, ain't it?" The young scout's gray eyes searched the Spaniard's swart face with the question.

"You misunderstand me, Randolph. I meant I shouldn't have changed my mind. It's a sign of weakness. I *meant* to blow his bowels out."

"I allow it would have bin a easier shot."

Don Pedro frowned broodingly. "I am an old woman. I have a tender heart. The belly-shot man dies so slowly. I can't bear to see a thing in such pain. Remember that, Mr. Randolph —" He unexpectedly turned the quick flash of his smile on Kirby. "That is *my* Achilles heel."

"Wal, Mr. Armijo," Kirby let the words come out slowly, the way they were forming in his mind, "fer a tender heart, ye've got a fair tough

135

heel. *Thet's* whut I'll remember."

With the flankers out on all sides, the train moved under forcing drive to the Big Bend of the Arkansas, rolled past "Hackamore Boy's Bend," as Sam had scathingly dubbed Kirby's late bathing pool, and turned west up the broad valley, following the right bank of the stream. The trail was hard sand along here, and level as a cleaned table. They made good time. When Don Pedro called the late noon halt at 2.00 P.M., they were a scant six miles from the Walnut Creek Crossing.

For Kirby, tension had been mounting all day. It was in his mind that something had to be done. Riding back to the halted wagons, now, with Walnut Creek but hours ahead, he knew that whatever was to be done had to be done quickly.

As he came in toward he wagons, Sam rode out to meet him, hand-signaling for him to wait up. The two got down off their mounts, squatting on a knoll about a hundred yards from camp. Sam had apparently been as busy thinking as Kirby. "Young un, I allow we're goin' to have to tell Armijo. Knowin' whut we do about Satank's ambush, it's got to be did."

"Ye still figger him clear on thet deal, Sam?"

"We simply got to figger he is, boy. After him gunnin' Tuss like he done."

"I reckon." Kirby's acceptance didn't come clean out, and Sam pressed him.

Current Check-Outs summary for Czarny, W
Fri Jan 04 13:36:55 CST 2019

BARCODE: 31184016344769
TITLE: The long trail back [Large type b
DUE DATE: Feb 01 2019

BARCODE: 31184015782571
TITLE: Santa Fe passage [Large type book
DUE DATE: Feb 01 2019

"Fur as I'm concerned, Armijo don't know a tarnal thing about this Walnut Crick *wickmunke*. And I allow he sure give ye the benefit of the doubt in thet gunplay this mornin'. Seems only fair we should pay him back."

*Wickmunke* was the Dakota Sioux word for trap, and Kirby nodded seriously at Sam's use of it. "I allow ye're right. And I got a plan, Sam. Popped into my head this mornin' — when Armijo wanted to leave Tuss layin' in the middle of the trail fer buzzard bait."

"I was wonderin' why ye was so hellbent fer loadin' Tuss's body in the cook wagon and totin' it along all this ways. Fur as I kin see, Armijo was right. He *would* of made top buzzard bait."

"My idee was thet we could use him fer better bait then buzzard."

"Sech as?"

"*Injun bait,* old hoss."

"How ye figger?"

Kirby grinned. "Never mind. Ye jest ride down and tell Armijo I want to talk to him, up h'yar."

When Sam returned with Don Pedro, Kirby did the talking. "Mr. Armijo, we got to do somethin' thet may run a leetle agin the current of yer Latin blood. We got to trust one another fer twelve hours."

"What's in your mind, Mr. Randolph?"

"I lied to ye about stayin' in camp last night."

"All right. I didn't lie to you about knowing that you didn't. Popo told me you followed McLawry, and I assumed from that that you were working in the best interests of all of us. However, assumptions don't save scalps. In this case your shadow had a shadow, Mr. Randolph. Popo's reputation as a tracker is legend along the South Trace, but his Latin heart beats a little less highly than that of the Anglo-Saxon. His gully was much farther away than yours. He was able to tell me only that there *was* a meeting between McLawry and the Kioway. No detail, you understand —"

"How come ye didn't leave me know all this last night?" Kirby's interrupting question was frost-brittle.

"I like you, Mr. Randolph. I wanted the story to come *from* you, not *out of* you. And I knew it would, just as it now has. It's all a matter of blood lines. Remember, Mr. Randolph?"

Kirby's answer, accepting the don's soft-smiled explanation, showed the bristle of his lifting indignation. "How come ye to include me with Tuss in thet pistol-brace this mornin', then?"

"Oh, that. Yes. A matter of simple curiosity, my friend. I wanted to see if your nerves were as good as your eyes advertise them to be."

"We've got an old American sayin'," Kirby nodded, "about whut it was got the cat kilt. Ever hear of it?"

"*Por su puesto,* but of course, señor! You mean

'curiosity'!" Don Pedro's child-bright smile was delighted with its owner's knowledge of American sayings.

"It's a bad habit, Mr. Armijo." Kirby, borrowing the don's own earlier phrasing, returned the smile only after he had honed its edges. "I suspect it'll get ye kilt one day."

"*Perfidamente! Touché* again. And now," the Spaniard's smile went as suddenly out as a wind-snuffed candle, "you were about to tell me what you found out that Popo did not. *Ne es verdad, señor?*"

" 'Verdad' as hell," snapped Kirby, fighting the growing anger of the awkwardness the elegant Spanish youth seemed always to engender in him. "Oncover yer eyes, *Patrón.* They're about to get flowed over with bad-news water. I smelled my skunk when Tuss didn't show no sign of gettin' his hump up at thet report of two hunderd Kioways in black grease and war feathers. Tuss was a old mountain man. He knowed Injuns."

"Go on. You make sense so far."

"I trailed him out. He had a powwow with thet chief which shagged me out'n the water yestiddy. I allow ye'd be interested in knowin' who thet chief was."

"Who?"

"Satank."

"That will be the young chief who's been such a terror the past two or three years?"

"It's him. He's top dog in the Arkansaw

Valley and he'll be the biggest Kioway ever lived, before he's fullgrowed." Armijo would have made one of the best monte players going, Kirby thought. He failed to bat a lid at the mention of Satank's identity.

"All right, then. Tuss met Satank. What followed?"

Kirby quickly told him, and at the end of the telling Don Pedro sat quietly for a space before asking abruptly, "What is to be done?"

"I allow we all three agree Tuss got us into this tight." The young scout's mild gray eyes traveled over both his listeners. "So I reckon it's up to Tuss to get us out'n it."

"Mr. Randolph, you're losing me again."

"Ye'll find me in a minute." The gray eyes were a little less mild, the slow drawl a trifle drier. "Satank figgers the guns will be in the first three wagons put across the crick tomorry mornin'. And thet Tuss will be drivin' the fourth. The way I see it, thar's no call to disappoint him none."

"Mr. Randolph," the young don's smile was frankly admiring, "you're an evil genius. One would almost suspect you hadn't told the whole truth about your blood lines."

"Don Pedro," Kirby's voice in turn lightened momentarily, "ye're a smart man. Thar is a hole in my pedigree. My great-grandfather was whelped in Cadiz."

"*Señor Randolfo, salud! Un compatriota. Un caballero.*"

"A mountain man," corrected Kirby, unsmilingly.

"Have it your way. My respect for you grows."

"If ye two have got done with kissin' each other, let's get on." Sam's vinegary intrusion restored cooler weather, Don Pedro following its utterance with a string of salutary admissions and orders.

"You have been open with me. I can do no less with you. McLawry and I were running those guns on our own. My uncle is interested in a certain, ah, 'cultural' movement in Old Mejico. He financed the purchase of the arms. Naturally Blunt and St. Clair would frown on official association with such an enterprise. There was need for secrecy, you understand."

Kirby's reply was blunt. As long as the Spaniard was letting down his braids, a man might as lief give him the chance to shake it all loose. "I understand everything but why ye gunned Tuss. Ye didn't have to do thet."

"Naturally not. But business minds like that of the late Mr. McLawry's, and mine, run in related channels. One way or another, he would have had to be eliminated before the Mexican delivery. I believe you Americans call it 'the one-way split.' His suspicious absence from camp last night merely presented an opportunity to effect the erasure with some air of legality. I'm sure you 'foller' me, gentlemen."

"Way ahead of ye," grunted old Sam, rearing

141

off his haunches and grabbing for his mule's reins. "Let's ride."

"One moment, please." Don Pedro and Kirby rose with the former's request. "Mr. Randolph, I will wagon-boss the train for the remainder of the journey. You and the old man shall continue as scouts. We shall go on at once to Walnut Creek, corral the wagons and proceed with your admirable plan. I agree with you that so long as Mr. McLawry has given the pledged word of the white man to Satank, we are honor bound to redeem it. Any objections?"

"Ye make me tired with yer infernal Mex fancy talk," Sam's reaction was acid. "Ye make more out'n passin' the time of day then a white man would out'n a marryin' or buryin'."

"Mr. Randolph, you'd better improve your father's manners. He's not too old to be heel-hung back of a mule and dragged a few hundred rods."

"Let's roll," said Kirby, and that was all he said.

Under Kirby's orders, a casually normal camp was made that night. A number of unusually bright cookfires were built, one, especially magnificent, being set to blaze in the very center of the wagon square. Kirby wanted nothing to interfere with young Satank's unlimited view into this last camp of the white fools.

Toasting his long-cold shins in front of the center fire, broad back to the crossing of

Walnut Creek, big head slumped wearily forward on his hairy chest, squatted late wagon boss, Tuss McLawry.

Across the fire from Tuss, the tall wagon scout and his trusted gray-haired friend, along with Uncle Thorpe and most of the other skinners, sat hunkered over their coffee. The mood of Sam and Kirby was patently jovial, their talk unusually loud. Much boisterous mention was made of Satank and his yellow pack of Kiowa curs. Obviously the cowardly dogs had not dared follow up their attack on Kirby with one on the wagon train itself. Clearly their hearts were bad, those of the goddam-drivers brave as bears. Plainly there would be no more trouble from the Kiowas. They were gone. *Wagh! H'g' un!* The crossing tomorrow would be peaceful —

During this spirited broadcast, the young scout and his aging companion did their best to cheer up their silent comrade across the fire. Each took care to move around and pat the hunched giant on the stiff shoulder from time to time, and at least three times Kirby offered him a cup of coffee.

Finally, Kirby got up off his haunches and cleared his throat for the biggest speech of his career.

"Boys" — he announced, his voice somewhere around that of a gut-gored buffalo for volume and sincerity of feeling — "Tuss ain't feelin' too well tonight. Leetle tech of pistolitis in the mouth. Makes it hard fer him to talk. He asked me to speak fer him about the plans fer tomorry."

"Wal, whut about tomorry?" Sam bellowed back, reading his lines with clear relish. "It ain't no different then any other day, be it?"

"Oh, Tuss he don't mean jest tomorry." Kirby continued the overstaged bellowing. "Fact is, Tuss don't expect no trouble at all tomorry. But he's afeered them Kioways might sometime try to get at the stuff we got on them forty pack mules. He wants us to onload the first three wagons, pack their stuff on the mules, and put the mules' stuff in them first three wagons. Thet way even if the red sons do run off the mules, they won't get the valuable stuff we got on them, now."

"Wal" — old Sam again — "thet makes sense, don't it, boys? If them Kioways was to get their hands on the stuff whut's on them mules now, we'd all be dead!"

"All right!" Kirby dropped his bellow to a confident tone that wouldn't have carried over four hundred yards on a quiet night like this one. Fellow had to be careful. Might be Indians about. "Some of ye get the stuff out'n them first three wagons whiles the rest of ye get them mules in h'yar whar we got good light to onload them by. Soon's thet's done, it's fires out and everybody to sleep fer an extry early start tomorry! Oh, and one other thing, boys," Kirby called after the departing skinners. "Tuss allows he feels too peaked to set a saddle tomorry. Says he'll drive number four wagon, instead. Thet's yers, Laredo. Says ye kin ride his geldin' fer a day or two. Thet good enough fer ye?"

"Why, shore." Laredo, a black-bearded Texas skinner of uncertain temper, grinned evilly. "I reckon I ain't forgot how to straddle a cayuse. I allow I might be a shade creaky in the seat, but not nohow as stiff as old Tuss — !"

"Don't overdo it, ye idjut!" Kirby hissed, low-voiced. "This ain't no gut-cinch we're tryin' to girth up on them red sons, ye know. One tug too many and she'll bust — sure as buffalo chips draws flies."

With the shifting of the pack mules' loads to the three lead wagons accomplished, and the camp gone dark and quiet, the hours edged nervously past midnight.

The moon, fatter now by eight days than it had been when the Pawnees fired the grass at Cottonwood Creek, loafed around until after 3.00 A.M. before it gave up and slithered wanly down over the rim of the prairie. When it went, the dark clotted in behind it blacker than the unopened paunch of a grizzly. Hunched against the off wheel of the lead Conestoga, blanket-wrapped and chilled with the cold of the ground mists snaking up from the creek bottoms, Kirby nodded.

The next thing he knew was the sharp pressure just over the right kidney which a man trained in such symptoms generally recognizes as the point of a skinning knife held firmly in his back. The instant his mind registered this thought and before he could move in answer to the registration, the powdery voice was at his ear, the soft lips so close the warmth of their breath slid along his cheek.

"*A-ah! Heyoka!* Look out, fool!" The harsh Sioux words jumped at him, the pressure of the blade easing away from his back with them.

"Damn ye!" Kirby's snarled whisper held all the honest venom of a grown man who has been made a fool of by a wet-nose kid of a girl — and for the second time since being knocked into a St. Louis gutter. "I ought by rights to slap yer —"

"You ought by rights to stay awake!" The caustic jolt came laced around with a laugh low and female enough to wilt the whiskers of any man's indignation. "Where is your hand, Kirby?"

"Whut the hell's the matter with ye? Have ye popped yer head hobbles? By God, I ain't goin' to give ye my hand. Not unless I give it to ye alongside the head!"

"I wonder if you could talk if God quit letting you use his name? Give me your hand."

Kirby held forth his hand. In the predawn dark, visibility was limited to a short arm's reach. He felt the knife haft, warm from her grasp, come into his open palm. "*Nohetto,* there you are," said the girl. "*Oha,* wear it!"

"Wear it, hell. Whut's the idee? I got a knife."

"You have now," answered the girl, and Kirby, reading the implication, reached swiftly for his belt sheath. It was empty.

"All right." The ruffles of the mountain man's dignity were still starched. "Now ye've made an idjut out'n me. Whut do ye want?"

"I want to talk to you, Kirby. You've been acting —"

"We got nothin' to talk about," interrupted the scout. "Get on back to yer blankets. Daylight's comin' on."

"Kirby, you saw me with Don Pedro last night."

No answer.

"It wasn't the way you thought, *Wasicun.*"

Still no answer.

"I wasn't kissing him."

There are limits to the endurance of any young man twenty-six, feeling the way Kirby felt. "The hell ye wasn't!" His exclamation was short and ugly.

"The hell I was!" The denial came as quick as the charge, but it came like a caress for all its sharpness.

"I don't give a damn if ye was or if ye wasn't. I reckon it's true, whut I heered about ye in St. Louie."

"What did you hear about me in St. Louis, Kirby?" Again the caress in the voice and with it, now, the soft hand stealing through the

147

darkness to find his.

At the touch of the slender fingers, Kirby's hand trembled, the tremble spreading up his arm, racing around his heart, coming to rest in the core of his belly.

"Kirby. What did you hear in St. Louis?"

It shamed a man to be that way. It made him sick. Sweaty. Cold inside.

"They said ye was a breed." His voice sounded coarse and loud, strange even to his own ears. The words came and they were his words, but yet he wasn't proud of owning them. "Thet ye wasn't all white. Thet old Marcel ain't yer uncle, he's yer father. And thet yer mother was a Injun squaw."

He went on, plunging ahead recklessly, saying what he had to say, getting out what was in him that had to come out, and yet not liking the sound of it as it came. "I didn't listen to them. I kept my ears covered. I thought they was lyin'. Now, since seein' ye with Armijo after the way ye kissed me, I reckon they wasn't. Happen ye kin allus tell color in a woman. Happen ye kin allus tell a woman ain't clear white when she lays over fer every man whut is. Color blood flows thetaway. It's why a man wants a *Wasicun* woman when he starts to lookin' fer keeps."

Across camp, the sleep-thick voices of tired men muttered briefly, the 4.00 A.M. guardshift changing over.

"Marcel St. Clair *is* my father —" The words

were so low that any stillness less than that of the prairie at predawn would have lost them. "And my mother is a chief's daughter." The shadow of her, black against the growing gray, grew noiselessly taller. She started away along the wagon's side, paused once to call softly back. "I wasn't kissing him, *Wasicun*. He was kissing me!"

By the time Kirby got that idea soaked into his heavy skull, it was too late to call after her. He hunched back against the wagon wheel, miserable now from more than the chill of the fog or the bellyfrost of thinking about tying into two hundred Kiowas. What he needed now was old Sam. Where the hell was the old raccoon? He had been the one to tell him what was wrong with him up the river. Had told him to get busy and find himself a marrying-up kind of a woman. Well, he had found her. He had found her and she wasn't white. Maybe old Sam had the answer for that, too. Where was the crotchety old goat? He had ought to be through getting the rest of those wagons rigged for tomorrow, by this time. . . .

At four-thirty, Sam eased up to the lead wagon, found Kirby as he had left him, back-propped against a wheel. "How's she smell to ye now, boy?"

"Whut ye mean, 'How's she smell to me now?' " Sam was surprised at the quick way Kirby took into him, started to snap back at him, got himself a sudden hunch something was wrong, held sagely up.

"Whut ye suppose I mean, boy? I mean over thar beyond the crick. How's she look to ye over thar?"

"I'm sorry, old hoss." Kirby's words came in his old quiet way. "I thought ye meant somethin' else. I guess them Kioways has got me jumpy."

"Somethin' has," muttered the old man. "Though I ain't knowed ye to rattle too loud on account of a few Injuns. Ye heered a thing at all?"

"Nothin' from Satank. Set down and help me listen."

The old man squatted down, handing his lit pipe over to his companion. "I jest fired her fresh. Go ahead and have a suck. Happen thar's nothin' like terbaccy to quieten down a man's nerves."

"Thanks, old-timer. I reckon thar ain't." Kirby pulled thoughtfully at the old pipe for a full minute. "Sam, I got myse'f up to whar I'm needin' a mother's advice again," he said at last.

"Wal, I know ye ain't needin' no hints on how to sculp a Kioway, so whut's the gal done now?"

"Sam, ye recollect how ye done told me to come down the river and look myse'f up a white woman —"

"Hold up thar!" The old man's voice had

gone cranky as a warped windlass. "I ain't never told ye no sech thing, damn ye. I jest said a woman. Thet thar 'white' business is yer own doin's."

"All right, a 'woman.' Leastways, I've found her."

"I allow a blind mule could have see'd thet from taw. I could have told ye when ye was layin' in thet gutter in St. Louis. And another thing, boy. Ye ain't ridin' single saddle on it, neither. Thet gal is plumb gone on ye. I meant to talk with ye about it. It's goin' to make ye trouble. Ptewaquin was tellin' me thet Don Pedro and the gal had it out, proper. Seems he wants to marry her and told her so. Then she up and tells him she's yer squaw — and she said *squaw*, boy. At thet, he grabs onto her and kisses the billy-be-hell out'n her. Jest as he does, some galoot comes up through the dark to talk to Don Pedro, and he has to let the gal go. Ptewaquin didn't see who it was, but —"

"It was me, Sam." The young scout's admission was abject. "Goddam it, it was. I ain't got sense enough to spit downwind."

"I allow ye ain't," nodded the old man, soberly. "Ye allus was clumsier then a cub bear."

"Sam, whut's a man to do? I allus sweared I was goin' to get myse'f a white woman, and h'yar I am with another damn color gal."

"Ye convinced fer sartin she's color? Ye remember I done told ye she warn't."

"I called her a damn squaw fer kissin' Armijo and dug at her about what the trappers was sayin' in St. Louie about Marcel bein' her old man, and her maw bein' a Injun. I troweled it on a foot thick. She never said nothin'. Jest sat thar. Finally, she gets up and says, 'Marcel St. Clair *is* my father and my mother *was* a chief's daughter.'"

"Is thet all?" Sam's simple inquiry seethed with contempt. He had never been able to see Kirby's convictions on color; he forgave the boy only because he allowed a little age might change them. After all, Kirby was a Southerner, and the color line had been built into his bones.

"No." His companion's words smoldered with self-scorn. "She told me she wasn't kissin' Don Pedro. Thet he was kissin' her."

"Wal?"

"Wal, she left before I could think of whut to say."

"Thinkin' never was yer long suit, son. I allow ye'd do better without worryin' whut hue a gal's skin be. They're all the same color inside, ye know."

Kirby grinned in spite of his misery. "I don't reckon many mothers would put it jest thet way, Sam. But it comes out even when ye add it up."

"Sure does. Only trouble with ye is, ye cain't add."

"I aim to start learnin', right now," said Kirby, grimly.

"Wal, not *right now*," Sam grunted. "Right now ye've got a pack of two hundred Kioways to wade through. Leastways, ye will have in about a half-hour."

Kirby nodded in response to the old man's disagreement, both of them falling silent, letting their eyes probe the lifting darkness. There was light enough now for a man to see, faintlike, halfway across camp. The Conestogas still stood in their hollow square, tongues out, as they'd been parked the night before. Nothing had been moved, with one peculiar exception. Every wagon stood team-hitched, its four span of sleepy mules full-harnessed, ready to roll. A mighty close eye, given broad daylight, could have seen one other thing. The lead team in each hitch was picketed down, hard and fast. The need for staking those leaders was the biggest gully in the wagon-trace of Kirby's plan. And there was no track around it and no way to cord it over.

The drivers who would ordinarily have been on the boxes of those twenty-one Conestogas had something a whole hell of a lot tougher than a mule to skin that morning.

They had a wolf. A red one. Breed of Kiowa. Name of Satank.

Kirby vowed the minutes were crawling after one another so slow a man would swear he could nigh hear them sucking their feet out of the mud of that last half-hour. Still, the start had to be just right — enough light for a mule skinner to see a Kiowa across an iron sight, not enough for a Kiowa to see tie ropes and picket pins across a mud creek.

"Ye still figger them to try it, Kirby?" Sam's question was plainly asking for a negative re-assurance.

"Hell, Sam, ye know as wal as me thet if ye give a Bow and Arrer Injun a whiff of rifle-iron smell, ye cain't head him."

"Wal, I was jest askin'." Sam's statement labored under a wrap of resignation. "I allow ye're right as warts on a hawg's belly."

"Shhh!" Kirby's warning hiss was followed by long seconds of intent listening.

"Whut'd ye hear?" Sam's query shook with Kiowa fever. "Shet up!" Kirby accompanied the order with an elbow jolt in Sam's ribs that like to knocked the little trapper clean out of his skins. "I thought I heered Injuns talkin' —"

In answer to the stated thought, a fox barked three hundred yards up the creek. Its mate yapped back from an equal distance downstream. Out on the plains, directly across the creeping ground mists that hid the creek bottoms, the *pee-weet, pee-weet* of a sleepy plover made known its owner's indignation at the fox yipping. The querulous chuckle of a disturbed prairie hen answered and agreed with the plover. Back in the sandhill gullies beyond the mists, a whole chorus of coyotes began a snarling bicker.

"Ye ain't jest whisperin', ye heered them

talkin' " nodded Sam, drily.

"It's light enough." Kirby's announcement came suppressed, harsh. "Let's roll!"

The two figures arose, slipping around the side of the wagon away from the creek. Cupping his hands Kirby bellowed in a voice designed to carry a day's march down the trail, "Roll out! Roll Out! Catch up! Catch up!" Immediately the morning gloom swarmed with the moving figures of men and mules. By the use of much excess shouting and harness-jangling, the *arrieros* made the hooking up of the teams to the first four wagons sound complicated enough to pass for the assembling of the whole train. In minutes, the last tug was fastened, the last harness snap checked. Loping swiftly down the line, Kirby halted at the number four wagon.

"All set, Laredo?"

"All set heah." The lean Texan nodded to the bolt-upright figure of Tuss McLawry lashed on the wagon seat. "He'll stay on."

"All right, remember, hold up a leetle to let the others get those first three wagons clean up the far side before ye barge into the crick." Passing back up to the head of the train, Kirby paused at the number three Conestoga. "Ye all set h'yar, Huff?"

"Yeah."

"Everything all right inside thar?" Kirby's question went with his head, in through the puckerhole back of the driver's box.

"Cozy as a big bung in a leetle jug!"

The answer sounded good to Kirby and he grinned. "Happen I'll give ye six sons a chance to pull that bung in a few minutes." At the number two wagon, the same questions went to young Cal Friday and his hidden litter of hard-bitten whelps. The answers were as fast and cheerful. "Now remember, Cal, keep close up. These three wagons has got to keep together. Happen the Kioways kin split us apart over thar, we're done."

"They ain't goin' to get twixt me and Sam. Jest so Huff keeps up's all ye got to worry about." Back at the lead wagon, Kirby found Sam on the box, stone pipe going full-blast. "Ready, Samuel?"

"I allow, Mr. Randolph."

"How's everything inside?"

"Fine as a broomtail colt's brush!"

"Sam, cuss it, have I fergot anything? I'm nervouser'n a chippy in church!"

"Naw. Let her rip, Kirby." The old man spat and grinned.

Kirby didn't answer. Across the creek, the mists were lifting. The grayness, thick as wool minutes before, was thinning as quick as a man watched it. Another ten minutes would bring a wonderful shooting light. A breeze blew up from the creek hollow, hitting his face damp and cool, making him know by the quick chill of it that he was sweating like a hog butcher in frost time. He threw his hand to his mouth, rolling the cry down the wagon line. The creek bank seized its echoes, multiplying them, hurling them afresh up and downstream, out across the open prairie, into the trapping ranks of the silent sandhill gullies.

"All set! Stretch out! Stretch out! Hooray fer Santy Fee!"

"Gee! Gee! *Hee-yahh!*"

"*Arriba! Arriba! Adelante!*"

"Haw thar, damn ye! Whoa! Whoa."

"*Hee-yahhh,* dammit! Hike! Hike!"

Three mule skinners, one old beaver trapper, one green trail guide, twenty-four mules and one very dead erstwhile wagon boss did their level best to create the illusion of a full twenty-five-wagon train taking the trail.

It was a fair job of selling, and Satank bought it.

Kirby put the Spanish mare down the creek bank, splashed her across, took her up the far side. She was fresh, wanting to go out ahead like she had every morning since this big *Americano* had ridden her. But Kirby held her down, close to the wagons, waiting for that first rush and splash that would tell him Sam had taken the lead Conestoga into the creek.

Behind him now the first splash hit the crossing. Sam was in. Followed two more splashes. Cal and Huff were in. Trace-chains jangling, axles squealing, snorts, hoof thuds, whipcracks, curses. Sam was up the bank and out, rolling his Conestoga right behind Kirby. Hee-yahh! Harrup thar! Cal was up. Hike! Hike! Lay into it, yuh bastards! That would be Huff. Up and rolling. All three of them right behind him now.

There it was. The fourth splash. Laredo had Tuss's Conestoga in. "Whoa theah! Hold up, goddamit, you're mired in. Whoaahh! Hold up them other wagons, boys, Tuss is stuck tight, heah. Hold 'em in, Tuss, dam yuh! Whut the hell's the mattuh with yuh? Cain't yuh heah nothin'?" That was it. The fourth wagon. In and stuck, fast. Now!

Ahead of Kirby the prairie lay flat for miles. To his right, more of the same. On his left squatted the low sandhill gullies. Those sandhill gullies, now, that's where it had to come from — and that's where it did come from.

Laredo's mid-creek yell had no more than bent the grasstops on its way in among the shallow gully ridges than it was picked up there and flung echoing back. Only the echo sounded a hell of a lot more like Kiowa wolf howl than it did a Santa Fe skinner's shout. Even as Kirby drove his moccasins into Bluebell, the gullies split open and began spitting out a red vomit of Kiowas.

The hostiles were on top of the Conestogas almost before the skinners got them stopped. Kirby barely had time to haunch-slide Bluebell in alongside Sam's rearing mules and go diving in through the puckerhole back of the driver's box. Then the Kiowas were on them, swarming and snarling like a pack of village curs closing in on a pile of fresh buffalo guts. They literally engulfed the three motionless wagons, burying them under an avalanche of neighing ponies and screaming riders.

But as this multi-hued horde reached the waiting Conestogas a notable and unnatural phenomenon took place. It was neither the time nor climate for five-thousand-pound freight wagons to go to noisily budding out. Nevertheless, the three wagons did just that.

It is sure the prairie never before beheld quite such a spontaneous burgeoning of unsuspected life.

White Osnaburg top sheeting found itself as suddenly flung off as water from a wet dog's back. All around the edges of the bright blue wagonbeds of the Conestogas, gorgeous black blossoms with stabbing flame-orange centers and whistling lead stamens began bursting into riotous bloom.

While laboring mightily to supply his share of the black smoke and bright fire blossoms, Kirby couldn't help admiring the effect of the cheery gardens beginning to grow around the booming Conestogas. The loveliness of the plots was especially enhanced by their swiftly growing borders of quiet red bodies.

Momentarily stunned by their reception, the Kiowas now pulled away to reorganize. They had expected no resistance at all. Had run into all that could conveniently be put up by twenty-three salt-tanned mule skinners and two hardlot mountain men, firing free and fast from limitless stacks of loaded rifles.

But now it would be different. This time it would be different. This time they were ready. This time Satank knew what he was going into. No loose mass charge, this time. *Wagh!* This time they would hit the *Wasicun* in waves. Fifty to the wave. Satank and his fifty, first. Of course. Then Yellow Fox. Then Bad Liver. Lastly, High-Shoulder-Wolf. All ready? Are the hearts all brave? *KyHeda-bH!* Let's go to fight!

And go they went, Satank first, as promised, his splash of howling riders smashing squarely at Sam's wagon. Kirby fired, threw a gun away, grabbed another from the pile in the middle of the wagonbed, fired again. Sam was doing the same, as were the seven skinner's who had been hidden, with a hundred of Don Pedro's smuggled Holy Irons, in Sam's wagon. The other two Conestogas, in turn, each armed and manned alike — one driver, seven hidden teamsters, a hundred guns — were breaking out their barrages as Yellow Fox followed Satank in, leading his braves at Cal's wagon, and Bad Liver followed him, taking his frantically yelling pack down onto Huff's vehicle.

High-Shoulder-Wolf waited.

The Kiowas' second try was better than their first. Half a dozen of the crazy devils actually got into the wagons and had to be butt-clubbed to death. It was hot and nasty for about three or four minutes, and Kirby was so busy grabbing and firing rifles, ducking arrows and lances and repelling club and axe-armed "boarders" that for those fateful minutes he had no chance to know whether his teamsters were winning or losing the wild fray. Then he began to see the attack breaking up.

One hundred and fifty is a lot of Kiowas to handle at lance-length, but two dozen good shots with three hundred rifles stacked and loaded to hand can down a sinful lot of redskins. Especially when the range was so close Kirby allowed a man could spit the red scuts to death. Leastways he almost could when he was doing that spitting from back of a three-inch, oak-plank wagonbed!

The red assault wavered, began to lap back.

It was then High-Shoulder-Wolf quit waiting. It was then The-Wolf-With-The-Tall-Withers came barreling in, the rattle of his ponies' hoofs on the dry ground serving to rally his failing companions around the Conestogas, rallying them and throwing the whole Indian surge, reinforced by his fifty fresh braves, back against the arrow-spattered wagons.

As they came, Kirby gave a groan and yelled at Sam. "Dammit! As though we ain't got enough trouble! Lookit yonder. I told thet damn fool to stay in the crick no matter whut."

"Yonder" was back toward the creek

crossing, and "thet damn fool" was Laredo, the Texas skinner, blacksnaking his eight braying steeds and two-and-a-half-ton chariot directly toward the beleaguered wagons. Sam's answering yell was as loud as Kirby's but a shade more cheerful.

"The son of a gun'll get hisse'f kilt, same as ye're goin' to. So let him come, whut do ye care? The more the merrier. Goddam. Did ye see me get thet un? Shot him right through the belly as he was pullin' a bow. The ball twisted him around so's when he let fly, the errer go'd squar into the buck next to him. Hit the red son right in the side of the head! *Hiii-eeee-yahhh!*" Sam finished off with the Oglala Sioux panther scream, and Kirby grinned.

"Save yer breath, old hoss. H'yar comes Satank agin!"

"Hell! Ye're crazy about them comin' again. Lookee thar. By God, they're goin'!"

Following the old man's wild-flung gesture, Kirby could see that the outer ranks of the hostiles, led by young Satank himself, were pulling away, upvalley — away from the careening approach of Laredo's Conestoga. "Sam, they're afraid of Laredo's wagon. The sons must figger it's full of men and guns like these three!"

"Ye're right! Sam, old hoss, ye're right! Hooray fer Laredo!" By this time the Texas skinner had hauled his plunging hitch to a stop alongside Sam's wagon, and the old man yelled at him. "Fer cripes sake keep yer top canvas tight. If them Kioways see ye ain't totin' a load of reinforcements, they'll come back on us like a bellyful of Taos chili!"

"Like hell!" Kirby's denying shout was exultant. "They're pullin' their lodges fer keeps. Lookit them scuts go! Laredo, dammit, ye're a hero!"

Kirby's asseveration regarding young Satank's plans proved right. With a wit and brevity of decision which spoke well for his already considerable reputation as a red field commander, the Kiowa chief had suddenly remembered a previous engagement elsewhere — a previous engagement he would worry about making as soon as he could put about ten miles between him and the *Wasicun* devils in those four blue goddams back there.

As Kirby's accolade went to Laredo, the swart Texan uncovered his canines with what passed for a grin down his way. "Yuh-all got a hero heah, but it shore ain't me. No suh. Me, I was jest fixin' to climb down off'n thet drivuh's box and hit the hell foh the corral afoot, when some jaspuh speaks up behind me, cool as a mason in Mobile. 'Drive right on up thet fah bank, mistuh,' he says, 'and keep agoin' till yuh get alongside Mistuh Randolph's Conestogah.'

"Unduh the circumstances, I drove — seein' as how I don't nevah argue with none of three things: a gun, a mule, or a *woman!*"

"A woman!" The combined exclamations of Laredo's listeners, paced by Kirby and Sam,

163

echoed in disbelief.

"Yeah. A ordinary, two-laigged, female woman. Ma'am —" Laredo's tough voice went gentle on him as he turned to the puckerhole behind him. "Yuh-all kin quit proddin' me in the liver-lights with thet Hawkens, now. We're heah. Wheah yuh said. Right alongside Mistuh Randolph's wagon."

Followed a silence then, while all eyes, now conscious of the black barrel poking into Laredo's shortribs, watched the badly shaking weapon slowly withdraw and disappear into the Conestoga. A moment later, Aurélie's dusky face appeared in the puckerhole, the green eyes wet with tears, the low voice uncertain. "Oh, Kirby, I'm sorry. I-I just wanted to — Oh, I'm sorry, that's all. I'm just sorry!"

The silence could have been sliced with a square spade. Young Cal Friday blew his nose. Sam coughed. Kirby blinked and narrowed his eyes. "Hell, ma'am." The young scout's voice was so low that nobody caught the tremble in it. "It ain't no crime to run off a couple of hunderd Kioways, singlehanded. I allow ye ain't done nothin' wrong, more than likely savin' twenty-six white men their scalp-hair."

# 10

New wagon scout Kirby Randolph found his big hands full that bright May morning following the Kiowa attack at Walnut Creek. First things were taken first.

Left over from the out-of-season blooming of the mountain man's four-wheeled flowerbeds were half a dozen injured mules and three still-crawling savages. These were quickly singled out and shot, the mules first, as befitted their prior places in the hearts of the skinners. Next, the train's minor wounded were cared for. With the exception of Uncle Thorpe, these amounted to nothing more serious than lance slashes and arrow scratches, abraded skulls and powder burns. But the former had taken a razor-headed war arrow squarely through the bone and cartilage of his right knee.

While Cal and Huff held the old man's arms, Kirby cut the head of the arrow off behind the knee and pulled the shaft out from the front. Uncle Thorpe winced, got up, hobbled a few steps, and allowed he was as good as new. Kirby, watching the way he put his teeth in his lip when he said it, reckoned the oldster wasn't well just yet.

With Thorpe on his feet, the rest of the train was brought across the creek, the guns reloaded on the pack mules, fires set and coffee boiled. After that, Tuss was planted shallow, without a reading, and the wagons stretched out and got to rolling.

Sam, heading the train, the late afternoon sun slashing into his squinted gaze, anxiously searched the prairie ahead. Kirby should be back. He'd been gone all of four hours. The wagons would have to be halted and corralled up before long. Dammit now, why did a body Sam's age have to have a wetnose like Kirby to fret over? Suddenly the old man stopped frowning, started grinning. The south wind, coming up the trail from out of the low swale which hid its next mile, was packing the most elegant voice in Sam's world.

Kirby cantering up out of the swale a moment later, broke his song to shout at the scowling graybeard, "Hey! Stretch them out, old hoss. We got clear rollin' two mile ahead to the purtiest campin' ye ever see'd!"

Waving the teamsters to pick up their pace, the young scout pulled in alongside Sam, spending the next jogging hour in telling about the growing beauty of the country beyond. When he had run down, Sam thought a minute, then asked, "Ye didn't see nothin' of the Kioway? It seems damn peculiar they ain't tailin' us."

"I ain't said they ain't," replied Kirby. "I allow they are. I jest ain't see'd no sign of it, thet's all."

Sam scowled. "Anything else strike yer rovin' eye? I mean exceptin' how all-fired purty the country is?"

"Wal, yeah. Country's powder-dry up ahead. Ye kin raise dust enough to choke a short dog by spittin' in the trail."

"Wal?"

"Wal, thar's plenty buffler, too. I seen loads of sign and two, three big herds, fur off. They was all driftin' south, not grazin' much and not beddin' none. Hard to tell from the distance, but appeared to me they was bein' drove."

"Naw!"

"I reckon. We'll know tomorry, sure."

"Whut ye figger?"

"Like I said — country's bone-dry. Next water south is Ash Creek, whar we're campin' tomorry night. Thar's water in the Arkansaw. Left to themse'fs, I'm thinkin', the buffler wouldn't hardly be leavin' it."

"Thet how come ye figger they're beein' hazed? Whut's the idee, ye suppose?"

Kirby looked ahead, scanning the rise of the prairie beyond the trail. "Drift a big herd two days without water. Then sundown of the second day they get upwind of Ash Crick. They're smellin' water, they's a jillion of the shaggy critters, and the only thing twixt them and a good drink is twenty-five wagons and four-hunderd-odd mules. Ye figger it from thar."

Sam was silent for several seconds, his ragged beard following the thought-twists of his mouth. "It ain't hard," he said, finally. "We're campin' dry tonight, and by tomorry our stuff'll have to get to thet water, too. I jest hope ye're wrong about them buffler bein' drove, boy!"

"We'll know tomorry," repeated Kirby, turning in his saddle to wave up the wagons. "Yonder's our spot fer tonight."

The following day they made the remainder of the nineteen miles to Ash Creek, their flanks, point, swing and drag, being covered the entire way by shoal after shoal of nervously drifting buffalo.

Since early morning they had been winding through one immense herd of the surly brutes. It was a tricky, touchy business, requiring the utmost in care and knowledge of their habits to avoid stampeding the drifting thousands into a rushing jam that could flatten every wagon and human in the train in the course of a handful of bellowing minutes. Kirby knew the black-horned devils as few men did, knew that in sailing his Santa Fe schooners through such a vast, restless sea of them, he was making an un-avoidable but very dangerous tack.

A buffalo had a built-in dislike of being headed, he knew, and would go far to avoid crossing the trail behind the wagons. Instead he would try to press on ahead of the lead wagons, increasing his speed accordingly. In doing this he soon picked up the speed of the whole herd, the bulls in the rear beginning to run to catch up, pushing their fellows ahead to greater speed, and in short order, if the wagon guide were green or his caravan inexperienced, starting a first-class stampede.

And when you get close to a hundred thousand wildeyed monsters, each crowding a ton in weight, galloping blindly over and through you, you've got yourself a *real* stampede. Fearing this, Kirby had kept the wagons at a crawl all day, keeping the pace down where the leaders of the menacing escort could easily keep ahead of the caravan.

By midafternoon their progress had slowed to a practical standstill and, as Sam joined Kirby at the head of the stalling train, all doubt as to the origin of the great herd's paralleling movement had been dispersed. Not a feather tip nor a pony print had been seen since daylight, but the mountain men now *knew* what they had only suspected the night before.

"How do ye see her now, son?" The old trapper's narrowed eyes swept the vast brown tide lapping in on them from every point of the prairie compass.

"Ye don't have to ask me thet, old-timer. Them bulls bin walkin' into the wind all day. Thet means jest one thing."

"Yeah." The old man's answer was short. "They're bein' drove, all right. Damn them lousy Kioways."

"Wal, Sam, drove or not drove, we got to get through them to our water. Yonder's Ash Crick, two mile to the left, thar."

"Yep. Ain't nothin' fer it but to swing left and head fer thet crick, Kirby boy. We could drift from h'yar to the Rockies before the black buzzards might open up to let us out."

"Uh-huh." Kirby's grunt was absent-thoughted, his scowling gray eyes studying the surge of the great stream passing on their left. They had to go through here, somewhere. And they had to go quick. "Sam," the young mountain man's voice cracked with tension, "I'm goin' to swing the wagons right h'yar. Either they're played out enough to split and let us through peaceable, or they'll start runnin' on us. We ain't got no choice, nohow." With the words, Kirby turned, giving the backward handwave that would turn the train left and south into the very belly of the rumbling herd.

They reached the creek without further incident, the herd, seized by one of the unpredictable impulses common to cattle, wild or otherwise, parting as meekly as so many muley cows to let the wagons rumble through without so much as a tail lift or dust-paw challenge.

Over the objections of older heads than his own in such matters, Kirby ordered the wagons parked in an unorthodox open V, the point aimed in the outer-prairie direction from whence the buffalo must come, the open end of the letter backing on the creek. He selected a sharp bend where the stream looped back tightly on itself to form a pocket of good-grassed land, thus achieving a defensive position which had the glummest of the skinners nodding their heads in approval. This young rooster was no ninny. He would do to ride the trail with.

After he got his wagons the way he wanted them, parked longways with the tongues in, thus protecting the tongues and obtaining the widest possible V, he ran a reinforced picket rope across the open base of the wagon triangle.

He then instructed Popo to fasten the best mules in the herd, figuring eight to a wagon, to this line. The little Mexican at once pointed out the impossibility of stringing two hundred mules on a hundred-foot picket line. "It's got to be done," insisted Kirby. "Even if we got to put the devils in harness to do it." And that was the way it was finally done; each eight-mule hitch being snubbed to the flimsy line by its leaders. It was a crazy, dangerous picket, forming a packed-solid phalanx of four lines of fifty mules each, but clearly the best they could make to halfway guarantee holding on to some of the mules.

The rest of the stock, over two hundred mule

spares, were tight-bunched in the grass pocket behind the V. Half the *arrieros,* under Don Pedro, were detailed to hold this loose herd, the other half, under Popo, stationed among the picket mules. The best of the saddle stock was brought up and tied to the rears of the two end-wagons of the V.

Checking the finished layout, Kirby shook his head, turning with the grimace, to the last remaining task.

Everyone working, Aurélie and Ptewaquin included, the company set about throwing up a bulwark across the neck of land in front of the wagon-V. When darkness halted the work, they had created, with axe, shovel, mattock and blasphemy, a breast-work of rifle pits across the entire neck. Behind this firing line they dug in, two men and a stack of Armijo's rifles to every twenty feet. In between each rifle post a dry-twig and buffalo-chip fire was laid, the lighting and refueling of these to be the assignment of Aurélie and Ptewaquin. As an afterthought, and at Laredo's hard-bitten suggestion, every wagon in the V was cross-roped and staked down, drum-tight as a circus tent. It was a precaution that was to bring many a heartfelt blessing onto the evil-grinning Texan's head before the light of another day rolled up.

By the time all this was done, and a hasty supper wolfed down, it was 9.00 P.M. For the next hour things were quiet, Kirby and Sam lying in the outer line of rifle pits, listening for the sound they knew would precede any sudden break in the buffalo's behavior — the shattering war whoops and night screeches of the Kiowa.

Meantime, up and down the creek as far as the ear could hear, the sounds of the immense herd watering and wallowing could be heard. There was sinful little wet water, Kirby allowed, and one mortal lot of dry buffalo. But if nothing happened to jump them, they might get watered by morning, and without wrecking a solitary wagon — that is, maybe they might. By the sound of things, by the tremendous uproar of pushing, shoving, bellowing, blowing and bull-roaring going on along the creek, even that outside chance was a thin one.

With each passing hour the sounds of strife among the huge animals grew. Those already in the stream would not get out of it, those behind them forcing in regardless. And behind the ones pushing at those already in the water were the uncounted tens of thousands of those still shoving in from the dry prairie. The milling, pawing, lowing and challenging was incessant, the dust pall thrown into the air by the churning animals so thick a man saw things as through a heavy rain. Kirby shuddered. Cripes! Just the noise of their unseen grinding and fighting was enough to make the ground move under him. Out there in the blackness, for miles on both sides, the water-wild behemoths were crowding and shoving in. And the wagon camp's little creek bend stuck right out into the middle of that roaring, shaggy horde, with all the assurance of a six-foot sandspit trying to outstare the piling face of the Arkansas in peak flood.

For a while the ring of lit fires served to steer the vanguards of the herd, on around the campsight, but by midnight it had become necessary to begin shooting into them to split the buffalo off and away from the bend. From then until three, the men maintained a steady fire, not rapid but regular, aiming at nothing but the noise and the darkness, not trying to kill buffalo but only to keep up a constant reminder to the advancing herd that humans had preempted this tiny point of land.

The little string of warning fires helped in this direction, too, serving as a visible boundary for the crowding bulls to see and split away from. Aurélie and Ptewaquin kept the pinpoint flares in faithful blaze, while Kirby and Sam began to rove the rears of the riflemen, hawkeyeing the ring of dull light furnished by the little beacons. The purpose of this vigilance was to spot the first glint of polished horn or gleam of squinty black eye which would warn of some particularly foolhardy brute having ignored the firelights and rifle flashes to come on in, regardless. These occasional individuals were especially dangerous, since each of them constituted a potential spearhead. Where one could go, others would follow.

As these singles loomed up, froth-mouthed and head tossing, Kirby and Sam shot them, both firing at the same animal, making sure he went down where he was, quick and quiet.

About three-thirty there seemed to come a lessening of the advance, the men in the pits grabbing quick turns for the first pipe since supper. Kirby and Sam hadn't shot a single for ten minutes and it looked like the worst was over. "Sam, I think we've did it!" Kirby, feeling the lift of his second major trail victory in twenty-four hours, was jubilant. "They're slowin' up, sure as hell's hot."

"Mebbe bufflers is like Injuns — they're thar when they ain't thar." The old trapper wasn't just ready to start celebrating.

"By Tophet, Sam, we've turned them. By damn, we have! And without losin' one lousy mule!"

"Happen ye're countin' yer teams before ye get them hitched agin. Me, I don't like it. My God, boy, listen to them out thar! Thar's a million of them yet to come and we still got the Kioways to hear from."

As if to refute Sam's pessimism and bolster Kirby's elation, the next five minutes got even quieter. Then, in another five minutes of continued easy breathing, the settling herd split of its own accord to pass peacefully along both flanks of the wagon-V, and even old Sam was ready to concede Kirby his victory.

Then it happened.

First the little chip fires began winking out, half of them gone by the time Aurélie came panting up to Kirby, the other half going while she talked. "We're out of chips, mister. No more fires tonight."

She had been "mistering" him ever since he'd cut her with the color-line slur back at Walnut Creek, and Kirby, not wanting to hurry his hand and being too dog-busy anyway, had let her get away with it. He hadn't even been to thank her for the crazy dash with Laredo's Conestoga that had broken up the Kiowa ambush. Now, looking in frank admiration at the flashing green eyes and high-flushed color of her, he figured this was as good a time as any to start putting his wedge in.

"Don't worry none about it, Miss St. Clair, 'honey.'" He grinned. "We got them whupt anyhow. Ye kept yer fires burnin' when we needed them. We're out'n the buffler bull-rushes, now."

"Thanks, mister." There was no answering warmth in the acknowledgement. "Are you guaranteeing us a quiet night from here, in?"

"Unconditional, ma'am. The next sound ye hear will be Mr. Randolph's charmin' voice hollerin', 'Stretch out fer Santy Fee.'"

As a matter of hard fact, the next sound Aurélie heard was neither Mr. Randolph's voice, nor was it charming. Neither was it cheerfully calling, 'Stretch out for Santa Fe.' What it *was* doing was screaming. And what it

176

was screaming was *"Hiii-yeee-hahh!"* And who was screaming it was Satank, War Chief of the Arkansas Valley Kiowa.

"The next sound *you* hear," Aurélie's acid hiss went to Kirby, splitting the momentary silence following the Kiowa chief's war cry, "will be my little feet running like hell for the wagons!"

"Not a bad idee, ma'am." Sam moved to the girl's side. "Mind if I jine ye?"

"Please do!" The girl grabbed the oldster's gallantly proffered arm, flashing him that snowtooth smile that always managed to jump Kirby's heart. "Shall we go?"

"By all means! Give my regards to the buffler, Kirby boy!" With that, the two of them hit for the wagon-V, leaving the young scout to ponder his failings as a prophet — which same ponderings proved mercifully short. Seconds after the echoes of the first Kiowa screams died away, the ground under his feet began literally to quake and roll.

The subsequent burst of whoops and yelps from the hazing Indian riders were immediately drowned in the terrifying rumble of the onrushing bison. Those bulls were coming now and they weren't ambling and grunting and stumbling like they had been for the past six hours. The mental blocks, stunned by Satank's first scream, began falling into place in Kirby's mind.

God Amighty. Those bulls were *running.*

Wheeling, Kirby raced along behind the resting riflemen, now all alerted by the Indian yells and building buffalo noise. "Stampede! Stampede! Hit fer the wagons! Roll out! Scatter back!"

Twice he ran the length of the lines, yelling at men who were needing very little yelling at. Each grabbing a desperate armload of rifles, the entrenched teamsters leaped out of their pits and went high-rolling for the wagons. Kirby, delaying his own retreat until the last man had jumped and run, made it into the wagons a short three pony lengths ahead of the first bull to come crashing into the parked Conestogas.

Luckily, the first wave of buffalo to come driving in consisted of forty or fifty scattered front runners, rather than the solid sea wall of the main tide of the herd. "Into the wagons!" shouted Kirby. "Pull the top sheets and fire down on them from above. Ye cain't hit nothin' firin' from between them wheels. Get on top! Get on top!"

Half a dozen teamsters had sprung to the wagon seats along the point of the V at Kirby's first shout, and these, reinforced by Sam, Kirby, Ptewaquin, who handled a better gun than most of the men, Aurélie, who amazed Kirby by matching the giant Sioux squaw shot for shot, and Don Pedro who had come running up from the mule herd, got an instant stream of hot fire going down into the first of the shaggy invaders. The range was point-blank, the supply of loaded guns ample, the marksmen, sharp.

By the time the main front of the herd hit, the shooters had piled up twenty to thirty dead bulls around the point of the V. The bulking bodies of these dead bison helped a little to break the sorce of the main herd, but even so, there was no stemming them. On they came, falling and crashing over the bodies of their fallen fellows, stumbling full tilt into the rocking, shuddering wagons.

And down they went, the desperate teamsters firing at muzzle-length into their black faces, humping shoulders and thrashing flanks. God bless those stake-down ropes, now. The wagons bucked and groaned and splintered under the rending impacts of the blind-running bulls. But with God's help, and Laredo's ropes, they held!

In the end, the barrier of dead and down buffalo beyond the point of the V saved the wagon spread. The pushing herd, its original momentum slowing perceptibly, could no longer surmount that shambles of mushy carcasses. More and more they began to split around its pulpy abattoir. And ten minutes after the first headlong rush, they were streaming by both flanks of the wagon-V, shunting off north and south to plunge in twin cascades of heaving, hoarsely lowing black torrents, over the steep banks of Ash Creek.

The choked mass of them in the narrow

stream beds became shortly impassable, this sending the following thousands into a still wider split, with the result that twenty minutes saw the danger really and finally past. The dazed and shock-stupid men climbed stiffly down off the loaded wagons, threw their guns into the dirt of the wagon yard and followed them with their weary, unnerved bodies. They just sat or squatted or lay there, too nerve-shot and played out to even talk.

They were hardly beginning to recover their shaky tongues to congratulate themselves when Satank, pushing rapidly in on the heels of the herd he had stampeded, split his Kiowa in a sudden two-pronged, war-whooping rush around both sides of the wagon-V, driving pell-mell past its flanks and down on top of the mule herd behind it.

The screaming Kiowa went so close past the wagons that even in the dark and twister-thick haze of dust, Kirby spotted two or three old friends: Yellow Fox. Bad Liver. High-Shoulder-Wolf. There they went and there wasn't a damn thing a man could do to stop them. Kirby ground his teeth, whimpering his helpless rage, even as he went stumbling across the wagon yard to fire after them.

It was no use. Satank had outmarched them.

By the time the exhausted men could get themselves off the ground, scramble for their guns, get up on the end wagons of the V and fire over the picketed mules' heads, it was all over. The Kiowa just hit the loose herd and kept on going — taking most of it with them. The terrified *arrieros* managed to hang on to their serapes and forty head of their braying charges, but for all practical extents and purposes, Blunt and St. Clair's caravan was out of the mule business.

# 11

About everything that could be broken on a wagon was found to be splintered or sprung that morning following the buffalo stampede at Ash Creek. About noon of the third day, Kirby got the battered train rolling again, making the six-mile drive to Pawnee Fork for the caravan's seventeenth camp since leaving Council Grove. At this point they were one hundred and fifty-three miles from the Grove, two hundred and ninety-eight from Westport, and had made, Kirby frowningly calculated, a slow ten-mile-a-day average. Furthermore, from where he sat, hunched over a small fire waiting for Don Pedro, Sam, Laredo, Popo and Uncle Thorpe to assemble for a council, they had mighty slim hope of improving that speed.

The other faces which presently joined his around the fire were equally long. Don Pedro led off. "Well, Mr. Randolph, what do you think of our prospects, now?"

"I dunno, Don Pedro," said Kirby, frankly. "Thet's why I called ye all fer this powwow. It looks to me like we're up the crick." He paused to look around the firelit circle, missed old

Thorpe Springer. "Whar's Thorpe, Sam? I told ye to fotch him."

"So ye did. But he wouldn't fotch. He is right sick, boy. Thet cussed leg's goin' black on him, near up to his waist."

"I'll look at it, later." Kirby's frown deepened. "Why didn't the old fool speak up? He probably ain't bin keepin' thet hossmanure poultice on thet leg at all."

"Yes he has, too." Sam informed him, worriedly. "But I tell ye one thing, boy. Hot hossmanure dressin' or not, either thet old man is goin' to lose thet leg or we're goin' to lose him."

"We'll see," was all Kirby said, turning abruptly to the business at hand. "How about the wagons, Laredo? And the teams?"

"Mules are in fair shape but we'd best handle them Conestogas with a kiss and a prayer. We ain't got a stick of hardwood left big enough to splint a broke toothpick."

"Ye got any suggestions?"

"Yeah. I cain't keep my teams rollin' without I get some spares to spell off my lame ones and my harness-galled ones." Laredo's bright black eyes, flickering sharply at Don Pedro, clearly mirrored his Texan's dislike of the Spaniard. "I got to have them mules of yo'n, Mistuh Armijo — one way or anothuh."

Kirby, watching the young don as the tough skinner braced him, saw the finely arched black brows lift slightly, and relaxed when the Spaniard's answer came in an amused tone. "Well, Laredo, you may have them. No need to be favoring me with your hard looks." Don Pedro spread his long hands in a gesture of compliance. "The guns they are carrying can all be put in one wagon."

"All right." Kirby intervened, sensing the tension growing across the fire, despite the don's purring words. "The guns go in the first wagon and Laredo gets his forty spares." The mountain man's face was as flat of expression as a bargaining Indian's. Ignoring Don Pedro's mocking smirk, he addressed himself to the silent Texan. "Anything else, Laredo?"

"Naw. It makes me no nevuh mind what Armijo does with his damn guns." The Texas skinner's drawl went as straight into the young Spaniard as his black glance. "Me, I jest work this heah train."

"All right. Everybody's blowed off, now." Kirby's words stepped carefully into the eye-locked silence. "Whut are yer orders fer tomorry, Mr. Armijo?"

Don Pedro sat quiet for half a minute, staring into the fire, a rare frown sitting his thin features. When he spoke, he kept his tones as cautiously impersonal as Kirby's. "It's the better part of a hundred miles to the Ford of the Arkansas, and at our present rate that means ten days. I'm satisfied that within that time we shall all know a little more about each other and our remaining prospects." Coming easily to his feet, he smiled the old, gracious smile. "And now, good night gentlemen. If there are no more glares and insults to be exchanged, I have a little matter of, ah, personal business to attend to." His glance here flicked to Laredo. "Something a trifle more fragrant than your, ah, you will pardon the expression, señor, 'gamy company.' "

Kirby saw the gleam stab Laredo's narrow eyes, came to his feet, following the Texan to his.

"Whut does 'gamy' mean, mistuh?" As Laredo's question went to Don Pedro, Kirby went to Laredo, gliding in behind him, quick and light as a mountain cat.

"It means, hombre," the young don's level voice was delivered without smirk or smile, "that you smell bad. In a word, Laredo, you stink."

Watching Laredo, Kirby saw the clawed right hand tense, knew the next instant would send it diving for the low-swung pistol at the Texan's hip. Across the fire, Don Pedro stood waiting, his handsome face surveying Laredo with the same detached languor that had preluded Tuss's execution. Kirby knew nothing of the Texan's gun speed and didn't intend to find out at the possible expense of his top skinner's life. His own right arm, hanging long and loose at his side, flashed out in sudden and blurring life.

Don Pedro, his eyes on Laredo, was outmatched. He scarcely had his hand on the hooked butt of the Spanish pistol when he found himself in an admirable position to determine what Laredo's flintlock horse pistol looked like, viewed bore-hole on.

"Get away from it," rasped Kirby, keeping the gaping muzzle of Laredo's weapon swinging a six-inch arc around the compass point of Don Pedro's navel. "Take it off'n him, Sam." The old trapper, already ahead of the command, was around the fire, his hand starting for the Spaniard's holster.

"No need, Mr. Randolph. No need —" The young don stepped back away from Sam's reaching hand, at the same time taking his own hand off the pistol butt. "The situation has gone flat, Randolph." Kirby caught the "Mister" omission. "No drama left. Not for gentlemen like you and me. Though I must say, Don Pedro, smiling deprecatingly until now, grew serious, "you are very quick, Mr. Randolph." There was that "Mister" back in again. "I make only the reservation that barring the interfering necessity of my having had to watch Laredo, we might have had a closer outcome."

"We might," said Kirby, still holding Laredo's gun on the don. "Ye kin try watchin' *me* next time. Thet is, if Laredo don't outwatch *ye* meantime."

The Spaniard shrugged, and Kirby concluded, "Ye kin cut yer stick anytime. And keep yer hands from wanderin' on the way out."

Turning to go, Don Pedro smiled again. *"Mil gracias, señor.* As for Laredo, I meant only to improve his manners. Perhaps a ball in the arm or shoulder. *Quie'n sabe?* A captain must have the respect of his men. *No es verdad?"*

"Ye meant to kill him," said Kirby, flatly, not offering to elaborate the bald contradiction. Don Pedro sighed, bowed slightly, made his graceful way out of and away from the fire's jumping light.

"The low-down Mex buzzard!" Laredo's snarl included Kirby in its snapping bite. "I'd of killed him sure if yuh hadn't of grabbed my gun off'n me."

Kirby tossed the weapon back to the Texas skinner. "Mebbe so, Laredo. Me, I alow ye're lucky to still be suckin' live air. Ye seen him agin Tuss."

"I seen him." Laredo was still sulking, his unvented anger trying to find a way out on Kirby.

"Wal, ye seen a fast man, then."

"Yeah, I reckon." The skinner, prodded by his respect for the tall young mountain man, grudged the admission, coppering it with a tacked-on qualifier. "But all the same, yuh should have left me be. Theah was no call fer yuh to go to mixin in."

"Sure," nodded Kirby, dismissing the *impasse* with a measured grin. "I reckon thet's right, Laredo. Now whut ye say we get Uncle Thorpe up h'yar and have a look at thet leg? Ye and Sam tote him over. I'll build up the fire and heat up the iron-jest in case. Ye'd best roust out Cal and Huff and have them to come over, too. Old Thorpe's apt to be grumped up as a goat-bit bull."

They brought the old man up to the fire and laid him on the clean blanket Kirby had pegged down where the light from the flames would strike it. Huff and Cal, Laredo and Sam, squatted, wince-faced, as Kirby peeled the matted rags off the old teamster's leg. Thorpe himself lay white and muttering with the pain of the thing.

"It ain't bad, Kirby boy. It really ain't. Feels much better then it did yestiddy. I'll be around soon. Won't be sech a burden to ye, then. I —"

Kirby near puked when the last wrapping came away from what had once been a knee. The sudden upwafting stench of the rotten flesh and the green horse-droppings of the compress turned his belly over with a flop that shoved his supper clean up around his tonsils. It was a minute before he could look at what he had uncovered.

The flesh of the upper leg was a deep liver-red, from just below the knee to about halfway up the thigh. The foot and lower leg were an odd white-gray color, turning a bruised yellow in places, and Kirby knew before he touched them that they were gone. The knee, swollen twice-normal, was broken open like a ripe melon all around the arrow wound, the proud flesh cringing back from the edges of the splits in thick gray curls. In the wound itself seethed a nest of fat screw-worm maggots.

The firelight blotted out for a moment and Kirby looked up to see Popo reaching him an earthen jug of mescal. He took it, nodding silently, poured an iron cup full of it down the protesting old man. "Hell's fire, I don't want thet greaser bile. I feel puny enough as it is!"

"It'll numb ye a leetle mite, Uncle Thorpe. I got to do some cuttin' on yer leg."

"Whut ye goin' to do, now, Kirby? Whut ye goin' to do, boy?" The old man was whimpering a little, struggling up to see what Kirby was about. The big scout pushed him gently back, the flat of the huge hand forcing him down easily.

"Nothin' but a leetle cuttin' and slicin' to let the pizen out," he reassured the trembling old-ster. "Same as ye'd slash a festered-up saddle boil on a mule. Give him another can of that mescal, Sam. I got to go get me somethin' out'n the cook wagon."

"No ye don't. I saved ye the trouble." Sam, standing behind Uncle Thorpe, held up the two-foot meat saw.

"Well, go ahead and give him the mescal," nodded Kirby. "We ain't got all night."

By now the old man was feeling the jolt of the first huge gulp they had put down him and took the second willingly enough. Kirby waited half an hour, during which time he and the others took turns small-talking Uncle Thorpe's mind off his bad leg and lacing him with additional wallops of Popo's mescal. At the end, the old man, more sick than drunk, but groggy in any event, began to ramble on about Tuss and Clint and Armijo's gun mules. When he looked up at Kirby and said, "Say, whar the hell's Clint, anyhow? I ain't see'd him all day," Kirby figured they had got him about as far as they could on the rotgut.

God, he hated to do it. Hated to take a man's leg away from him. Hated even to touch the damn thing. Or look at it. Cripes! It stunk like a dead dog that had just been turned over after lying in the hot sun three days. Grimacing, he nodded to Huff and Cal and Laredo.

Feeling the men seize him, Uncle Thorpe struggled up. "Shet up, Thorpe!" Kirby, sick-nervous now, barked his orders at the oldster. "I'm startin' to cut now and ye're goin' to feel it. I jest don't want ye grabbin' my knife hand or kickin' thet leg around."

The razor-honed skinning knife slashed around the top half of the thigh, quick as a streak of light. Thorpe screamed, arching his body crazily. The powerful skinners pinned him brutally. Looking intently at the foot-long cut he had made, Kirby saw the meat in it looked wrong, dark and thick and sort of gummy and mushy. Again the knife flashed, six inches above the first cut, and again the old man's hysterical scream shattered the nerves of his holders. But now the leg meat was fresh and firm, the blood bright and free-running.

Thorpe began to sob and shudder, but lay fairly quiet. Kirby was to the bone in seconds, circle-cutting the meat all around it with a speed and skill gained in the taking off of countless buffalo rounds. He was surprised, though, how much tougher the live human muscles cut than the dead animal ones.

Throwing the knife on the blanket, he reached for the saw. At the first grating snag of the blade in the living bone, old Thorpe came up off the blanket bringing all three of his restrainers with him. His eyes bugging with agony, white lips snarling, his scream was more than Kirby could take. "Dam ye, ye're takin' it off! Naw, Kirby! Aw, Lord A'mighty, boy. No no! Please —" The mountain man's balled fist sledged into the crazed oldster's jaw, breaking the pleading scream sharp off. The old man slumped limp as a neck-wrung rooster, and Kirby sped the saw in sickening, tooth-edging cuts.

"Sam, grab me thet flange iron out'n the fire. Hurry up. His cussed blood is shootin' out like water through a bullet-holed bucket."

Working automatically now, Kirby shoved the blackened, gangrenous log of the severed limb, rolling off the blanket. Laredo jumped cursing from the thing as Kirby stood aside for Sam, tight-mouthing his orders. "Plunge it on them veins first. Them big ones."

The broad iron, spitting-hot, hissed like cold water in bubbling fat as it went across the pulsing stump. Sam kept it running around the bloody pulp until the flange went from apricot to cherry-red to ash-gray. The searing metal cooked the open flesh to a smoking brown.

"All right, Sam. Thet'll do. Hand me thet tub of tallow, Laredo."

Scooping the rancid axle tallow in gobbing handfuls, Kirby plastered the seared stump thickly. Stepping back he nodded, white-faced, to Sam. "Wrop it up tight with them tore clothes. Then wind a chunk of canvas around it and truss it up gentle-like. I'm goin' to be sick."

# 12

The next morning found Kirby and Sam riding scout far in advance of the dilapidated caravan and talking, small wonder, of Indians.

"It appears," Kirby was saying, "like young Satank has dusted the country."

"Likely he has," Sam agreed. "And with all them mules danglin' from his coup stick, he kin afford to. Thet was a neat trick. The red rascal's got brains and innards, both. *Woyuonihan*, I respect him. I respect all of them. They're great people."

"I allow ye're the original red-lover, Sam. Me, I side with Cap Marcy. . . . 'It ain't no use to talk honor with them. They ain't got no sech thing in them. They won't show fair fight and they kill and sculp a white man wharever they get the best on him, and if ye treat them decent they think ye're afeered. No, the only way is to invite them all into a big feast and then kill about half of them. Thet way the balance will sort of take to ye and behave themse'fs. . . .' Now thet's the way old Cap seen them, and thet's the way Kirby Randolph sees them!" Kirby bobbed his head with a great deal of conviction and Sam, looking at him with his mouth corners screwed down into his chin whiskers like he had just bitten into a green persimmon, slowly wagged the head of his inner thoughts.

This obstinate cub was sure set against color, especially Indian color. Too bad, too. Save for his contempt of color blood, there wasn't a sharper young one on the frontier. Happen the boy could learn himself that blood was red, no matter the color of the skin that was laid around it, he would finally be a man, full grown.

The hundred miles from Ash Creek to the Ford of the Arkansas would have taken the sap clean out of a fresh-sawed stump. Sitting now, hunkered to the coals of the ninth fire they had made since losing the mules to the Kiowas, Kirby glumly reviewed the journey.

It had taken them three days to pull the thirty-three miles to Coon Creek. The first camp out of Coon Creek, heading for the Caches, thirty-six miles beyond, they had buried Uncle Thorpe. The old man had lived four days, his leg apparently starting to heal. Then on the morning they had left Coon Creek, when Kirby had taken the rags off the stump to change them, he had smelled it beginning to rot again. He had wrapped it back up again, saying nothing to the oldster. But at noon camp Thorpe was talking to Clint again and by span-out time that night, he was dead.

Next day had been clear and beautiful and they had made a good camp that night. The following morning three Mexicans and two skinners were down sick and Sam, diagnosing the trouble as scurvy, had warned Kirby that they would have to lay over soon for a buffalo feed or the whole company would be down. Meantime, half a day was spent gathering prickly pears, and mashing them and boiling them into a bitter pulp which Sam forced down every gagging member of the train with the dire admonition that "scurvy was one painful son of a gun of a way to die. And thet short of fresh humpmeat and hot buffler *boudins*, pear pulp mashed and boiled was the onliest way to fight it."

An all-day buffalo scout at the Caches had netted nine thousand piles ot dead-dry chips and exactly one bone-clean bull skeleton. Then for the past two days it had rained steadily again, holding their miles down to a measly seven or eight a day.

Right now, judging from the way the moon had her pocky bottom wedged among the cross-river sandhills, it was crowding 1.00 A.M. Unable to join the rest of the camp in its grave-quiet slumber, Kirby had given up trying, rolled out of his blankets, stirred up the fire, thrown on a handful of wet chips, humped his lean belly up to the stink and the smoke, and crouched down to do himself some worrying.

And what was worrying him wasn't busted

wagons, trail-muck rains, fresh meat or scurvy, or even digging old Thorpe under. What really had him down was a little billet-doux Sam had brought him after night-supper.

The young scout had sent the white-haired trapper over to Aurélie's fire to drop a hint in Ptewaquin's huge ear that the tall young *Wasicun* would make talk with the little *Shacun* lady. Nothing could be guaranteed, of course. The *Wasicun* was, after all, a warrior. But it might be gathered that if the little *Shacun* behaved herself, showing proper respect and becoming modesty, the *Wasicun* might possibly be in a mood to tender some peace talk.

Sam's return from this truce-feeler had been prompt, the answer he bore, roundabout but clear and cold as lake-ice.

*Ha-ho, ha-ho!* Ptewaquin thanked the *Wasicun*. He was indeed a warrior. Even a chief. *Tahunsa*, they were cousins, Ptewaquin and the *Wasicun*. But the little *Shacun* would not talk with the tall white warrior. She had changed trails now. She was going to live in the great lodge of the dark man. The thin one who smiled so much and rode the fine black stallion. Even no later than this very night Ptewaquin had heard the little *Shacun* tell him that she would share his great lodge at the Trail's end. *Nohetto.* There you were!

Cripes! Hearing that Aurélie was going to marry Don Pedro and go to live with him for keeps in the Governor's mansion in Santa Fe was enough for Kirby. More than enough. Way more. Damn her anyways and all of them that carried color. They were all alike. Wild. Crazy. Spooky. Scary. Quick to twist into a man or away from him. Slow to go away from his mind. Once they got you, they had you. They had you and they held on to you. Held on to you like this cussed Aurélie was holding on to him right now. Propping his eyes open. Keeping his nerves tight. Not letting him ease down. Not letting him sleep. Pulling his mind and his hands back onto that creamy face and the full, live warmth of the rest of her. Pulling his nose back to the wonderful smell of her. His eyes to the peach curve of that dusky cheek, the heat lightning of the gleaming teeth, the green fire in the smoking glance. His ears to the passion-parted lips of her, burning moist on his cheek, and to the throaty, panting words of them — *Oh, Wasicun! Wasicun!*

# 13

They started early, having a long last day's drive between them and the Arkansas Crossing. They had a fine morning and a good road, the best of both they had hit so far. Noon found them halted on a beautiful little stream which wandered into the Arkansas from the north. They had made smart time, near nine miles, had only six left to the Crossing. Kirby ordered the mules unhooked for a two-hour graze and rest.

Shortly after span-out, a lone horseman showed up, jogging their backtrail. The stranger was a smallish man, inclined to look a little pudgy, brown-haired, round-faced, altogether a very mild-appearing fellow.

After the first quick glance, Kirby dismissed him as a greenhorn traveler without better sense than to ride the trail alone. Calling over to Sam, who was busy grinding a handful of skillet-roasted beans in the coffee mill, he opined superiorly. "We got company, Sam. Tinhorn sport a'ridin' the trail alone."

As he looked up to confirm his young friend's casual diagnosis, the old man's eyes widened. Turning the most scathing of motherly snarls on the ignorant cub by his side, he snarled. "Tinhorn sport, huh? Ye wetnose fool, thet's Chris Carson."

"Kit Carson!" Kirby breathed the name the way a Texas sprout might worshipfully whisper "Sam Houston!" or a Mexican urchin, "Santa Ana!"

"Sure, Kit Carson, ye featherhead idjut!"

Further punishment from Sam was averted by the famous frontiersman's arrival at the fire. "*Hau*, Sam. Whut ye doin' down south? The Pied Noirs run ye out?"

"By God, I *am* glad to see ye, Chris. Get down! Get down! I was jest grindin' the beans. We'll have a can of fresh in a jiffy. This h'yar's my boy, Kirby Randolph. Kirby, meet Kit Carson." Sam leered vindictively. "Ye've heered of Mr. Carson, ain't ye, young un? He's the Injun fighter."

Unshot by Sam's arrow, or at least feeling no pain from the wound, Kirby put out his hand, a grin as broad as his drawl going with it. "Howdy, Mr. Carson. This h'yar's a real treat. Sort of like shakin' hands with Jesus, or Jed Smith."

"Oh, I reckon it ain't as bad as all thet. Happen ye've got a sprinkle of salt acrost yer own tail jedgin' from the looks on ye."

"I heered ye was workin' fer old Blunt up to Fort William. How come? Whut ye doin' up thar?" Sam's question, interrupting the complimenting, turned the discussion onto the straight trail of business, bringing a quick nod from the famous Scout.

"Sort of keepin' a eyeball peeled on the Injuns, happen ye know whut I mean, Sam."

"I allow I do. Give ye much trouble do they, in these parts?"

"Considerable." No word-waster, Mr. Chris Carson.

"Mostly Kioways and Comanches, ain't they?" Sam's question maintained the high quality of the oral economy, producing a slight qualification in the other scout's answer.

"Wal, yes, some Kioways. But mostly Comanches. And I allow anyways ye figger them, the Comanches are the lowest Injuns God ever hung a warbonnet on. It ain't no lie whut they'll do to a white man. Or a woman or a kid, either. Happen ye get one in yer sights, leave him have it in the belly. I like Injuns and I know them. Most's fine. But damn my soul, ye cain't live with them Comanches. I'd gut-shoot the buzzards quick as I saw them anywhars."

"Ye mean Blunt and St. Clair's expectin' trouble from the Comanches and are payin' ye to let them know when it's comin'?"

"More or less."

Sam's understanding head-bob was brief. "Ye out lookin' fer any special trouble? Right now, I mean?"

"I was."

"Whut ye mean, ye was?"

"I done found it a'ready."

"Whar?"

"Behind ye. I allow ye're gettin' old, Samuel. Ye've had Injuns on yer tail since leavin' yer last night's camp."

"Naw!"

"Sure. Not many, mebbe, but enough. And a real salty chief."

"The hell! Me and Kirby figgered them cussed Kioways had gone home. Son of a gun, I hate to let a Kioway outfigger me like thet."

"Ye didn't," observed Carson laconically. "It's Comanches follerin' ye."

"Cripes," said Sam, and, having said it, seemed satisfied to sit in squint-eyed and thoughtful silence.

After a minute, Kirby, self-assurance outbidding reluctance, picked up the old man's end of the conversation. "Ye say Comanches, Mr. Carson? Ain't this a leetle out'n their range? I thought we was in Kioway country as long as we was on the Arkansas. Ain't the Comanches supposed to run mostly on the Cimarron?"

"Naw. It's all the same. The two tribes is thicker then buffler scum in a bull waller."

"Ye was sayin' they got a big chief along. Who's thet?"

"Canadian River Comanche. Big giant of a feller. And a *bad Injun*. Heads the raidin' bands thet works the Texican settlements fer white captives. He's collected some scandalous ransoms."

"Whut's his name?"

"Kioways call him An-gyh P'ih. Thet comes out 'Heavy Foottrack' in their lingo. 'Big Foot' in ourn."

"Big Foot!" Kirby's exclamation jumped out excitedly. "By cripes, we heered of him clear up on the Powder. Ye sure he's the one thet's follerin' us?" The young scout had had enough hostiles to last him a spell; he hoped their famed guest might be guessing at the chief's identity.

"No missin' it, boy. I'd know thet 'heavy foottrack' of his'n, anywhars. And it jest so happens thar was a moccasin print as big as a mule's bottom, sprang alongside thet crick ye camped on last night. Oh, I alow Big Foot and me knows one another, all right."

"I allow ye must." Kirby backed off, suddenly remembering the great scout's awesome reputation. "Ye got any idees why he's follerin' us? He kin see we ain't got enough mules to fuss about."

"Wal, yeah. Old Blunt he was worried about the gal — Miss St. Clair. Whut with the name Big Foot's got as a kidnap and ransom chief, Blunt he figgered I'd best mosey down and have a look fer yer caravan. This h'yar *is* the train with the gal in it, ain't it?"

"Yep." Kirby's answer was short, carrying no offer of elaboration.

"Whar's the Spaniard? Don Pedro, ain't it? Santy Fee Gov'ner's nephy, or somethin' like thet. Whar's he?"

"Over thar by thet leetle white spread of canvas whar the big Injun is cookin'." Sam supplied the information, seeing Kirby wasn't going to.

"Thanks, Samuel. I'll amble over and tell him he's got Comanches on his tailpiece. Mebbe *he'll* know somethin' about how come."

"Happen he does, ye won't find it out." Sam nodded sourly. The visiting scout threw his coffee grounds in the fire and got up. "All right, old hoss, I'll see you boys along the trail. I suggest, meantime, ye get yer train rollin'. Thar'll be a bright moon tonight, whut the folks out h'yar calls a 'Comanche moon.' And they ain't bein' romantic when they calls it thetaway, neither. Ye won't want to be travelin' in it. Them red sons dearly love a bright moon to work by."

Toward nightfall, the weary (and by now, wary!) train pulled a long, climbing cross ridge, to look down on the long awaited halfway point of the journey. The Arkansas Crossing at last!

While the squealing wagons lurched and groaned past him over the brow of the rise, Kirby pulled Bluebell off to one side and looked down on the spot so perilously gained in earlier Trail annals, and to prove so swiftly fateful in his own history. The banks of the stream were level and fairly open, the various cut-downs and wagon approaches clearly marking all the numerous fords. There was no one main crossing, Kirby quickly saw, but as many as eight or maybe even a dozen, most of them above the small island in midstream, which marked this historic spot on the Arkansas. The famous "Ford of the Arkansas" was in reality a literal maze of wagon ruts for hundreds of yards above and below the island. The island itself was a pretty thing, the south side and lower end of it gracefully draped in green-lush willow timber. Kirby noted that a small camp was pitched on the open end of the island and, even in the poor light, from the conical structure of the tents, he called it for a Spanish outfit, Mexican really, and probably a military one.

They made their own camp on the flat, close up to the stream, receiving, by the time he and Sam had boiled their coffee and fried their pork, an unexpected caller. Don Pedro made known his errand without wasteful flourish. Kirby couldn't remember having seen the boyish don so jubilant, naturally wondered why. And found out quickly enough.

"Boys," this familiarity was a mild shock in itself, "I've had a stroke of luck. A double stroke. I've sold the cursed guns and been given the marriage promise of Señorita St. Clair!"

Much as he wanted to kill the handsome youngster, Kirby knew the don's visit wasn't inspired by the chance to gloat. He was a strange breed of cat, this Don Pedro, and a man couldn't exactly hate him. Kirby couldn't, anyway. He was elegant and overbearing, superior and highfaluting. He was a tight-pants dandy, probably as cruel as any Spaniard, kept his nails too clean, shaved every day, brushed his teeth with grit and ashes, prayed seven days a week and wore a cross around his neck. And had eaten off Spanish plate with a settlement knife and fork every last meal from Council Grove. Still, when you got through faulting him, you knew you weren't horsing anybody but yourself. This black-browed sport was all hombre. And a man who was half-smart better believe that he was.

"Wal?" Kirby tried to make it sound like a simple question and not like he was calling the don a dirty name.

"Congratulations, comin' and goin'," said Sam, covering quickly for Kirby's bluntness. "We fer sure won't miss them blamed guns, though I allow I've sort of tooken a fancy to Aurélie."

Don Pedro laughed again, his white teeth flashing in the gloom. "I'm sure we all have, old man," he said, and saying it, stared flatly at Kirby. The young scout had no time to pick up the challenge as the don went ahead, talking to Sam. "And in your particular case, for her big Sioux friend too, eh, *Anciano? Caray!* May *Dios* grant me your powers when I am your age. *Hijo!* That night on the Arkansas you nearly caved the back of my tent in! *Madre!*"

Sam floundered around looking for an answer, awkward as a blind bear in a bramble patch. Kirby helped him out.

"Whut ye want, Don Pedro? We're plumb tuckered and aimin' to get some shet-eye."

Ignoring the sullen address, the Spaniard bowed easily, his voice having all the patent restraint of a proud man speaking under studied control. "I would like you both to be my guests. I have been asked to invite you especially." He paused to grimace the last sentence toward Kirby, went ahead smoothly. "You have seen the camp on the island. It is that of my uncle's business associate, Colonel Juan Vicarrez, sent along with a detachment of Taos Indian Militia to locate us. Uncle feared we might have encountered some trouble. *Caray! Some* trouble? He puts it mildly, eh, *compañeros?*

"Well, Colonel Vicarrez is delighted. He will take delivery of the guns here and now, tonight. And he insists on fêting me. I demurred, of course, but he had heard about Señorita St. Clair and me and, *pues,* well, you know how these Spaniards are, señores. He would not be satisfied.

"And I, in turn, shall not be satisfied unless you are my guests. Particularly you, Mr. Randolph. I would like you to study how the Latins display courtesy and chivalry — in its proper place, at the *banqueta* and over the wineglass. I insist, señor."

"I ain't goin'," said Kirby, angry at himself

206

for letting the girl's whim upset him so, wanting, really, to attend the Mexican celebration.

"Señor —" The velvet voice stiffened. "*Por favor.* I have asked you like a gentleman —"

Sam, eager to lap up the wine of Old Spain, threw in his hurried weight. "Aw, c'mon Kirby. Fer the luvva Pete. Whar's yer sportin' blood? Lord Amighty, I should think ye would —"

"Will *she* be thar?" Kirby hadn't meant to say that at all, was surprised to hear his voice asking it. Damn! Why did a man's thoughts have to go running out his mouth?

"*Por supuesto,* but of course."

Kirby heard the don's answer without listening to it. He wanted the Spaniard to go away. Quick. He was getting mad now. His gut was closing up hard, like a fist. The small of his back beginning to squeeze in tighter and tighter. "Get him out'n h'yar, Sam. Go on, hurry it up!" The command came side-mouthed and sibilant, jumping the old man to his feet with its ugly vehemence.

If Don Pedro heard it, he gave no sign, but Sam knew the rare sound of his protégé's voice in real anger, and he knew enough to act fast when he heard it. "Uh, Don Pedro, I allow the boy's plumb wore out, like he says. Let's me and you get on. Happen this un says he ain't goin', why, he ain't."

"But he was asking about the señorita. As though that might change his mind. After all, it was her request that he join us. Come along, Randolph —"

"I said I ain't goin'." The voice was as flat as the snap of a broken bowstring. "Now, get. I don't want to turn ugly about it, mister."

"As you will." Don Pedro laid the words down most carefully, so as not to fracture the thin ice of their composition. "A courtesy refused is an insult offered. *Buenas noches,* Mr. Randolph. Come along, Old One. You shall taste such wines as you never dreamed could grow in a grape!"

Kirby watched the flames in the fire, trying to get them to show him what Aurélie might look like over there at the fandango on the island. He kept seeing her face, but that was easy. Any man who had lived out of doors knew that night fires were full of faces. It was harder, though, to get the full figures to show up. He peered more intently into the cheery glow of the cottonwood logs, the shouting, laughter, singing and guitar-playing from the island spurring his imagination.

She had fancy clothes, he knew. He had seen those rawhide trunks in number three wagon. As old Marcel St. Clair's daughter, she was a rich girl. There would be no end to the finery and fooforaw she had brought out from St. Louis.

But what would it be tonight? Silks? Crinolines? Velvets? Probably some of each, one of those Spanishy-Frenchy get-ups. Mantilla, bolero, swirling skirt, little Morocco slippers. Yep, that was it. There it was in the fire, now. She was beautiful! Especially when she flashed that smile. And that voice, too. Low, easy, soft in the throat. Real female. All female. The kind of a voice that went into the pit of a man's belly like a hard blow, left him wondering what had struck him, left him weak and on the edge of being sick, yet made him feel strong to want to bury his hands and face in every part of where that voice had come from.

"Kirby — !"

Whoa. Hold up, boy. That voice of hers, calling his name out of the fire, just then, had been a little too real. Made a man wonder if he hadn't been on the prairie too long, spent too many nights talking to shadows and looking into fire faces. He had best poke up the fire and roll in. A man didn't want to get like old Sam and the others. By God, he wasn't that far gone yet —"

"Kirby! Answer me!"

He looked up then, startled. Closing his eyes, he counted ten, opened them again, still saw her standing there.

"*Hau, Wasicun.*" Her powdery voice shivered the tall scout clean to his moccasin soles. He came to his feet, not answering her, just standing there, staring back. The fire had been as all wrong about the way she was dressed as he had been about where she was.

Kirby had seen a thousand Indian girls on a hundred May nights look just the way Aurélie St. Clair was looking now. She had nothing between her and the warm breath of the river air but her moccasins and a simple Sioux camp dress. The rounded grace of the slender arms, bare to the boy-straight shoulders, shimmered copper-red in the lingering firelight. From beneath the hem of the doeskin, the full curve of the bare calves tapered into the chisel-cut ankles.

"*Hau,*" he answered, at last, his deep voice matching hers for softness. "*Hohahe,* welcome to my tipi."

She slid around the fire and past him, into the shadow of the wagon behind them, past the prying light of the flames. Kirby was after her in three long steps, asking no questions, expecting none.

She was waiting for him there in the blackness, no gloom deep enough to hide the lambent green eyes, the copper glow of the flushed cheeks. Her arms came reaching for him as he bent to take her in his, the coiled seekingness of them weaving around his burning face and corded neck with a melting warmth that turned his kiss into a fury.

They clung thus, trembling and moving blindly while the earth floated beneath them and the stars swam crazily above. After a dozen sobbing breaths, she broke her mouth from his, buried her face in his shoulder, wept softly.

"Kirby —" Her voice, small and weak, seemed calling from far off.

"Yes, *Wastewin?*"

"Kirby, we've got to talk. I must talk to you, *Wasicun.*"

"All right, honey. Whar'll we go? We cain't get nothin' said around h'yar. Camp's still wide awake."

"I walked out in the dusk tonight. Found a little place. Above the island. A little stream coming in —"

"Yeah. I mark the place. Seen it from the hill comin' into camp this arternoon. Crick forks in from the north. Lot of willow timber and a leetle sandspit whar she jines up with the Arkansaw."

"Yes, oh yes. That's it, Kirby. Meet me there in half an hour. We can't go together."

"I reckon not, honey gal. I'll be thar."

She stood looking up at him, lips parted. Standing on tiptoe she kissed him quickly on the mouth, the words rushing with the lips to caress him. "Kirby, Kirby. Oh, *Wasicun,* I do love you so!"

She was gone then, around the wagon, circling through the dark, keeping the hulking bodies of the other Conestogas between her and the remaining company fires. Watching her fade noiselessly away, Kirby muttered half aloud.

"Cuss it, she sneaks around like a Pawnee, talks like a Sioux, and makes love like a

Arapahoe. And by cripes, I'll have her anyways! I'll have her if it takes the last gasp I got. If I have to spend the rest of my life gruntin' Sioux and strappin' cradle boards on thet god-beautiful back of yers, Aurélie gal, I'm goin' to have ye fer my squaw. God he'p me, I mean it — and color be damned!"

Kirby, following the sandbanks of the Arkansas west toward the creek fork, felt fit to whip a dozen bears. It was one of those *nights* and a blind man couldn't miss it. Late May, warm, the moon fat and just edging up behind the sandhills beyond the crossing. The air tepid and fragrant and just moving enough to bring a prairie man the smells he lived on. Warm sand, new grass, old hay, gray sage, fresh water, damp loam, naked rocks, willow pungence, woodsmoke and simple ozone. Just pure, unadulterated prairie air. Air that got down in a man and tasted so mouth-watering good he would swear he had eaten his belly full of it, instead of just breathing it into his lungs.

A night like that and air like that made a man feel the way he was put together. Made him suck in his breathing slow and deep, to make him know his chest was wide and powerful. Made him flex and twist his arms as he walked, that the loop and roll of biceps and forearm could tell him that here were arms that could cradle a child or break a man's neck, easy either way. Made him stride long and bent-kneed, feeling the whole singing play and counterplay of the forces that were in him repeating the thought at every step: this is the hour and the night to remember. Feel them *now,* man. And remember them. There may be other nights with other wonders. Other hours. Minutes. Seconds. But these *exact* ones will never come again!

The sight of the creek fork ahead slowed the scout's racing thoughts, threw them out of the whirling channels of rare introspect, into the straight stream bed of customary reality. He turned up the creek bank, ears tuned, eyes searching.

Ahead lay a high cutbank, sheltered along its top and upstream edge by crowding willows. At its base lay a tiny white beach, closed in by the bending willows. She was waiting for him there, standing centered on the little beach, her braided hair glowing ash-silver in the moon-light.

As he approached, she reached beneath the bank to bring forth a buffalo calf robe. This she unrolled and spread at his feet. *"Woyuonihan, Wasicun.* I honor you, white man. *Hiyota ka,* come and sit down." By the mock bow she gave him and by the way she said *"Wasicun"* (it could be said a dozen ways), he knew the mood of the wagon-shadow was gone. Here was the cryptic, keen-humored *Shacun* back again.

Kirby wouldn't have known a Roman from a Rumanian. But he knew enough about Indians to savvy that when you were in their country, you did as they did. Here in this willowed-in rendezvous on the middle Arkansas, he felt, somehow, that he was in Aurélie's country. Returning the bow with equal mock ceremony, he smiled. "*He-hau*, well, well! The leetle *Shacun* knows the rules. She is not *waohola sni*, not without respect. *Ha-ho*, thank you."

He lowered himself to the soft curl of the robe, squatting on his haunches, Sioux-fashion, Aurélie sinking to her knees by his side. She held something out to him and he saw the dull glint of a stone pipe bowl in the moonlight. He took it, nodding acknowledgment while she brought a smoldering punkstick out of a little rawhide carrying bag.

With the pipe going, he settled down, cross-legged, handing it gravely back to the girl. She took it, blew a puff in the directions of each of the four winds, and one straight upward to Wakan Tanka, the Great Spirit of the Dakota Sioux. With the return of the pipe, Kirby, in turn, blew a puff toward the stars, muttering, "*Tunka sila le iyahpe ya yo*, Father, receive my offering." Aurélie greeted the little prayer with a moonflash smile, and he knew he had pleased her. After a moment she began to talk.

"Something has happened, Kirby. I'm not going to go through with my promise to Don Pedro. I can't now."

"Why not? Whut happened?"

"It was something I didn't know when I told

him I would marry him. Something I really didn't know myself until tonight. But now I know, and I'm afraid."

"I don't foller ye. I guess I'm jest dumb."

"When he came to me tonight and told me about the celebration over on the island, the first thing I did was ask him if you were going to be there. I don't know why. It wasn't in my mind to do that. But when I opened my mouth those were the words that came out."

"Yeah. I guess we got it fair bad. I done the same thing. Same way, too. Wasn't thinkin' about ye but blatted out about ye."

"He was angry." Aurélie went on, passing Kirby's statement. "Stomped away, proud as only a Spaniard can. Then he changed, the way he does. Smiled and bowed and said he would go personally to invite you. When he came back and said you had refused to go, I told him I wasn't going, either. I know he was furious but Sam was with him and he never let on at all. Went away, arm in arm with Sam, laughing and talking as natural as anything. He's a devil Kirby. He scares me."

"He scares me, too," said Kirby, simply. "But I don't see whar thet gets us. Ye ain't refusin' to marry him jest because ye're ascairt of him."

"No, that's not it."

"Wal, whut is then?"

"Kirby, when I spoke right out about you to Don Pedro, I knew I had to quit lying to myself. I knew that no matter how you might feel about a halfbreed girl, I couldn't do anything about the way a halfbreed girl feels about you."

"Yeah, I know. I guess ye got it figgered how I feel about ye, too, ain't ye?"

"Yes."

"And thet it don't make no difference no more, about the 'breed' part of it? Ye know thet, too, don't ye?"

"I think so, Kirby."

"I allus had my mind clamped down on the idee I was goin' to get me a white woman. I reckon, now, my heart knowed better then my head, all along. It started tellin' me how I felt about ye when I was layin' in thet gutter in St. Louie. And it ain't quit tryin' to hammer it into my thick head thet ye're my woman fer a single damn minute, since."

"When did you *really* know, Kirby?"

"Tonight, I reckon. Last night, when I heered ye was marryin' Armijo, I jest give in like a whupt yeller dawg. My pig head started to tellin' me all over again thet ye was still a breed. And rotten. And crazy. With no more morals than a Mandan. I was still listenin' to it, I guess, when ye come to my fire tonight." He paused, raising his head for the first time, and seeing the moonbeam flash of the running tear before she could duck her face to hide it.

His voice came to her as slow and gentle as the big hand which followed along behind it to lay on her shoulder. "But honey, when I looked up and see'd ye standin' thar acrost from thet

216

blaze tonight, I knowed my ears was covered fer good. I'll tell ye, gal, I aint' never goin' to listen to my head again. I don't know much about love, Aurélie, but I allow it ain't give to many to feel like we do about one another. Ye're jest a kid, really, but I ain't never see'd no more of a woman growed. I got nothin' only a hard life to offer ye but if ye'll have me I'll go down the trail with ye till we cain't neither of us see to foller it no more."

"Kirby, oh, Kirby! I'll ride any trail with you. You know that. But I still haven't told you everything about me. Maybe you won't want me to share your trail after I tell you who —"

"I don't want to know nothin'. I've allus understood a woman's got herse'f a right to change-up her mind. Thet's good enough fer me, Aurélie."

"Kirby, I've got to tell you."

"The hell. All ye got to tell me is thet ye don't love Don Pedro."

"I don't love him, Kirby. I don't have to tell you that."

"Yeah, I reckon even I ain't thet dense."

They sat silent then, a long time, his great paw patting her shoulder, stroking her bowed head, playing with the thick braids of her hair. Funny how when a man and a girl started talking about love they stopped making it. Times like right now, with the moon fat and sassy, the river running quiet and nothing but the grassfrogs and crickets presuming to argue about it, a man could just sit and look at a girl, patting her shoulder and smoothing her cheek and forgetting all about her body, and his, too.

When Aurélie looked up, she was dry-eyed, the quick smile that was such poison to Kirby's backbone playing around her mouth corners. "Can you swim, Kirby?"

"Thet's a hell of a question."

"Want to? Now, I mean. You're not scared?"

"To swim? Me scared? Whut's eatin' ye, gal?"

"Well, I just thought — oh, you know. Last time you went in swimming, you nearly didn't get out. I thought maybe —"

"Oh, shucks, thet!" Kirby's laugh was quick to catch up. "C'mon, let's go. Satank ain't within three hundred mile. And besides. No two hunderd Kioways is goin' to keep me out'n thet crick, if it comes to follerin' *you* into it!"

Aurélie, her head cradled in the warm laxness of Kirby's arm, stretched languorously, feeling the goodness of the long relief ease slowly down her arching oack.

Kirby, one knee up, the other angled carelessly into Aurélie's soft side, idly pressed his back down into the robe, reassuring himself that he was still lying on firm ground, not floating in space as he felt. The moon, slanting low now over the crossriver sandhills, was in his eyes.

And a little of it in his heart.

There was no woman in this world but the

slim, dusky one by his side. He knew it now if he never had before. Maybe for other men there was other worlds. He didn't know. A man could set his store by a sight of different things, likely. For some it was books, like as not. Or maybe battlefields. Or just a big bellyful of food. For him, it was this woman.

Well, maybe there *were* other things, but he had never found them. They had yet to show him a better reason for a man being alive than just being the right man for the right woman at the right time.

"Kirby —"

"Yeah, honey?"

"What are you thinking?"

"I'm thinkin' it's gettin' late."

"Not that — You know I don't mean that!"

"Wal, mebbe it's turnin' cool."

"Kirby!"

"Smart, ain't ye?"

"Just a woman, Kirby. What was it?"

"Wal, it was jest somethin' I've allus thought about. Thet out'n all the things in the world, thar ain't really nothin' past a man and his woman."

"You mean if they're really right for each other. Like you and me."

"Yeah. Like ye and me."

"It's funny, Kirby, I was thinking that, too. Not just like you were, maybe. But the same thing, anyway."

"It works all over the world, I reckon,"

nodded the scout, stretching to greet the strength that was beginning to come back into him. "Look at old Sam and thet Sioux ox, Ptewaquin. I reckon mebbe the old coon would be tyin' his pony out front of her tipi flap if they was up in Oglala country."

"Kirby — I wonder if you'll ever tie Bluebell in front of my tipi?" The girl's question echoed a wistfulness that wasn't lost on the mountain man.

"I figger to. When the time comes."

"Oh, I hope it comes soon, *Wasicun*. I want you in my lodge. I promise you your pipe will always be in its rack and your moccasins mended."

"It'll mebbe come sooner then we know. Somehow I got a feelin'."

"When, Kirby?"

"I dunno, *Shacun*. Mebbe in a month. Mebbe tomorry. Depends on a couple of things. Mostly on Don Pedro, I'd say."

"I'm afraid of him, Kirby. When he finds out about us, especially about me, he'll —"

"Wal, don't fret yerse'f frantic." Kirby kissed her gently. "I allow we kin handle him if it comes to thet."

"He's very dangerous, Kirby. You know that, I guess. Not open and strong like you, maybe. But, well, he's —"

"Yeah. I know. He's inside-dangerous." Kirby had stood up with the slow words. "I bin watchin' him, don't worry. Come on, Aurélie, honey. We got to drift."

Arm in arm they moved down the bank of the Arkansas. Above the island they separated, the girl to continue on along the bank into camp, Kirby swinging wide, inland, to come in across the open prairie. Before they parted, Aurélie leaned quickly up, putting her cool lips on his chest where the open collar bared it.

Bending his head, Kirby kissed the fragrant hair, let his cheek lie in its waving warmth. She nestled into his arms, turning her head so that her cheek lay over the driving beat of his heart. They stood a moment thus, wordless, then she was gone, running lightly through the cotton-woods and on down the moonlit bank below, leaving him to ponder the queer, pagan ways of this Indian girl-child of his.

Back at the wagon, Kirby had no more than rolled into his blankets than Sam came cat-footing it up through the dark. Not content to let the old dog lie down to a deserved sleep, Kirby sat up and launched cheerfully into him. "Sam, old hoss, throw a few chunks on them coals. I got news fer ye thet won't wait till mornin'."

The old trapper merely nodded, stirred up the fire, threw on a handful of cottonwood limbs, opined drily, "Must be a big night fer it. I was jest goin' to roust ye out. Got a fair to middlin' piece of gossip fer ye, too, Casanovy."

Ignoring his companion's answer, Kirby, no

master of suspense, let the oldster have it square-on. "Sam, ye was right about Injuns and color-blood all along. I got to admit thet. Me and Aurélie's done made it fer keeps tonight. She told me it's me she loves, and by God I love her. We're goin' to marry up, proper." The young scout's excitement spread into a reaching grin. "I hope thet idee don't onsettle ye none, Mother dear."

"Oh, *I* ain't onsettled none by it —" Agreeably surprised as he was by Kirby's ebullient revelation, Sam had a source of his own from which to draw enjoyment, suspense, as always, seeking and wallowing in company. "But I allow ye might be. Happen ye was half-smart, thet is."

The coffee of Sam's affected complacency shortly began to filter through the thick strainer of Kirby's mind. "I don't foller ye, old hoss. Whut have I got to worry about?"

"Oh, nothin' special. Jest thet yer gal seems to be havin' herse'f a big night tellin' tales about yer love affair. Last I seen of her she was blabbin' to our Mex friend."

"Hold up, Sam! Ye ain't sayin' thet Aurélie was blabbin' about her and me to Don Pedro?"

Sam cut him short. "I ain't sayin' nothin' else. Armijo and me come acrost the river jest as she come walkin' down the bank. He started climbin' her about whar she'd bin thet hour of the night. And mister, she don't climb worth a damn. She up and told him whut fer,

222

ye'd best believe me."

"Whut did she say?" Kirby wasn't exactly nervous he reckoned, but a man gets edgy about being in love. Especially if the girl went to talking about it to the other fellow.

"Wal, I couldn't rightly say, seein' as how she was layin' him out in Spanish mostly." Sam measured his statement very thoughtfully. "But I got the drift. Ye couldn't miss it, whut with the Sioux signs she threw in. Thar was somethin' about whut he could do with his uncle's mansion in Santy Fee, his ranches, his hosses, his bullion, his elegant ancestors and a few other things. I swear thet gal's a wonder. One minute she's duckin' and crawlin' around coy as a pet cat. And the next, she's spittin' and clawin' like a crazy panther."

"After she told him she wasn't going to marry him, whut happened?"

"Seems he jest stood thar a minute, sayin' nothin' and grinnin' easy. Then he up and grabbed her and let off another batch of Spanish thet added up to 'How the hell come ye ain't?' She looked him squar in the eye and let him have it. 'Because I'm marryin' Kirby Randolph!' she says. 'And how come I'm marryin' him is thet I love him. I've always loved him. *Sabe Usted, primo hermano?*' "

"Whut did he do then?" Kirby asked the question like a man dazed by a hard blow on the head, moving his mouth and making words, but not thinking them.

"I dunno. About thet time I was backin' away. But before I got out'n earshot, I heered him say, 'Congratulations, *querida*. It is all fer the best. Ye'll make a fascinatin' widdy. *Hasta la proxima.*' "

"Whut ye reckon Armijo will do?" Kirby was thinking now, his words low.

"I figger him to come lookin' fer ye. The average hombre would give up, oncet ye'd beat him to the bedstead, but not thet buzzard. He'll come arter ye, boy."

"When ye figger he will?" Kirby asked the question idly, poking at the fire with a speculative moccasin toe. A shower of red sparks ballooned upward — and with them Sam went suddenly rolling, hip over shoulder, under the wagon. His answer came hissing from behind the covering shadow of the rear wheel.

"Right now, boy. Watch him close. H'yar he comes. Don't let on ye know a thing. I'll lay whar I be. I don't think he see'd me." Glancing up with the old man's warning, Kirby saw the gracefully lounging figure of the Spanish don approaching across the camp ground. He came to the fire's edge, bowed slightly, addressed Kirby with his gentlest smile.

"*Buenos noches, señor.*"

"Whut do ye want?" Kirby stood up, muttering his words deep in his throat.

Under the wagon, Sam, hearing that throat-sound, stiffened. It was a way the youngster had, letting that hollow growl get into his voice.

224

It had an animal sound to it, that growl, a sound Sam had always likened to one he could remember an old dog wolf making when he had come on him caught in a fox set, up in the Bad River country. If a man knew Kirby Randolph, he knew what that throat-growl meant. Happen he didn't hear it often, and happen when he did hear it, it wasn't loud or showy. But if he knew the boy, he knew what it meant.

Kirby never looked for trouble and would make a long trail to walk around it. But when it cornered him, when there was no way out, no way to go around or back off, that trouble better come walking up mighty soft and with its eyes for sure wide open.

Don Pedro neither heard nor cared for Kirby's growl. But he was walking soft and keeping his eyes open. "I want you, señor." The smile didn't vary the least mocking curve.

"All right —" The animal sound still purred in Kirby's throat. "H'yar I come."

As the mountain man made to step around the fire, Don Pedro flashed the double pistol on him. Kirby stopped, his moccasins almost in the fire. "Ye aim to use thet thing?" His query meant just what it asked. There was no fear in it, no contention, no backing off, no going around. It was just the straight-on request of the gambler asking the price of the game before buying into it.

"I do, Mr. Randolph. Indeed I do. I am going to shoot you like I should have shot Tuss — in the gut. Only you are not to have the chance Tuss had. No chance at all. Remember? I told you that before. You're not armed and men of your blood would call it murder. As you did with Tuss. In your eyes he was murdered. But in mine, señor, *executed.* The word implies the carrying out of a due sentence of guilt. I excused myself on these grounds with Tuss. I shall of course apply the same high sense of justice in your case. *Comprende Usted?*"

Kirby crouched wordless, without motion, every nerve in him keyed to the next second.

"Very well." The thin smile was still on the don's lips, long-gone from the slant black eyes. I shall count before I fire. I enjoy the suffering before the actual pain is felt. Once I have shot you the finish will come at once. You have my word. Three, I think, makes a pleasant count. *No es verdad, amigo? Pues —*

"One . . . Two . . ."

Up in the beaver country a man learns to make many useful noises. To call like a crow or a whippoorwill. To whistle like an elk, to chatter like a magpie, bleat like a Big Horn, whicker like a wild stud, growl like a grizzly, scream like a panther. Usually, if he is an old one at it, like Sam, he can do them all pretty well. But always he has a favorite. One noise he makes best of all, and prides himself mightily on. In Sam's case, Oglala admirer that he was, this favorite noise was the panther scream. With its combination woman-in-labor, bowel-knifed squaw and guts-drawn-alive screech, it would lift the hair off a dead dog. Or, as the case might he, off the neck-nape of an elegant Spaniard.

"Thr—" The don's final count was begun, and no more than begun, when Sam let go.

*"Hiii-yeee-hahhh!"*

The Oglala panther scream leapt out from under the wagon and pounced on the Governor's nephew like a live thing. The Spaniard's fiddle-tight nerves snapped so loud Sam swore he heard them go. Kirby, timing the move a hair behind Sam's awesome screech, drove his right moccasin into the fire, kicking a flaring splatter of burning wood, live coals and choking ash up into Don Pedro's face.

The Spaniard fired twice, fast and blind. But the shots, triggered into where Kirby had stood when Sam's howl broke up the soirée, missed by feet. The twin echoes were still banging around under the wagon when Kirby's knee pile-drove into the pit of the don's groin, jackknifing him forward to bring his chin smashing into Kirby's right fist. It was a slicing, cross-swinging blow, not clean and flush-on, and while it nearly tore the Spaniard's jaw off and sent him spinning into the ashes of the fire, it didn't finish him.

Clutching his groin, face fish-belly-gray with the painsickness, Don Pedro struggled to rise.

Kirby let him get to his knees before he kicked him. When it came, the huge foot whistled with the throw of two hundred and ten pounds behind it, crunching viciously into the soft ends of the ribs, directly over the heart. The young don's breath exploded in a piercing burst. His head, arms, shoulders, all seemed to sag and melt aimlessly. He pitched straight forward into the burned-out ruck of the fire, not even the gentle motion of breathing marring the stone stillness with which he lay.

"By damn, I think ye've kilt him," muttered Sam, scraggly beard wagging a worried circle.

"No, I ain't," said Kirby, the old Virginia softness moving back into his voice. "I ain't kilt him, Sam. But I wisht I had."

"Whut do ye mean, boy? Ye ought to be glad ye didn't!"

"I mean, now I got to kill him anyways. Sure as a wet dawg stinks, I got to kill him now, Sam."

The old man paused, bright little eyes puckered in thought. "Yep, boy," the admission dragged with reluctance, "I allow ye do." Another pause stretched ahead of the conclusion. "And happen likewise, I allow ye will."

"Happen," nodded Kirby, and said no more.

When Kirby awoke it was lead-gray in the east and the towering form of Ptewaquin, Aurélie's Sioux shadow, was bending over him. *Ha ye'tu mani,*" said the Indian woman, "I have been walking in the night."

"*Woyuonihan,*" nodded the mountain man, sitting up, "I respect your eyes. *Nas'i s'ni?* What appeared in your sight?"

Quickly the squaw told him. When the Spaniard awakened from his beating, he had sent for his servant, Chavez the Comanchero, the little brown frog who had been here at the Crossing awaiting his master's arrival from the east. The two had talked and Ptewaquin had heard the mention of a name which had a bad sound to Indian ears. An-gyh P'ih, Heavy Foottrack, the Comanche!

"Big Foot!" The name burst from Kirby's clamped lips. A bad sound, indeed. There wasn't a red son on the Prairie with a harder-earned reputation in a nastier profession: ransom-grabbing white victims out of the Texas settlements and the Santa Fe Trail traffic.

Aye, the squaw had nodded, Big Foot. Well, the little brown one had departed, very suddenly. And he had departed *south*. Across the Jornada, the Desert Crossing. Toward the Cimarron. Toward the land of the Comanche. Toward Big Foot. *Iyu'ha*, that was all. Ptewaquin had thought the *Wasicun* scout should know.

As the slit-eyed giantess turned to go, Kirby quickly reached out to place his hand on her shoulder. *"Ta ye' e'ca' no we,"* he murmued, earnestly. "You have done well, Mother."

An hour after the next night's cookfires had burned down, Ptewaquin came again to Kirby's fire. *Hau,* Ptewaquin gave greeting. And would the *Wasicun* scout go now to see the Spaniard? Chavez the *Comanchero* had returned from the Jornada, his eyes very big with excitement, and the Spaniard had immediately wanted to see the wagon scout.

At Don Pedro's tent, Kirby noted that the young hidalgo moved with difficulty, placing his feet gingerly and hunching his body carefully, as a man might, say, who had been gut-kicked something fierce and recent. Beyond that physical one there was no other reference to last night's affair, Don Pedro saying what he had to say, direct and level as usual, his first words shooting Ptewaquin's story about Chavez and Big Foot, dead center, leaving Kirby without any support for his suspicions of Chavez's business with the Comanche leader, except his own dislike of Don Pedro.

"Randolph, we're in trouble. My man, Chavez, who has a brother among Big Foot's band of Comanches, met me here at the Crossing with a story he had heard from some Comanchero traders at Blunt's Fort. That story was that Big Foot was waiting at the Lower Cimarron Spring beyond the Jornado to ambush the train and abduct Miss St. Clair. Last night I sent Chavez to visit his brother. Tonight he has returned. The story is true. The Comanches are waiting for us across the Jornado."

Kirby, his racing mind returning at full gallop to that long-past day he had ridden into the Blunt & St. Clair camp at Council Grove, found himself suddenly remembering the dark fears there expressed about just this danger by little Popo Dominquez, the *arriero*. The mountain man hadn't thought Popo was talking idly then, and he didn't think the don was, now.

"Go on," he grunted, noncommittally. "I'm listenin'."

"My plan is a simple one," nodded the don. "If you can better it, I am ready to listen, of course."

"Go on," reiterated Kirby, flatly.

Don Pedro would take the St. Clair girl, along with her Sioux guardian and all the Mexican *arrieros*, and leave tonight, riding hard on up the Arkansas for Blunt's Fort. There he would obtain additional Mexican guards and bring Aurélie over Raton Pass and down the mountain route of the Santa Fe, meeting up with Kirby and the wagons at Mora River Crossing, where the mountain and desert branches of the Trail came back together. Kirby and Sam would of course stay with the train, taking it across the Jornada by the regular route. Forewarned as they were, they should be able to sustain any Comanche attack. Don Pedro respectfully suggested that it would be well for Kirby to leave early, scouting the way for the wagons, riding well ahead of them. *Así, no más*, it was that simple. Did Señor Randolph see it any more clearly?

It developed that Señor Randolph did not. After a brief discussion of details, the mountain

231

man arose to depart, saying he had best mosey over and say his goodbyes to the girl.

"*Por supuesto,* but of course!" the young Spaniard was his complete smiling self again. "Are not such enforced separations the very headiest wines for the further heating of true young love?"

"I'll be damned if I know," grunted Kirby. "I ain't the true young type."

# 14

Five minutes after Don Pedro had arisen to bow and smile his departure from the campfire, Kirby ordered the teamsters rousted out. They listened sullenly as the big scout talked.

"Armijo has give orders thet we're to head on acrost the Water Scrape. We'll pull out ahead of daylight so's we won't have no trouble with the Cheyenne.

"I understand thet since the big rains of 'thirty-four thar's wheel ruts markin' the trail clear acrost. Ain't no danger of gettin' lost no more. Laredo, ye know the Trace better then me. I'm leavin' ye to head the wagons. Armijo has bought hisse'f a yarn thet Big Foot and them Canadian River Comanches are layin' a *wickmunke* to grab Miss St. Clair, so he's takin' her and ridin' fer Blunt's Fort tonight. He figgers thet by the time Big Foot finds out we ain't got the gal with us, he'll have her safe in the fort. Then he'll pick up a Mex escort and bring her over Raton Pass and join up with us where the Blunt's Fort road comes back into the Trail at Mora River Crossin'.

"Me, I dunno. I don't trust the Mex but I'm

runnin' his train and I'm takin' it acrost in the mornin' on his orders. Any man don't like thet kin squeal now. I'm aimin' to roll at four o'clock."

Nobody spoke, and nobody had to. Kirby could read face sign as fast as hand. The skinners were going across with him but their silence was the kind that dropped in gray and fat ahead of a southwest twister.

"Ye'll cook three day's food tonight. It's fifty mile acrost the Scrape and I'm told thar ain't six buffler chips twixt h'yar and the Cimarron to light a blaze with. Every wagon will carry a five-gallon water keg. Every man jack of ye will water his own hitch durin' the night on this side, and I allow ye had best guzzle them till their guts bust. Sam will scout jest ahead of ye, with me way out in front. Any questions?"

"Yeah." The affirmative came in Laredo's arid drawl. "Whut's the ideah of yuh scoutin' so fur ahead? We know the Comanche are waitin' fer us. Cripes, they bin trailin' us, ain't they? And we bin told Big Foot come acrost last night with the Comanchero. We bin told other things, too." His emphasis was tied onto Kirby hard and fast by the narrowed glance that went with it.

"Sech as?" Kirby's question crawled flat as a snake's track.

"Sech as yuh bein' in cahoots with the Comanche to h'ist the gal and hold her fer ransom. I allow all the boys would feel easier if yuh just rode with the train, Mistuh Randolph."

"It's none of yer damn concern, Laredo, but ridin' out ahead ain't my idee." Beyond a sudden, tight lumping of his lean jaw, the mountain man gave no sign of his surprise at the content of Laredo's grim charge. "Don Pedro ordered it done and he's payin' the bills. Any more questions?"

There were none, the men filing away in the darkness as lip-tight as they had come up ten minutes before.

Kirby sent Bluebell splashing across the Arkansas at 3.00 A.M. Behind him no fires warmed the bowel of the new day, and the wagon ground lay quiet under the motionless shadows of pre-dawn. But smaller shadows moved cursing among the hulking Conestogas, and the thin jingle of trace chains spiked the nervous snuffling of the mules, to give the lie to the apparent stillness.

Across the stream, the scout paused to survey the crowding blackness of the sandhills ahead, then swung the mare around the base of the first of them.

Minutes after he disappeared, another rider drew rein at the same spot. A short, squat rider, this one, sitting a tough Spanish mule. He waited until the sandhills swallowed the soft clopping of Bluebell's passage, then put the mule hard left, cutting into the hills on a narrow side trail. A late moon ray, wanly lingering along the deserted track, took a second from its passing to light the rider's face. It was a wide, flat face, vacant-looking under its immobile, toothy grin, and brown and warty as a wild sow's bag — *Chavez, the Comanchero!*

The sandhills ran five miles before opening out to the pancake flatness of the Jornada proper, and as Kirby broke the mare out of their dragging, fetlock-deep sand onto the baked clay of the Water Scrape, the sun was still two hours away. For six hours then, he put his mount across a lie of ground as dead and blasted as a burned planet. At first the mare went steadily enough but at ten o'clock became eleven and eleven inched toward noon, he felt her starting to go rough under him.

The heat, beginning to hammer into his broad back the minute the sun cleared the sandhills at seven, had by midday become unbearable. By one o'clock, Kirby's face, normally sun- and windburned an oak-brown, showed dead-skin gray in the colorless brass light. His eyes, their serous fluid varnish-set by the stifling waves of ground heat, stared unblinking along the rutted tracks of the Trace ahead.

At two, he was chilling and vomiting, his eyes no longer able to find the horizon. Where sand and sky should meet was now nothing but a continuous blind flare. Bluebell's failing walk became a sprawling stumble. Escape or retrack was impossible. And in the molten vastness flanking him on every quarter, a sowbug couldn't have found shade enough to squat in. A man could go ahead, or nothing.

At three, he shared the last water in the paunch-skin bag with Bluebell, stripped the saddle off her and left it propped in the middle of the Trace. Across it, he laid the ten-pound Hawkens, along with his shot pouch and powder flask. If all went well, Sam would find the abandoned gear and bring it along. If not, Kirby wouldn't need it again — ever.

He began to walk, leading the mare, his only burdens the clothes on his back, Clint's flintlock, his Sioux skinning knife. By four, he knew he was not going to make it. He had gone a scant two miles, must still have twenty-five left to the Cimarron. The mare was played out, done. He could crawl maybe another three, four miles without her. Unless —

He dropped the reins. Stood swaying, looking at the mare. His hand came up, the pistol in it wavering along her neck, searching for that spot behind the ear. Dead and down, that pony could give him shade, meat, blood to drink — life. The Spanish mare threw up her head, flared her nostrils. Kirby tightened his grip on her forelock, began sliding the flintlock muzzle into place behind her ear again, and suddenly found his dulling mind registering the fact she had winded something.

Lowering the pistol, he followed her ear-pricked gaze. If it was Indians, she would be whickering. And happen she had smelled water, she would be moving.

It was game, then. The mare had winded game of some kind. Maybe a buffalo, by Tophet. If there was game, there was water. Especially if there was buffalo there was water. Follow the way she was winding. That was what. Quarter out along the line she was staring. This way. She was looking this way. Out along here, away from the Trace.

Kirby went two hundred stumbling steps, seeing nothing. When he looked around to check his position with the mare's, she was gone. All right, she was gone. But where the hell was he? And where was the Trace for that matter? Damn. Mustn't get away from those rain-washed ruts. Lose them and a man was sure done. He tottered back toward the ruts, one hundred yards, two hundred. Where the hell were they? Where was he?

As suddenly as he wondered, he *knew* where he was. And where he was, was nowhere. Lost. Gone. Dead. He lurched on, as a man will. Going ahead. Or was it backwards? Or sideways? No matter. He was going.

Six steps he went, stumbling over nothing, sprawling into the waiting sand. Funny how a man's body would be all done and his guts all gone, and his damn brain still hammering at him to open his eyes, take another look, try once more. And how a man would do it, too.

How he would open them again, just like Kirby was doing now.

Wait a minute. That wasn't sand. Not that stuff, by cripes. Sand didn't come in a round swirl piled up like a blue-mud beehive. His hand went out, clawing for the stuff, his fingers getting into it and coming back with a green-stinking gob of it. He smeared it, still slime-wet from its recent passage, across his mouth and into his nose. Buffalo dung! A whole beautiful, sloppy stack of it. And wet. Still wet in this sucking heat.

That pile of dung wasn't ten minutes old.

They said faith moved mountains. Maybe so. It was hope that moved men. Hope opened a man's eyes as Kirby's were open now, straining red and wide at that line of bull tracks weaving toward the mounding sandhills ahead. Hope made a man know that when he found that bull he would find water. Dammit, hope was what a man lived in — even when he was dying in despair!

When Kirby topped the last sand rise and saw the bull, the shaggy brute was lying down. And that was all. The trail ended there. But where was the water? The sand hollow in which the bull lay was dry as the dust in a mummy's pocket. No, by God, it couldn't be. Yet Kirby knew it was. Knew that the buffalo was as lost as he.

Even as hope went out of him, it flickered in a brief spasm. He saw the picture of a man and a horse sharing the last drops of life in a waterskin, a mountain man's waterskin — the green-cured paunch of a buffalo bull! The flint-lock barrel wavered and circled. Kirby couldn't remember hearing the report but he saw the bull come lurching to his feet, saw him stagger a dozen paces, plunge, buckle-kneed, back into the sand.

In ten minutes of painful crawling, he was up to the creature, burrowing under the enormous head. Lying on his back, he sawed weakly above him with the skinning knife. When at last the jugular was open, the thick blood came belching out, flooding his face and chest with its sickening sweetness. His mouth sought for the severed artery as helplessly as a blind beaver kit's for the dripping nipple, the searching jaws continuing to work spasmodically at the raw pulp of the thing long after it had ceased to yield its clotting fluid.

Kirby awoke to the dazzling blaze of the desert stars. The night about him was as cool and soft as summer wind. His mind was bell-clear.

Finding the knife where he had dropped it under the bull's head, he opened the belly, carefully working out the precious stomach paunch. It was half full of a brackish slime that had once been water and Kirby lay and nursed at the crawling stuff for many minutes. Then he hacked away a ragged chunk of hump meat, chewing the blood carefully out of that. Shortly, he felt good enough to go back in the belly and get out the liver. He ate a pound of this, drank some more of the paunch slime, lay back, closed his eyes. The strength came up in him in pumping waves and wth it his mind began to move.

At moon-up, he stuffed his shirt with strips of humpmeat, made a backpack of the water paunch, and set out along his backtrail. The desert was white-lit with moonblaze, the tracks he and the bull had made leaping black as ink marks from the blotting sands. It was no trick to run their line back to the spot where he had fallen in the bull dung, but it took an hour to unravel the crisscrossing maze he had made after Bluebell disappeared. Finally, he ran it out, coming squarely over the spot where his moccasin prints fanned away from the mare's hoof-marks.

Again he made speed, for the mare's track was glass-clear. He had not run it two hundred yards before his heart began jumping. The prints were running due south by west and apparently not faltering. Another quarter-mile and the tracks still ran true, no swinging, no wandering and still due south by a little west. By cripes, his thinker had totted up the proper sum this crack!

Back by the dead bull, lying in the black, waiting for the moon, he had allowed that if he backtracked and trailed the mare she might go to water, granting she had not died of the heat before sundown. A man could soon tell, once he got on her trackline, if she was heading somewhere or just rambling. If the prints strung out straightaway, especially if they strung out south by west, he as good as had his gutful of Cimarron water.

After a mile he was going in a shuffle trot, a rare grin cracking his lips. The mare's stride had picked up and lengthened. She knew where she was going now, mister, and so did Kirby. She must have whiffed that water as soon as he had left her, right after she had smelled the bull. That would explain how come she was gone when he had looked back. That and the cussed heat-dance that made it so a man couldn't see to swear on it, over fifty yards. But the hell with that. That mare was going for water and that meant the Cimarron. He would have his bare-blistered face under a foot of cool sandseep before the moon sank. A man could thank God for a few things about now, and Kirby did.

"I allow I owe ye one, mister." His eyes left the trail to sweep the wheeling stars. "Happen I hit the Cimarron ye kin share the credit with a blue roan hoss thet kin lay a string of tracks fer twenty mile, straight, on nothin' but a stray whiff of water smell. And with an old he-goat named Sam, who kin teach a man to read mouse sign acrost bedrock, blindfold. And mebbe so with six years of Sioux learnin' up the Mini Sosi. And with a pile of wet chips smack dab in the middle of sixty mile of sand."

It was broad day when Kirby topped the last of the cherty hills beginning to front him, and saw what Bluebell had winded so many hours before: a tumble of weird whitestone hummocks littered with bright-hued pebbles, shouldering in along the course of a dry river bed and buttressing the finest sight a man ever saw — the spreading cattail marsh that rimmed the green-scum pond that was Lower Cimarron Spring.

Even as he ran stumbling for it, Kirby realized the mare was not around the waterhole. Wondered why as he flung himself on his belly to suck at the bracky sludge. Found out when, two minutes later, he raised his eyes from the fetid pool to take his first good look around.

"*Hohahe*," grinned Big Foot, speaking Sioux with a commendable accent, "welcome to our tipi."

Kirby didn't move off his belly; he lay flat and still while his chin dripped scumwater and his eye traveled stride for stride with his galloping thoughts. He could see eight of them, his working knowledge of the red brother's tactical mind telling him he had at least twice that number out of eyetail range, behind him.

That was nice. Nothing between him and getting back to the wagons but twenty-five or thirty Canadian River Comanches. And Big Foot, grinning at him there across the pool.

That red son alone would be enough to tie a man's nerve strings into a knot he would never get untangled. Six foot eight if he was an inch, the outsize vulture, and that ugly he made a blushing beauty out of Satank.

"If I had knowed ye was comin'," the mountain man's grin measured the Comanche's, hard line for hard line, "I'd have boiled a dog." Then in Sioux, he added, "*Wonunican,* excuse me. *Mini ya. Hin yanka.* I am thirsty. You will have to wait."

He drank slowly, having no fear Big Foot wouldn't be there when he was through.

So that was An-gyh P'ih sitting across the rushes there on that skewbald studhorse. That was the famous Heavy Foottrack, eh? Sitting there with a mouth big enough to slide a watermelon in sideways. With a nose you could store a small dog in and still have room for a litter of pups. With a jaw as long and muscle-lumpy as a jack mule's. Well, let him sit. As long as a man was taking his last suck he might as well make it a good long one. As he drank, Kirby heard the hoof thuds of the moving ponies. No mountain man would have to look up to know they had split, four and four, were coming around the waterhole to flank him.

When he did look up, the scout was surprised to see that the Comanches had not unslung their bows, were slouching on their ponies, loose and easy, waiting for him to finish. Damn it, there was something here that didn't figure.

Happen a bunch of hostiles caught a *Wasicun* scout at a desert waterhole with no horse and only a popgun pistol on him, they had ought to feather his hide in a hurry. These red sons were just sitting there, slack-tailed and stupid.

Kirby stood up, spat a sneering mouthful of water on the ground, sucked in his empty paunch, belched disdainfully.

The eight sand-carved Comanche visages split in as many appreciative grimaces. Touching the fingers of his left hand to his forehead, Big Foot grunted admiringly. "*Woyuonihan*, you have my respect."

"*Ha ho*," answered Kirby unsmilingly. "What do you want? Why don't you kill me, now?"

"Look behind you," shrugged Big Foot. "Your eyes will tell you."

Kirby turned, expecting the hill behind him to be crowded with Comanches, saw not a single one. But what he did see made sudden sense of two overdue puzzles: why Don Pedro had ordered him to scout so far ahead; why Big Foot's band had not feathered him up when he was belly-down at the waterhole.

"*Buenas dias, señor.*" Chavez's grin had not flickered a muscle since Kirby had seen him at the wagon camp the night before. "*Qué pasa?*"

" 'Qué pasa' my eye!" growled Kirby. "Ye know whut passes, ye greasy buzzard. And so do I. Real cute, ain't it? I ride out ahead of a train thet knows fer sure thar's Comanches ahead. I disappear and the Injuns *wickmunke* my wagons. My boys see me ridin' like a brother in amongst the Comanches. They already bin told by Armijo thet I bin in touch with Big Foot. Cripes! I ought to blow my own brains out and save ye jaspers the trouble."

Chavez stretched his grin one more tooth. "You are pretty smart, Señor. But not so smart as *El Patrón*. It is true, what you say. We will not kill you and you will ride with us like a brother, but not after the wagons, señor."

Kirby took that in his teeth and chewed it. When he spat it out the taste was bitter as bear gall. "The gal, eh? Ye're aimin' to use me some way fer gettin' at Aurélie St. Clair. Why, ye puke-faced damn —"

"Softly, señor. Do not strain yourself, please. You must favor your strength. For after we have used you to *El Patrón*'s purpose, An-gyh P'ih has even more pleasant prospects of his own for you."

Seeing they did not mean to kill him right off, Kirby took off on another scent line. Turning to Big Foot with a fawning show of hope, he asked, "What does the Brown Frog mean? Does An-gyh P'ih really place a value of his own on White Stripe's poor life?"

The towering Comanche looked down at him, thick lips smeared with the brush of contempt. "Ho, look you!" he called aside to his fellows. "See how The Belcher crawls now that he smells a chance for his mongrel life!" The watching braves nodded, adding their sneers to the chief's. "Hear me, White Stripe," the Comanche leader went on, pointing an arm the length and heft of a fencepost at one of his followers. "Do you mark this chief?"

Kirby studied the savage, surprised he hadn't noticed he was not a Comanche. "I mark that he is *Kae-kat'da-kih,* a Kiowa man."

"Nothing else?"

"No, nothing."

"You have it in your mind that you know a Kiowa chief called Satank?"

"Yes, White Stripe knows Satank."

"Then you still do not know this one?"

Kirby started to deny he did, but the name Satank rolled back the trail-miles of memory. Back to Walnut Crossing. Back to Ash Creek. Sure. He knew this one, all right. The wonder was that he had needed more than one look to remember him. "Ta-dl Ka-dei," he answered levelly. "Bad Liver."

"You may well say that name with your bowels loosening," nodded Big Foot. "For when I have done with you what the Spanish Chief has paid me to do, Ta-dl Ka-dei will take you back to Satank. And with An-gyh P'ih's blessing. There seems to be a little matter between you and him and the Arkansas River."

*"Aiii-eee!"* Kirby winced. "I recall it well. My horse slipped. I did not mean to push Satank in the water. *Wonunican.* It was a mistake. You may tell him it was a mistake."

"Aye, it was indeed," agreed the Comanche.

"But you may tell him yourself. Satank will understand. He is noted for his love of the white brother. Being especially fond of *Wasicun* goddam-scouts who knock him into the water in front of a party of his picked braves —"

Chavez edged his mule forward, interrupting the chief's oration. Speaking rapidly in Comanche, a tongue Kirby followed but poorly, he harangued Big Foot. By the accompanying hand signs, the watching scout understood that as far as Chavez was concerned the conversation was well past being done.

Apparently the chief was in agreement, for he turned to his men, lashing at them with sudden short phrases of the bickering Comanche dialect. They snapped back at him, putting Kirby in mind of so many snarling village curs, but falling to his orders quickly enough, the six of them getting behind Kirby just as Chavez emerged from a near bend in the river channel leading the missing Bluebell. Kirby swung up on the mare and Chavez tied his feet securely under her belly. His hands were left free, a stout lead rope being run from the mare's neck to a tie ring in the cantle of Chavez's saddle. Getting aboard his mule, the Comanchero signaled Big Foot that he was ready. The Comanche nodded, reined his pony alongside Bluebell.

"*Hopo!*" He grunted the Sioux go-word at Kirby. "*Hookahey*, let's go."

"*Waste*, good!" The scout made his voice inveigling, the smile that went with it obsequious. "White Stripe is eager to ride with his Comanche friends. Eager to hear how savagely and with what cunning An-gyh P'ih plans to seize the red-haired squaw. To know what sly plan the wily fox's brain of Big Foot has —"

Big Foot's answering smile was the spirit of warm appreciation. Kirby saw the great arm coming, couldn't for all his trained speed, move to avoid it in time. It crushed into his neck, just missing the face at which it had been aimed. The blow was like one from a giant-swung wagon tongue, nearly tearing his head off his shoulders. He was still conscious as the following smash came crunching in — saw the clubbed fist whistling down on him, big as a beanpot, hard as a millstone. He felt the searing, instant pain of it explode across his ear and the side of his head, remembering nothing more.

Looking at the bloody-headed figure flopping across the withers of the startled Bluebell, Big Foot turned his paint stud away and summed up his whole Comanche's viewpoint of the situation in a single, backflung English phrase to the leering Chavez.

"Goddam. Him talk too much. Quiet now."

# 15

That ten-day march with the Canadian River Comanches, dogging the main track of the Santa Fe Trail south and west, up the Cimarron, across to the Canadian and down to Point of Rocks, was one for any mountain man to remember — and Kirby never forgot it.

It began with a two-day brush with six trappers from Blunt's Fort caught out in the prairie flats west of Middle Spring of the Cimarron, continued with a full day's stopover at Big Foot's base camp at Willow Bar on the same river and a hair-raising, all-night buffalo barbecue among the nomad Ciboleros, the wandering Mexican buffalo hunters, far south along the Rabbit Ear River, and concluded with a murderous attack on four white herders from Santa Fe and their five-hundred-head herd of top-grade Spanish horses.

The horseherd runoff ended the recreational aspects of the Tshaoh outing. A man with any kind of an Indian nose at all could smell that the slitmouth sons were getting down to payoff cases now.

A few miles downtrail, with dark coming on

apace, the savages left the Santa Fe at a wild-looking spot called Point of Rocks, pushing the stolen herd across trackless country to ford the Río Colorado — the Canadian River — well above its regular crossing on the main trail. Here the taciturn horsemen ate the last of the fresh buffalo ribs brought from the *Cibolero* camp, rested and watered their new livestock. Shortly they hit out again, driving what they wanted of the horses, abandoning the rest.

There followed a forced fifteen-mile night march, attended only by feeble starlight and the lonely crying of coyotes, to a junction with what figured to be the lower fork of the Canadian. Here, the marauders turned west, following the course of the new fork up into a country as rough and rocky as any Kirby had ever ridden. Inquiring of Chavez, whose emptyheaded company by contrast to that of the sullen Comanches he was learning to enjoy, he discovered the hostiles had two good reasons for the detouring cutoff.

First, the main trail reached the regular crossing of the Canadian just a few miles beyond Point of Rocks. Here were stationed (sometimes!) the Mexican Customs Guards who met the incoming wagon outfits, inspected and taxed their loads, and gave them military escort on into Santa Fe. *Hijo!* That was why Point of Rocks was the unwritten boundary for Indian depradation along the Santa Fe. The Comanches just did not work past Point of

Rocks, señor. A sort of gentlemen's agreement with the Mexican Government, perhaps. *Dio sabe!* No matter, it was the way things were.

Secondly, the westward-climbing course of the stream they were following, Ocate Creek, led into the Blunt's Fort road to Santa Fe. The *Señor* would recall that this was the road down which Don Pedro would bring the flame-haired Señorita. Aha! That brought a spark, eh? *Por Dios!* One should hope so. All they had to do now was follow Ocate Creek to the Blunt's Fort road. Then take that road north to a place called Vermejo Creek. Remember that name, señor. Vermejo Creek. That would be a place to see. And there were going to be some real things to see when An-gyh P'ih went in at that place to "seize" that girl away from Don Pedro. And the señor would be in the best place to see them, eh? *Ya lo creo!* Indeed, indeed. And in the rigft place to be seen, too, eh? *Jesus Maria!* Right in the front rank of the Tshaoh attack. Right between Big Foot and Black Dog, just as *El Patreón* had ordered. That was the plan, *niño.*

The distance? Oh, not much, señor. Thirty miles, no more. That roundabout sneak had added some time but there was no hurry now. Lots of time. Big Foot always gave himself plenty of time to avoid things like Mexican Customs Guards. Never rushed things, that chief. Always a careful one. A real big planner. *Hijo!*

Forty-eight hours later, Kirby had his chance

to see *how* big and *how* real.

At 1.00 A.M. the Comanches stopped to
water and graze the stolen herd. The warriors,
excepting the half-dozen detailed to hold the
herd, threw down their worn buffalo robes and
greasy Three Point blankets and dropped into
the trained slumber of the nomad soldier. This
time Kirby, anchored to Chavez by a horsehair
rope and flanked by the assorted snores of a
hundred Comanches, had no difficulty joining
them.

He awoke to a day and place as beautiful as
ever a mountain man dreamed. There was no
mistaking the dry bite of that air, the swimming
blue of that sky, the water-clear sharpness of
everything a man looked at from a juniper cone
six feet away to a snow peak sixty miles. No
confusing the cotton white of those clouds, the
thin carry of the lonely shrill from that eagle
speck painted motionless above yonder crag. If
they had less than six thousand feet under them
Kirby would miss his guess. By damn, they
were up high, and judging from the noisy race
of the narrowing stream pounding its way back
along their last night's pony tracks, were going
higher with today's march.

That march, the sun cool and glass-bright
the whole of the easy-shuffling way through the
endless quiet of sky-high red rock and blue juniper, had Kirby's mountain-hungry eye swinging to every quarter of the compass. The hours

went on hawk's wings, hushed and silent, the winding track of the Blunt's Fort branch of the Santa Fe Trail curling in out of the cobalt northern peaks — about 2.00 P.M. crossing the Trail, the Comanches turned north. The late afternoon haze brought them to another beautiful mountain stream which Chavez identified as Vermejo Creek.

The name put a chill up Kirby's long spine that drew his belly in like green rawhide.

Vermejo Creek, far northern tributary of the Río Colorado. Vermejo Creek, its crossing of the Blunt's Fort road a mile off there in the purple east. Vermejo Creek, pre-agreed site of Big Foot's date with destiny — and with Don Pedro — and green-eyed Aurélie St. Clair.

Vermejo Creek, end of the trail for Kirby Randolph.

That first night on Vermejo Creek was a faithful tracing of the previous one on the Ocate Fork. Kirby spent it laced cozily to Chavez, surrounded by the same ugly bevy of sleeping braves. The following morning he was awakened by a now familiar prodding in the rear.

"*Arriba,*" nodded Chavez. "An-gyh P'ih wants to see us."

They found the chief squatted on a rock spur jutting high over the tumbling creek and giving unlimited view of the rolling country to the north. With him were Ta-dl Ka-dei and two wolf-grinning subchiefs. Horsehead and Crazy Legs. Big Foot and Company were in good spirit.

Splitting his face with the third grin Kirby had seen there since meeting him, Big Foot waved the captive scout to a seat in the chosen circle. There followed then through the usual conglomerate of hand signs, broken Sioux and butchered English, with Chavez bridging the rougher spots with his sibilant Spanish, what must have been the longest Comanche speech on record. It was addressed principally to Kirby and delivered with the patent pride of one gifted field commander explaining a particularly juicy tactical situation to another. Its expanding translation left the white scout groping for some place to set a solid thought in its quagmire of belly-queasing revelations.

. . . In the first place let it be understood that White Stripe was to listen carefully that he might understand the sort of craft required to make a name as lofty as Big Foot's in a career as touchy as Santa Fe Trail raiding. Toward this end it was necessary that the white scout get it clearly in his head the exact way the plan went, as originally agreed between An-gyh P'ih and the Young Spanish Fool. There had been some minor touches added. . . .

Kirby saw Chavez's eyebrows go up on that reference, guessed the chief was naming Don Pedro and that the Comanchero did not cotton to the implication. However Chavez was old at this game, made no further sign, and went along with his end of the translation.

... The Young Spaniard had offered a price in gold for the abduction of the St. Clair Chief's daughter. This was to happen thus. The Spaniard, coming down the mountain road from Blunt's Fort, would make a very loose camp on Vermejo Creek. Then Big Foot would ride in and scatter the few Mexicans who would be the girl's guard. The Spaniard would fire his gun, making a great show of fighting, but Big Foot would get the girl and ride east to hide out on Ute Creek, leaving the Mexican guards free to go back to Fort Blunt and spread the alarm. Riders vould then go out to Taos and the St. Clair Chief would come, bringing the gold for the girl.

*Wagh!* The Spaniard would then "escape," make his fearless way to the fort, offer to risk his life once more by contacting the Comanches and arranging the ransom. It was that simple. The Spaniard would be a real hero and probably get the pale squaw for his tipi into the bargain ...

Chavez, evidently in the dark as to the working details of his master's plan beyond its Vermejo Creek rendezvous, nodded with vacuous pleasure as the Comanche finished, inquiring with careful tact if An-gyh P'ih had not forgotten something. A little thing to do with the open-mouthed *Wasicun* prisoner, there.

... Yes! Big Foot had almost forgotten.

When the attack on the girl's camp was made, the Spaniard had insisted that White Stripe be right up there in front with Big Foot and Black Dog. All the Mexicans would see him. Everybody in New Mexico would know that the white goddam-scout of Blunt and St. Clair had ridden with the Comanches that stole the girl. That he had plotted all along, even as the Young Spanish Chief had said, to steal the girl and make a big ransom. . . .

So far in the story Kirby's surprise had come from the fact the chief would choose to tell him of the plan at all. He had known all along that Don Pedro was going to pay that ransom and make himself the big he-coon in the deal while fixing it for Kirby to wind up low hound in the dogpile.

But bigger surprises were building. Another mouth was getting ready to drop, dumb-open. And where that other mouth was going to be sagging was in the pock-pitted mask of the frog-faced Chavez. Now was to come the professional touch. Now was to come the Comanche part of the deal. The little "added something." And its coming watered up Chavez's bandy knees so had he didn't dast to stand for fear of falling. Big Foot began to talk. And long before he had finished the Comanchero had ceased to translate, sitting gray-faced and putty-mouthed under the crooked forking of the giant Comanche's tongue.

. . . Now then, White Stripe was to understand he had heard only the Young Spaniard's part of the deal. Now came An-gyh P'ih's part. And would the *Wasicun* scout forgive Big Foot for having just thought of it? Had his part of the plan come to him sooner, he could have spared his friend White Stripe a long ride. As it was, here they were, and Big Foot's belated idea was this. Did White Stripe see those peaks over there? Those were the Spanish Peaks. And that peak beyond them was Raton Peak. And in between them came the Blunt's Fort road. Down that road, no later than tomorrow, possibly this very morning, would come the girl.

See how close those peaks were? Well that was how close the girl was. And she was coming, never fear. Black Dog and six scouts had left before dawn to ride up there and make smoke when they saw her. Soon the smoke would come. And here was Big Foot waiting on this rock. . . .

The chief paused for breath and to savor the meat taste of the thing. Switching his slant gaze from Kirby to Chavez, he played his Comanche hole card.

. . . So, Comanchero, what do you suppose has happened to your patron's plan, now? Listen. The attack will go right here. We will take the girl and your master. As he said to do. Then a little change. Just a touch. Just no escape for the Spaniard. That simple. What do you think of that, Comanchero? . . .

While the dull-witted Chavez was making up

his mind, Kirby had his plumb made. The slick, cagey buzzards. They had it figured simple and clean center. Sure, Aurélie was worth her weight in gold. So take her. But Don Pedro's heft could be counted in the same coin — and he weighed a hell of a lot more than the cat-slim St. Clair girl. Cripes, old Governor Armijo had half the gold in New Mexico. *Wagh!* Touch the fingertips in Big Foot's direction. Respect him. He was a real chief and a blue-chip trader to boot. If a St. Clair fawn was good pickings, an Armijo cub was better.

The slippery devils were aiming to hold Don Pedro for ransom, too!

Chavez had finally arrived at the same dry waterhole of thought, his tongue clacking with the dust of the discovery. "You mean to hold Don Pedro, then?"

"I mean that, yes," nodded Big Foot, heavy lips moist in the morning sun. "It is only good business. If one is good, two are better. Is that not a true thing, Cousin?"

"What of me, then?" The Comanche breed stumbled ahead, his empty smile capped by the frown lines cupping the sweat-beaded paste of his forehead. "What of your old friend Chavez? The companion of your campfires? The blood of your brothers? The —"

Picking his battered musket from the rock beside him, Big Foot skyed the piece, sighting casually along its rusted barrel, his easy words interrupting the breed. "Oh, him? Faithful

Chavez? He is just a little problem." The musket dropped with the words, centering squarely below the glistening frown lines. "Like a sick dog that is no good any more," smiled Big Foot, and shot the Comanchero between the eyes.

Chavez had been sitting close to the edge of the jutting council perch. The heavy half-ounce ball splattered his nose like a lead fist, driving his head back, toppling his slack body backward over the rock ledge. Kirby could see the fall but in the space of his held breath, the dull splash came up from below, putting its harsh period to the sentence of silence following the Comanche's shot.

"I never liked him," shrugged Big Foot. "Too greasy and sweating and smiling the whole time."

The far-flung puzzle which had claimed as its first fragment the arrival in St. Louis of a lonely mountain man aboard the Missouri packet *Prairie Belle* and which had gathered its ill-assorted pieces throughout the long weeks of wagon toil across the dreary plains of Kansas Territory, which had been designed by the strange beauty of a wayward halfbreed girl, colored by the passion of a reckless New Mexican hidalgo, cut apart by the tasseled lance of a Kiowa war chief, scattered by the crazy horsemanship of a Comanche trail raider, seized and fiercely held together by a hard-eyed Blunt and

St. Clair wagon scout, now fell into swift and final place.

An hour after the death of Chavez, with the stone pipe starting its fourth round of the silent group on the sunlit ledge above Vermejo Creek, the aquamarine drop of the sky behind Raton Peak broke into a climbing bloom of cottony smoke blossoms.

Instantly the pipe stopped passing, the five sets of eyes narrowing with the squint of far-sighting.

The smoke puffs broke in a series of three, two, five, followed by a long pause and a repeat of the complete series. Big Foot nodded to Horsehead where the subchief squatted by a knee-high cordon of neat-laid greasewood twigs. Horsehead nodded back and put his hand out to Crazy Legs. The latter handed over the smoldering pipe and Horsehead knocked its live embers into the calloused palm of his hand, transferred them carefully into the base of the greasewood pile. Here a little blowing and a handful of dry piñon needles quickly had an orange flameburst growing.

Horsehead arose, threw an armload of green juniper on the blazing greasewood, at the same time flipping a filthy red blanket over the burning pile. The flame hit the green foliage with a sucking hiss, belching up a clot of gray-white smoke.

Twirling the blanket, Horsehead broke the column into three close puffs, then kicked the whole fire over the cliff, dispersing the leftover smoke with quick, fanning sweeps of the blanket.

As Kirby watched the three smoke balls climb up out of the flanking hills, Big Foot held a grunted discussion with Bad Liver.

"*Aii-eee*, did you read that, Ta-dl Ka-dei?"

"No." The Kiowa was his usual solemn self. "I read Horsehead's all right. His work with the smoke is very clean, that of an artist. Black Dog is careless. Was it two, three, four he sent, or what?"

"Three, two, five."

"Oh, then everything is good. They are coming."

"Yes, they are coming. But not tonight. They will only just get here tonight. Tomorrow, early. We will go in on them then."

"Well now, with this new plan of yours, you will not need White Stripe. Is my tongue straight?"

"No, we won't need him. You want to start back now, Ta-dl?"

"Yes. I will take White Stripe and go. Right now, I mean. It is a long way. Satank will be wondering, already."

Hearing his Comanche name, Kirby quit watching the smoke, went to listening and watching the hand signs between the Kiowa and Big Foot. What he picked up in the next few seconds trailed his mind clear back to Lower Cimarron Spring.

"Oh sure, you take him and go, old friend. Tell Satank we never saw his four hundred Holy Irons. But tell him I send him White Stripe, anyway. Say it is for the time I did not come for that raid in Texas. Tell him this, too. Tell him I got the girl and the Spaniard and sold them back for a real price. More gold than any Kiowa ever heard of. You tell old Black Face that. White Stripe is yours. Go on, now."

"I'll need a little help," shrugged Bad Liver. "I can't watch that one all the way by myself. I can't keep just these two eyes open all the way to the Arkansas."

"Oh, sure. Good. Horsehead and Crazy Legs will go. Now I am thinking it is too bad that Comanchero went over the edge. He was a good watcher. Too bad he wasn't all Comanche. We could have used him more. And say. Put White Stripe on that good mule the squat one left behind. I have had my eye on that tall blue mare. Leave her. She is a real horse."

There were wide spots in the trail of the chief's running string of barks but Kirby got the gist of it. Never long the man to be without some plan for the immediate future, he already had an idea stewing anent his projected return to Satank and the Arkansas Kiowa. And in the belly of that idea there was no room for the dead Comanchero's plodding mule. He was on his feet the moment he understood Big Foot meant to appropriate Bluebell.

The look of injured pride and incredulous disbelief widening the white scout's trusting gray eyes couldn't have been lost on a common pig, let alone a full-blood boar of Big Foot's elegant breeding.

"What wrong White Stripe?" the chief demanded, his glowering frown backing the hesitant English, slit eyes narrowing suspiciously.

"I claim *Woyuonihan*," responded Kirby, careful to keep his dignity limping with serious injury.

"Courtesy Rules? White Stripe claims Courtesy Rules on An-gyh P'ih? How so, Cousin?"

"Let me ask you a question," countered Kirby.

"Go ahead, ask it." Big Foot made the hand sign of assent, the scout nodding stiffly in acceptance, putting his words with patent pride.

"Am I a chief?"

"*Hau.*" The Comanche was quick with the admission. "A real chief. I have said it before."

"All right. Now. What will Satank do with me?"

"Take your hair. Naturally."

"Even so. Then White Stripe will be dead. Is that not so?" Kirby made the death sign in the air, Big Foot nodding in pleased agreement. "Very well, then. And does a chief ride a mule to *Wanagi Yata*?" He used the Sioux word for the hereafter. "Does he ride a damn longear to

The Gathering Place Of The Souls?"

Too long a setter of wily snares himself, An-gyh P'ih, not to recognize the snap of the trap steel when he had put his own huge foot squarely on a neat-baited pan. The Sioux-trained scout had trapped him. And Big Foot did not struggle. His was the typical Plains Indian's religious regard for the gracious Courtesy Rules, that stiff set of principles governing the treatment of friend and foe alike, and which was so at variance with their other, fiercer philosophies, serving as the unwritten but not transgressable law for the conduct of red War and Peace.

His slabface got blacker than the belly of coming thunder, yet his answer to Kirby's charge was a quick-shrugged, "Take the mare. Goddam. She is yours." Then a growling, begrudged admission. "*Woyuonihan.* A chief rides his best pony on that dark trail."

Kirby knew better than to get elaborate with his gratitude, giving the Comanche chief only the simple "thank you" hand sign, and a muttered *"Ho ha!"* in Sioux before turning to Bad Liver.

"Come on," the white scout gestured indifferently, "I am ready. *Hopo. Hookahey.* Let's go."

They set out in a northeasterly direction, Bad Liver leading the way, Kirby next, Horsehead and Crazy Legs bringing up the rear. The country was open, the way level and clear. It was 1.00 P.M. and high time for some tall thinking. Leastways, the scout allowed, for a man in his saddle, it was.

Regardless of old Sam's sour estimate that Kirby's brains were not located in his head, the young mountain man had not been where he had been and seen what he had seen without having picked up a fair smattering of frontier mathematics, particularly Indian algebra. Given a point to start from and a place to go to, Kirby thought he could figure the in-between spots about as quick as the next fellow. In this case you started from where you were — riding a strange country, your feet belly-tied under your horse, your horse lead-roped to the rider's in front of you. And where you were going — God seeing it your way — was back to the Blunt's Fort road and Aurélie St. Clair.

Meantime you had three damn good reasons to keep you from getting started.

Reason number one was a Kiowa chief who had ridden his first war trail before Kirby cut his second teeth. Ta-dl Ka-dei was past forty, of middle height, lean as a piñon. He was a light-colored, sullen Indian, totally lacking the ready humor common to his race. His blank, cut-rock face looked dumb as stone, fronted a mind as honed as an old axe blade. Looking at him, Kirby figured Bad Liver was a boy you didn't make more than one mistake with.

Number two reason was a Comanche

subchief of about Kirby's own age. Horsehead was a big Indian and homely as blue sin. The long, pony-nosed, slack-jawed face, which together with the roach cut of his coarse hair gave him his name, was set atop a body as muscular and heavy as a bear's. Horsehead talked slow, moved slow, probably thought slow. Figuring him escapewise, a man might reckon he could be got around. Providing you did your getting fast. But just be sure you got clean around him. Happen he got those grizzly paws on you, you were done.

Reason three was a barrel-chested little man with a prune of a head that looked like it had been parboiled in saltwater and sun-shrunk to half-size. Crazy Legs, with his bloated body, shriveled head and ricket-twisted legs, looked like a first-rate Comanche clown; was about as funny as a kick in the groin. In the bird-quick shift of the misshapen man's eyes, Kirby read real danger. Good things came in small packages most times. And once in a while, bad ones, too. Sizing him, Kirby decided Crazy Legs was a bad package.

Having totted up his men, the captive scout calculated his chances, and found them skinnier than a wet weasel. A man couldn't blow his break when he finally did make it, against hard cases like these. And he couldn't very well make any sets for them to step into, either. All he could do was to wait for the time and the trail to bring him his chance.

Six hours of monotonous, sun-drowsy trail jogging and a sudden blind turn in the climbing rock trace brought Kirby his.

At first they had encountered roughening country and a rising trail. The way had led through a growing maze of red boulders and thickening juniper scrub, the direction still northeast. Now, two hours later and a thousand feet higher, Bad Liver signaled a halt. Facing them was a fifty-foot rock slide. Beyond its top Kirby could see nothing but sky, judging from that that the trail topped out up above and most likely dropped sharply on the far side.

Bad Liver grunted a short word to the two Comanches, turned and put his pony up the scaly talus. Scare-footed and wary as a cat, the wiry Indian cayuse negotiated the slide, disappeared over its top rise. Horsehead nodded to Kirby, waved at the slide, proudly unveiled his secret command of the scout's mother tongue. "Him goddam hill. You climb all same fast Bad Liver."

"*Ho ha,* thank you," grinned Kirby. "And I hope ye fracture yer big red butt on yer turn!"

"Good! Good!" Horsehead accepted the compliment with swelling pleasure. "*T'ou-yh,* go ahead!"

Bluebell took the slide as nimbly as had the Kiowa's pony, coming out above on a sight that stole Kirby's wind. There was a level rock bench up there about thirty feet wide, and then there was nothing but one of the biggest holes in the ground Kirby had ever looked over. That canyon, hidden back of the rockslide climb, was at least eight hundred feet deep, its walls going down so vertically they appeared to be leaning in at the tops. Evidently the trail continued down its near face from the spot where Bad Liver sat his pony at the far edge of the bench. The captive scout did not wait to see.

Happen God wanted to write it out in letters eight hundred feet deep, Kirby could read *chance* as quick as the next man.

Heeling Bluebell, he got her switched onside toward the waiting Bad Liver. As soon as she had turned he began needling her with his hidden offside foot, sending her sidling toward the Kiowa as though she were moving through her own skittishness. Behind him, as he got the mare moving, he heard the scramble of the next pony coming up the rock slide.

Ten feet from Bad Liver, Kirby heard the Kiowa's sudden growl. "That's enough! Hold that pony! It's a bad trail over here where we go down."

"Whar *you* go down, ye slant-eyed buzzard!" Kirby dug his heels into the startled mare, leaping her into Bad Liver's standing mount with his soft-cursed answer. Eleven hundred pounds of Spanish mare drove, tall shoulder into scrawny rump, into eight hundred pounds of Indian pony. Ta-dl Ka-dei's fading scream was lost under his falling mount's terrified neighing.

There was a belly-wrenching moment during which Kirby had full cause to wonder if Bluebell were going to take him over after Bad Liver and his pony. Then, with the tiny, twisting images of the Kiowa and his mount five hundred feet below and still falling mirrored in his widened eye corner, he felt the shift in the balance of the clawing mare move back over the safe edge of the cliff.

If there were any time left now, it was all-fired short. Wheeling Bluebell, he hurled her back across the rock bench. Horsehead, coming up over the lip of the slide, his stout gelding off balance on the treacherous footing, was slower than Bad Liver. He did not have time even to yell out. Bluebell crashed, full-breast-on, into Horsehead's pony, sending the big buck and his mount, croup over Comanche, back down the slide. This time Kirby could not hold the mare on the bench, the two of them cascading on down the slide in the wake of the avalanche of rock chips and boulders set up by the falling Comanche and his pony. Stiff-legged and haunch-sliding, Bluebell did manage to stay upright the whole way, luckily keeping her hoarsely yelling rider unhurt and very much in the fight.

As much could not be said for Horsehead. Nor for Crazy Legs.

Fifty feet below, the second Comanche saw

Horsehead and his pony in time to get his own mount out of the way of their falling bodies and almost clear of the main stream of the sliding rocks. Almost but not quite. A knee-high wave of rotten granite and head-size boulders fanned swiftly out from the central fall of talus, knocking his little spotted mare's legs clean out from under her, sending Crazy Legs sprawling.

He was lucky. It went a little firmer with Horsehead.

The big Comanche had bounced onto the hardpan of the lower trail with force enough to stun a range bull, had still enough dumb strength to struggle halfway to his knees before his own horse, legs thrashing, body twisting crazily, had landed squarely atop him. Kirby heard the crunch and splinter of the bones above the noise of his own descent and knew they weren't horse bones popping like that. A second later Bluebell hit the hardpan, slid clear of the still moving slide, fell to her knees, and nearly went clean on over.

Bad Liver had been the only one of the three Indians with a gun, Horsehead carrying only a skull club and a short buffalo lance, Crazy Legs a hunting bow and three-foot war axe. Kirby could be glad of that, now!

Kneeing the stumbling Bluebell to her feet and swinging her hard around toward Crazy Legs, Kirby knew he had so far played in more luck than even a mountain man dast count on, thought sure his string was past due to snap.

And Crazy Legs nearly snapped it for him, too.

The little Comanche had fallen clear of his horse and the slide. Now, with the blue roan mare booming down on him, he snake-rolled out from under her rush, nocked an arrow in the roll, and let drive at Kirby's back as Bluebell's momentum carried the scout past. The shaft took Kirby low in the left side, hit a rib, glanced, came out clean in front, passing through the fleshy part of his left breast. The next instant he had the mare spun around and going back at Crazy Legs.

This time the Comanche got his arrow nocked and that was all. Bluebell's stabbing forefeet hit him in the shoulder, shattering the bone and throwing the loosed arrow wide and wild. Again her momentum carried her past the squat bowman, but this time when Kirby got her turned there was no nocked arrow waiting.

Crazy Legs lay thrashing and twisting in the trail, writhing like a runover rattler, his jerking body inching toward the war axe which had fallen ten feet away.

By now Bluebell was spooked bad. When Kirby tried putting her over Crazy Legs for the third time she swerved aside and bucked away. Turning her, the scout made his remaining best play, beating the crippled Comanche to the axe. He made it with a shade to spare, hanging far over the nervous mare's side, his bound feet holding him on, scooping the axe off the ground three feet ahead of Crazy Legs' spasming reach. It was but the work of a moment to slash the razor blade across the rawhide that bound his feet under Bluebell, leap off the mare and go cat-crouching back toward the crawling Comanche.

Crazy Legs died quick then, the axe blade parting his skull from pate to jawbone in one professional slice.

Turning to whistle up Bluebell, Kirby was startled to see a movement back by Horsehead's fallen mount and realized a second later that the big brave had somehow survived the impact of the pony's full weight and had just wriggled out from under the dying animal. Now he lay on his belly, groping and hitching around like a blindworm, his huge body paralyzed from the waist down, his peering face a featureless pulp. In agreement with his feelings in such cases, Kirby killed the suffering horse first. Then, a little sick from blood and shock, he picked up Horsehead's buffalo lance and drove it through the stricken brave's back. Horsehead rolled half over, clawed feebly at the lancehead where it came out in front, convulsed, coughed, slid back over on his belly and lay still.

Kirby sagged down where he was, vomited hard, lay face down and resting for twenty minutes.

When his head got clear he went after the arrow Crazy Legs had put into him. Breaking the shaft where it entered his back, he pulled it out in front, greatly relieved to know by the easy way it came through that he was not bad hit. Sure, a man would know he had had it in him, all right. But it wasn't any wound to keep a hard body from riding a long trail.

And he for sure had himself a long trail to ride.

Letting the wound bleed out, he gathered up Horsehead's knife and lance and Crazy Legs' axe. The bow, never having learned its use, he left. Legging up on Bluebell, he caught Crazy Legs' spotted mare, transferred over onto her, and set out on the backtrail, hand leading Bluebell.

He took it easy the first miles down out of the rough country they had entered earlier that afternoon. Eight o'clock and heavy dusk found him out on the level open of the plateau. At this point a man had best do some figuring. And he had best do it right, too. Happen he wanted to beat Big Foot to Aurélie St. Clair, he had better!

# 16

In a game where Aurélie St. Clair was all the chips in the middle of the blanket, a man hated like sin to plunk his whole stake on a string of Comanche smoke signals. But what was a scout in Kirby's buckskins to do?

According to that morning's smoke-talk from Black Dog, Don Pedro's company would now be in the ambush camp on Vermejo Creek. A man had to go on that. Lay his entire plot from there. That meant heading due west and hoping to hit the wagon road from Blunt's Fort, north of Vermejo, and follow it south to come down behind the Spaniard's camp. One thing was sure. He could no longer backtrail the pony tracks he and the Indians had made after leaving Big Foot's bunch. It was plumb night now and in an unfamiliar land. Either he cut across country and took his shot in the dark at hitting the wagon road, or he whimpered uncle and crawled off his horse right where he was.

Where Kirby came from, Uncle was a word you used solely in reference to your male kinfolk.

He set out west across the shadowed plateau,

holding Crazy Legs' mare in a high lope, hoping she had eyes in her feet for gopher holes and water cuts, and bottom enough to stick on the rolling pace for four hours.

She had. Midnight and the building light of the fat New Mexican stars brought them out, smack-dab, on the Blunt's Fort road.

Here he let the Comanche pony and Bluebell blow out for ten minutes, then swung them south and down the level track of the broad wagon trail. Two hours later, with Crazy Legs' spotted pony run clean into the ground, he spied what he had been scanning the night sky for — the star-hard outline, black against the hilly horizon, of the landmark spur above Vermejo Creek.

Now, hard onto a mile ahead of him must lie the Mexican camp of Don Pedro Armijo. And west of that another mile, under the jut-out of the spur, yonder, the Comanche hide-out. So far, mighty good. His string might be stretched somewhat but it was still of a piece.

Getting off the spotted mare, he took a careful feel of Bluebell, and found her breathing easy with only enough lather up to have her warmed for the real work. Next he did something he had to — unsheathed Horsehead's skinning knife and felt his way up alongside the drooping neck of Crazy Legs' good little pony. Getting in under her hanging head he put a lifting shoulder under her jaw, located the pounding jugular with his left hand, and slashed quickly through it with the knife in his right. He stepped back, spitting disgustedly as the hot sweetness showered over his face and forearms. The mare shuddered a little, staggered two steps, went to her knees.

The scout grimaced, spat again. A man hated a thing like that, but you couldn't leave a Comanche pony wandering night-free within winding and whickering distance of her friends in Big Foot's horse herd. Just the right pony nicker at the wrong time had lifted too many a white man's hair. Kirby did not aim to lose his the same way. Three minutes for a painstaking nose wrap on Bluebell and he was moving again, hand leading the mare, walking as softly as his thin Arapahoe footskins could take him.

Don Pedro's camp was in open country, right at the Vermejo Creek ford on Kirby's side of the stream. The starlight was good, the tents of the Mexican mule guard standing out clear and plain. Kirby had no trouble spotting the familiar white cone of Don Pedro's canvas with right next to it the equally familiar shape of Aurélie's and Ptewaquin's tent. Between him and the tents moved the grazing silhouettes of the Mexican mule herd. What wind there was blew straight and steady toward him, easing his mind as to the tricky chance of getting winded by the herd. It must now be a solid 3.00 A.M. Leastways, a man had to figure it was, giving himself a full hour's room in his estimate.

With first light at four and the Comanche attack in gray dawn half an hour later, a man didn't have any time to be standing around scratching his seat.

He led Bluebell around to the east of the camp, tethering her in the last of the piñon cover about a hundred yards downstream of the tents. Next he stripped to his loincloth and hurriedly cut his buckskin shirt into yard-long strips. Taking the strips and Horsehead's heavy-hafted knife, he shadowed out across the clearing.

There was no trouble. Don Pedro had followed his end of his bargain with Big Foot with real faith. There wasn't a guard posted and the don's tent and that of the women were pitched at a handy distance from the others — and at a handy distance from each other. In conscientiously striving to make it easy for Big Foot, the Governor's nephew had set it up spang center for Kirby.

Inside Armijo's tent, the mountain man lay on his belly and located the breathing. It came steady and regular. And it came alone.

Kirby, waiting for his eyes to soak up the bear's-gut blindness of the tent's interior, found his thoughts outrunning his straining gaze. By the time a man would breathe six times he could make out all that would ever be necessary of the blanketed form beneath him — still hung half crouched, hesitating, held motionless, he now knew, by something a sight thicker than tent-dark.

Times like these came often to a man who lived by the silence of a bare knifeblade and the proper placement of a paper-thin moccasin sole. But they never came easy. He tried telling himself it was the same thing which turned his belly about opening that tough little Comanche pony's throat, or about pinning Horsehead through with that damn buffalo lance. Knew, even as he was thinking it, that he was joshing nobody but Kirby Randolph.

This graciously smiling Spaniard had come to mean something to him. Something more than any white man he had bucked into or trailed along with. Something a man couldn't put his finger on, maybe, yet something he could feel like he had his whole hand wrapped around it. And wrapped hard. Not wanting to let it go. But to keep it and hold on to it.

Somehow it came to Kirby then. Way too far down the trail, for sure. Plenty too long past the middle of the day, for certain. But it came. And it came as sharp and clear as any thought he had ever had.

Above any man he had known, up or down the river, he wanted this quick-smiling, black-faced young Spaniard for his *friend!*

For a moment the crazy idea of waking the don up and bidding him in on the escape try bobbed to the surface of Kirby's mind. But the simultaneous memory of another swart skin and lightning smile put the idea sudden and deep under. Aurélie, by damn. Sitting here hound-dogging it over what a shame it was to leave Don Pedro for the Comanches, he had nigh forgotten what he came for. Cripes! Time was not only a-wasting. It was near plumb gone!

The Spaniard wouldn't come to any harm, anyway. Not as long as he was as good as pure Mexican gold to old Big Foot, he wouldn't. Hell, man. He had things to prove here tonight, Kirby did. Getting Aurélie away was the biggest half of it, but past that he had to make it clear for his own hide. Just let Don Pedro's plan come off and the whole damn frontier wouldn't be big enough to hide Kirby Randolph. Let alone that he would lose Aurélie into the bargain.

Providing he hadn't lost her already!

After that it was a thing any wetnose cub would have found simple. You took the loaded haft of the knife and smashed it back of the ear — once for certain — twice to make sure. You felt the body stiffen, heard the breathing break, felt the body sag, heard the breathing take up again. You were glad of that and then you were mighty careful with how you tied the hands and feet with your buckskin shirt laces. And how you stuffed the mouth with a plug off the flap of your loincloth. And cinched it down on the tongue with three wraps around the unconscious head.

When you got through you figured maybe the Spanish son would strangle but you knew he would stay where you left him.

Bellying out of Armijo's tent, Kirby crawled into his first hitch. Yonder there, silhouetted against the ground line in front of Aurélie's tent, squatted a hulking figure no man could miss. The Spaniard might sprawl his camp and the Mexicans might pound their brown ears. But where Aurélie St. Clair slept, there crouched Ptewaquin, the Ox.

Oh sure, asleep maybe. But asleep right square in the door-flap. And asleep like a Sioux. Snow-light. Cat-easy. Let a pebble roll or a weed stem scrape and a man would find himself for once under more squaw than he could handle.

Snaking to within twenty feet of the nodding giantess, Kirby wet his lips, pursed them with painful care. The sleepy bullbat twitter wobbled a little anxiously but it did the work. Ptewaquin's head came up, swung in his direction. The scout's whisper rode softly in out of the dark.

"*Tahunsa*, Ptewaquin. *Kola*. It is your friend out here, Ox Woman. Your cousin."

After a long pause the squaw answered in Sioux. "Who is it out there calling me friend and cousin? And by my true name?"

"It's me, White Stripe." Kirby paused uncertainly, added the hasty qualification, "Kirby Randolph, the goddam-scout!" There was no answer from the squaw, her silence forcing his move. "I'm coming in. Make no more noise!"

"Come ahead, you *Wasicun sunke*." The low words sounded like a she-bear muttering. "Ptewaquin wants to see you. And her gun in ready."

"Shut up!" hissed Kirby, crawling in out of the darkness, lapsing into tense English. "Get the gal out h'yar. Right now. Thar's one hundred Tshaoh a mile up this creek. They mean to hit this camp at dawn. Steal the gal and kill ye. The Spaniard plotted it with them. Now, hear me. And go do it. And put thet damn gun down!"

"Which Tshaoh?" grunted the squaw, keeping the rifle on him.

"An-gyh P'ih!" snapped Kirby, turning to pull the tentflaps, himself.

Aurélie, already awake from the whispering, beat him to it. Her tousled hair glinting in the starlight, green eyes smoky with sleep, showed in the opening as Kirby raised the canvas. Sleep-smoky or not, star-dimmed or otherwise, those green eyes needed but one look at that naked, gaunt body.

"Kirby!" The shaky whisper had only time to wander off the parted lips before the hard-bearded mouth was crushing them into silence. Long eyes closed, hungry arms straining, Aurélie came into the fierce kiss. The watching Ptewaquin blinked three times before the naked scout released the half-breed girl and began rasping the terse string of his adventures since leaving them at Arkansas Crossing, complete with Don Pedro's ransom plot and Big Foot's projected double-cross of the young don. "— And thet's the way she sets now," he concluded abruptly. "I got away from Bad Liver and come back h'yar fer ye." His eyes bored through the dark at Aurélie, his lean hands seizing her bare arms. "Ye kin believe thet and come along with me, gal, or ye kin set up a holler and get me kilt. One way or the other, I aim to try gettin' ye out'n h'yar. Whut ye say, Aurélie?"

"Oh, Kirby! Kirby! I'm going with you, man. I don't care about your story or about how Don Pedro makes out or anything else!" The tears fell in the dark, hot-splashing his forearm. "I just want to go with you, always, *Wasicun*. I've been like a sick dog without you. I'll never leave you again, Kirby. You can have every Cheyenne squaw in the Cut Arm Nation, too!" She came to him again with the choking words, and he took her hard and close, holding the fragrance of her soft hair against the filthy stubble of his clamping jaw. His words, quick and harsh, went to Ptewaquin.

"How about you, *Tahunsa?* Are your ears uncovered to this *Wasicun sunke* now?"

"My eyes see and my heart feels," said the Indian woman, following the words with a single, soft-spoken Sioux phrase that hit Kirby flat as the broadside of a swung axe. *"Etan'han yakaga witan'de."*

*Etan'han yakaga witan'de?* Good God! How

did that translate? "From this time on thou makest my daughter's husband?" Brother Moses! Did she mean that, full out? *Her* daughter's husband? Cripes! What a time to drop a rock like that on a man. Burying his amazement for digging up later, Kirby accepted the big squaw's allegiance. In a tight like the one they were hunkered down in, Ptewaquin was worth ten good braves.

"*Iho' hun,* well, Mother, listen. You know the Spaniard's big black stallion?"

"*Hau. Diablito.* That's the one."

"Thet's the one, yeah." Kirby lapsed back into English. "Ye know whar he is?"

"Tied on a picket line, back of his tipi. As is the spotted mare, back of our lodge, here."

Kirby had not noticed Aurélie's mare and now, following the squaw's gesture, caught the animal's trim shadow forty feet away. "*Waste,* good. Now listen. Ye go get the stud. He will know ye a leetle whar he would spook up at me. Get the saddle and bags and stuff the bags with food from the tent. Then hand-lead the hoss to those trees downstream, thar. My mare is down thar."

"*Hau,* anything more?"

"No. *Da'wi howo!* We must go right now!" grunted Kirby. "First light is near. *Hopo!*"

With the squaw gone, he and Aurélie made tracks for the piñons, the paint mare quick-stepping behind them. In five minutes Ptewaquin showed up with Don Pedro's nervous black stud.

"Watch him he don't whinny when he winds the mares!" warned the scout, his answer being a reassuring growl from the taciturn squaw. *Iho!* Well! If the black devil could even breathe noisy, it would be news to Ptewaquin. When Ox Woman put a nose wrap on, it was put on. Among her people, getting a horse out of an enemy camp was the first thing learned after walking. *Hookahey,* let's get out of here. *Hopo,* what are we waiting for?

"Foller me," nodded Kirby. "And fer God's sake hold on to yer hosses. We're goin' to wade the stream as fur as we kin. Happen one of them stumbles and takes ye under, hang on to him!" There was no further word, the two women following the scout and Bluebell into the busy rush of Vermejo Creek, Aurélie and the paint mare first, Ptewaquin and Diablito last.

A quarter of a mile downstream the creek entered a small gorge, getting way too fast and deep for wading. Taking advantage of a solid rock shoreline, Kirby led his followers out of the stream and along the base of the hills bordering the east side of the narrow valley which shouldered the Blunt's Fort road. Another twenty minutes of steady walking put them a mile downtrail of the ford. "Mount up," growled the scout. "And walk them hosses quiet. We got to pussyfoot it another two mile, anyhow. Happen any of them Comanche sons are awake, we don't want them pickin' up runnin'-hoss ground sounds."

The two miles gone, he kicked Bluebell into a rocking canter, Aurélie and Ptewaquin following suit. "Hold them on this rollin' lope fer a good two mile," Kirby ordered. "Then we kin open them up. And," he added grimly, "by the looks of thet sky back thar, we'd best do it, too!"

He had been right as late rain when he had figured back there before going into Don Pedro's camp that he had best make the time an hour later than it looked. Now it was getting toward four. And the rear sky he had just mentioned to the women was doing its distant best to warn them about it.

Behind the dwindling jut of the rock ledge over Vermejo Creek, it was fading a cool rosegray, swiftly blurring the blazing star field back of Raton Pass and the Spanish Peaks.

They reached Ocate Creek at noon and Kirby, scaling a four-hundred-foot escarpment while the women watered and grazed the horses, took a short look up the backtrail.

The look was short because the elevation, the clear day, the mountain man's good eyes and the Comanche genius for tracking horseflesh didn't add up to any need for a long one. Far to the north, a tiny dust haze hung over the Blunt's Fort road, snailing its thin way south even as Kirby watched.

He slid down the granite slope, his mind jumping ahead of his scrambling descent. His first plan, depending on a clear backtrail at Ocate Creek, had been to make a straight-out run for it, following the Blunt's Fort road due south to its juncture with the main Santa Fe at Mora Crossing. The dust cloud back there blotted out that chance.

His second shot was to double back here at Ocate Creek, following the creek on east over to the main trail, thus hoping to make it to the Canadian crossing and the Mexican customs guard Chavez had told him hung out there, taking the route of his recent night ride with Big Foot's band.

There was a third longshot chance, too, which prodded him to try the Ocate Creek way. If Sam had made it safe across the Jornada, lambasted the tar out of the mules all the way up the Cimarron and down to the Canadian, he could be rolling into Point of Rocks just about now. That was a chance a lucky jasper like Kirby might just dast hang on to.

It was a spot to sweat a man proper, and by the time he had got back down from his climb, Kirby had perspired plenty. Come a time like this, with maybe fifteen miles between you and an idiot bunch like Big Foot's, it didn't take a man long to work a lather up. Legging it down the last slope, the scout knew Mora Crossing was out and that he had to have time. Time that could be had only by risking a sneak for

Canadian Crossing. And by tricking up that sneak while they were about it, too.

Back at the creek, he ordered all the extra weight off the horses. With the animals stripped and the gear cached, Kirby barked his orders for the rest of it. Ptewaquin was to enter the creek, ride down it a mile, pull out and hold up. He and Aurélie would cross the creek, lay a plain trail down the Blunt's Fort road, split up and work back to meet Ptewaquin. The Indian woman grunted, waved, kicked the black stud into the fork and went splashing away.

Kirby grinned at Aurélie, reached over, took her hand. "Come on, honey. We got some tracks to make. Happen ye still want to ride the double trail with this man, ye kin start right now."

Aurélie squeezed his big hand and brought it up to the brushing caress of her lips. "Kirby," the green eyes swept him worshipfully, their usual brilliance dulled by the quick tear glitter, "I'm just so glad to have you back, I can't talk. You're never going to leave me again, *Wasicun.*"

"Not fer about ten minutes, anyhow," laughed the scout. "Come on, *wastewin.* Foller the leader!"

He put Bluebell to high-hocking it across the ford, Aurélie splashing the paint mare in her wake. For the next few minutes they rode in silence, then Kirby spied what he was looking for — an outcropping of hardpan granite running crosswise of the trail. "Hey, gal!" His voice, low and fast, snapped the words out. "Ye mark thet hardpan ridge running slanchwise of the trail up ahead?"

"Yes, what about it?"

"Wal, we're splittin' thar. No, hell! Don't slow yer pony. Keep her steady. When we hit thet hardpan ye swing east. Run it about a mile, cut back north and head fer the crick. If ye plot it right, ye'll come out about whar Ptewaquin should be. Anyhow, ye see thet ye find her. Ye got thet, now?"

"Sure, *Wasicun*. What about you?"

"I'm goin' west."

"Then west is my direction, too, hombre!" The girl's defiance was as quick as the flash in her eyes.

"Ye're goin' east and right now!" snarled the scout, the sudden rattle of the hardpan under their mounts' feet spiking his answer. "Swing thet mare left, damn ye. We'll be off'n this rock in a minute."

"You're not leaving me, Kirby. Not again, ever!"

Aurélie's startled mare leapt away to the left as the haft of Crazy Legs' war axe belted her alongside the neck. "Now ye keep her pointed thetaway!" barked Kirby. "And ride her damn rump off!" At the same instant he heeled Bluebell to the right, heading her west, his voice, carrying over his shoulder to the still hesitating girl, dropping from hard to soft. "Honey gal, I ain't leavin' ye. Ye ride like I told ye and wait up with Ptewaquin. I'll be along. Howsomever this trail splits, me and you are ridin' it fer keeps this time."

"Kirby, wait — !" Her call hit his broad back, twisting him around once more.

"Wait, hell!" he gestured, angrily. "Ye do as I say. Dammit, I won't have a squaw thet bucks me!"

She hesitated yet a moment, then flung her left hand to her brow. *"Woyuonihan, Wasicun!"* The words came cheerfully now, echoed by the clatter of the paint mare's hoofs heading east on the hardpan.

Kirby watched her go, clucked gently to Bluebell. "Mosey along, baby. And let me tell ye a secret. Happen ye want somethin' from a cussed Sioux gal, ye call her a damn squaw when ye're askin' fer it. *Hopo,* ye bone-rack crowbait. Hightail it!"

A half-mile west, Kirby cut north to Ocate Creek, put the mare in, waded her downstream across the Blunt's Fort road, and splashed on east in the water tracks of Ptewaquin and Diablito. Shortly, he saw a long rock bench rising away from the stream, south, guided the mare out on that, and swung her down the bank, hammering his heels, hard home. Five minutes later, Aurélie and Ptewaquin rode out of a rock cluster up ahead, waving him down.

Waving back, the scout eased Bluebell down, calling for the women to swing in and follow him. When they had galloped up, he put it to them, straight out.

The idea now was to keep moving. No more doubling around and laying split trails. From here they made their big ride for it. And no maybes. Save the talk and don't look back. Just keep a sharp eye on the trail ahead. Happen one of the horses hit a chuckhole or ran into a watercut, they were done. The way it was, with all three mounts in good shape, with the gain they could hope to get while Big Foot unraveled their split-up tracks back at Ocate Crossing, and with hard enough trail under them to hold down their dust fair small, they had a pack rat's chance.

With luck they could beat the Comanches to the regular desert route of the Santa Fe around Point of Rocks. There they would hope to find the Mexican customs guard or maybe a white freight outfit coming or going. Maybe even Sam with their own train. Failing all three, they would still have darkness to run for. And with darkness and the late moon, not having found help at Canadian Crossing, they might be able to slip the hostiles and get far enough south along the main trail to be safe by daylight. In any case, they weren't scalped yet.

Kirby rated the horses cautiously, loping a half-hour, walking fifteen minutes. He held to this change-off of gaits the whole of the long afternoon, knowing the trailing Comanches would be riding gallop relays, using the fresh horses they had stolen three days before — would be making two trail miles for every one he and the women piled up. It shrunk a man's gut to hold that check-rein gait but there was no other way for it.

Ahead now lay the high rise between them and the desert branch of the Santa Fe. Here the Ocate Trail left the stream where it plunged into a mile-long gorge, forcing the mounted traveler up and over the gorge shoulder, giving him a five-mile view of his backtrail. And letting him see ahead many another long mile down the wide-sloping plateau to the distant thread of the Canadian where it snaked out of the broken jumble of this Point of Rocks country. Kirby, topping the rise first, kicked Bluebell around to take his back look.

By the time Aurélie and Ptewaquin had brought their laboring mounts up the last rocky footing and turned to join him in his hand-shaded, westward squinting, the scout had already seen more than he wanted.

As Aurélie gasped and the squaw grunted, Kirby nodded wryly. "Wal, anyhow thar's only fifty of the buzzards. Big Foot must have left Black Dog and half the bucks back thar with Don Pedro."

"Not that it helps any," panted Aurélie, "but why would he do that? Maybe the others are circling south to cut us off from the Canadian Crossing."

"Naw," shrugged the mountain man, "they ain't. It's so Big Foot could use all the top hosses. Look close thar. Every last one of them bucks is leadin' a spare pony." It was true. Given a second look, no matter the dropping sun fought you square in the eye over it, a greenhorn could make out the doubling up of the tiny dots crawling the river trail far below. "Take a long squint at thet bunch in the lead, Ptewaquin," he ordered the squaw, "and tell me can ye single out any one of them thet looks special to ye."

The Sioux woman narrowed her eyes, holding her strong hands around them like copper-wrinkled binoculars. Watching her, her great head and frame molten-dyed in the late sun, Kirby was struck for the first time by the singular handsomeness of her hawk's features, and with their resemblance, even though grossly magnified, to the angular, high-cheeked cut of Aurélie's halfbreed beauty. He had had no time to query the girl on Ptewaquin's strange Sioux statement naming him as the proper husband for *her* daughter. Now, studying the red-bronze statue of the motionless woman, he suddenly knew he would never need to.

Ptewaquin had meant the statement, literally. She *was* Aurélie St. Clair's mother.

Shortly, the big squaw turned, rubbing her eyes to adjust them from the farsight strain. "One man, big. Bigger than Ptewaquin. He rides in front. On a red horse."

"Thet's all I wanted to know," breathed Kirby. "Trust An-gyh P'ih not to send a boy on a buck's errand."

"What did White Stripe say?"

"Your eyes are longer than *Wanbli K'leska's*, Mother. Who else could tell a pony's color across so much land? *Woyuonihan.* Big Foot rides a red roan."

*Wanbli K'leska* was the sacred Spotted Eagle symbol of the Dakota Sioux. The use of his name was a rare compliment. *"Ho ha,"* grunted Ptewaquin. "Thank you. *Hookahey,* let's get out of here."

*"Hopo!"* responded Kirby, spurring Bluebell down the slope. "We're gone!" The faltering hammer of the hoofs of Aurélie's and the squaw's mounts behind him tightened the scout's wide mouth. Between his own aching knees he felt the rhythm of Bluebell's tiring stride beginning to go rough. Ahead were still three hours of good daylight, many a long mile of open trail.

Glancing back at the stick-straight girl on the spotted mare, Kirby's heart turned over. Aurélie had caught the glance, thrown him a slim-armed wave, backed by one of the old heat-lightning smiles. Looking at that gold-skinned girl with her flying chestnut hair and snowflash grin made a man sick to the pit of his stomach to admit what he had to own up to.

And what he had to own up to was that time

and three tired horses were running out on Kirby Randolph.

Bearing north down the slope, Kirby angled their flight sharply east, the daylight letting him see that he did not have time to make the long swing north which he had planned would bring them in above the Canadian Crossing. Now he would have to run straight for the river, hit the trail below it, cut back north for the crossing.

Two hours later, he sighted the trail, suddenly close ahead. Taking a last look back as their stumbling horses left the long downslope to plunge into the cut-up rocks flanking the Trace, he saw the Comanche dust cloud rolling a scant two miles in their rear. Minutes after that, they were through the rocks and out onto the main trail, were walled in by the saw-toothed, south-pointing granite outcroppings, and would see the Comanches no more until they were looking at them over their rifle barrels.

With a full hour of daylight yet to go, the fugitives' sole remaining chance was their original best one of finding a Mexican Customs outfit on their side of the Canadian. On the level and going up the clear ground of the wagon road, the staggering horses seemed to find some last ounce of bottom and steadied up a hopeful mite.

As it worked out, they had only three miles to cover to the Canadian. And one way and another, kicking, beating and cursing their breaking mounts, they made it. Behind them, as they rounded the last rock-walled turn hiding the near side of the Crossing, the serrated granite ribs of their backtrail had been for the past ten minutes echoing the crazy, high-pitched coyote yammering of the closing Comanche pack.

From Kirby's position, riding last, the far side of the stream was screened by thin river brush. But the near side, where the Mexican Customs Station should have been, was bare and open, letting the three fugitives see everything clear and quick. And what they saw was nothing. Not a wagon. Not a tent. Not a single cookfire ash spot. Not a solitary horse dropping younger than last month's.

There wasn't a Mexican customs officer within forty-four miles of the main Canadian crossing.

The slobbering horses stood spraddle-legged, heads hanging, thick tongues slack between yellow teeth, heaving lungs, roaring. Their riders sat them like slumped statues. Able enough to see. Not yet able to believe. "Come on," said Kirby, dully. "We'll cross over, anyhow. Stream's only knee-deep. Bottom's hard rock, ye kin see. We'll hole up in them rocks acrost thar. I aim to put me a galena pill down thet damn Big Foot's throat if it's the last dose of lead I ever deliver."

"If you miss him, I won't." Aurélie's curving

mouth set hard on the promise, her green eyes meeting Kirby's unafraid.

"Good baby." The scout's dust-bearded face softened. "Looks like we'll hit the end of that trail together after all, honey."

"*Hopo!*" snarled Ptewaquin. "You can say good-bye in those rocks over there. Come on, let's go!"

The squaw first, Aurélie next, Kirby last, they drove their horses toward the ford, rounding the screening timber just as Big Foot's yelping horde broke out of the trail head three hundred yards in their rear. The next seconds spun around Kirby so fast he couldn't grab more than the first handful.

Big Foot's triumphant war whoop was drowned by Ptewaquin's exultant Sioux scream. Her cry in turn was echoed by one of the same tribe and brand from Aurélie, the three simultaneous yells being overlaid by a fourth piercing challenge of an identity that electrified the weary scout. Jeepers Murphy! There was only one tribal yell like that in the whole damn west — the Oglala panther scream!

And only one brass-lunged old buzzard in the world to holler it just that cat-squalling way.

The next instant Bluebell had lunged him past the river timber, brought him the sight which had set Aurélie and Ptewaquin to screeching. Across the river, the Osnaburg top sheets of its Conestogas, ghost-white in the deepening hill shadows, squatted the tightest parked, most welcome wagon corral any Comanche-shagged trail scout had ever dreamed.

Aurélie and Ptewaquin had already made it across the stream, had their horses stumble-running for the wagon square, when Kirby finally got his own yell working. *"Hii-yeee-hahh!* Sam! Sam, old hoss!"

"Sam, Sam, my foot!" the old scout bellowed back, Hawkens waving frantically. "Ye looked ahint yerse'f lately? Get on over h'yar, ye damn chucklehead!"

Not bothering to look, Kirby got.

Ten seconds later he was inside the square and Big Foot's braves were breaking around the edge of the cross-river timber.

The Comanches were halfway across the shallow Canadian before they realized what they had galloped into. By the time Big Foot had haunch-slid his red roan to a water-showering halt in midstream, the first ten-gun volley from the parked wagons had crashed into his packed followers, emptying five hostile saddles and adding one ounce of galena lead to the weight of each of the owners of several others. Deep voice splitting with fury, the Comanche chief screamed at his braves to break and run for it, setting them the prime example by driving his roan back through their piling ranks before the first of them could even bring their squealing ponies under control.

Kirby, cursing wildly, grabbed Aurélie's rifle

as the girl started it for her shoulder, snapped a shot at the disappearing back of the Comanche giant, cursed again as he saw the chief spin in his saddle, clutching low at his right side. That was a hit all right but not where he wanted it, damn it. A man could tell by the way the big son had twisted that he hadn't drilled him center. Worse than that. As Big Foot spun to Kirby's shot, another rifle boomed in the scout's ear, another curse joining his own as the second slug ripped across the river, whined over the slumped chief's shoulder, and thudded into the arched neck of his plunging roan.

The horse went down, headlong, its neck broken by the heavy ball, the wounded Big Foot being thrown clear and still kicking into the trail beyond. The next second his fleeing braves had scooped him up and borne him out of sight around the bend timber, and Ptewaquin's delicate growl was burning Kirby's guilty ear. "Damn. You bad shot. Make Ox Woman miss!"

Kirby's disgusted answer was lost in the crash of Sam's second volley, delivered the moment the panicky turning of the hostiles showed the old man he had no need to hold a reserve fire. That second volley, splattering into the careening backs of the Comanche rear guard, emptied no more saddles. But from the half-dozen high screeches and sudden slump-overs accompanying the arrival of the lead among the last of the red riders, Kirby allowed there would be tall wailing in some six Comanche lodges before the week was out.

That ended the Canadian Crossing fight. Destined to go into Trail history as a great battle, its actual casualties were five known Comanche dead, a baker's dozen wounded. Among the white forces the sole casualty was the hard side of Kirby's skull where he had banged it on a wagon tongue in his hurry to get into the dirt on his arrival at the square — which was not strange since from first to last of the impromptu collisions, the Indians, so far as anyone could remember at the moment, had not fired a solitary shot!

Kirby, knowing his frontier fellows as few of their own number did, expected that by the time the train reached Santa Fe the toll claimed by the whites would have stretched a mite: probably up to as many as twenty Comanches killed, including Big Foot, naturally, and well over fifty wounded. But what of that? In every Indian fight Kirby had ever been a party to, the white men had killed and wounded more red-skins than the total number they had against them to begin with. It was wonderful but that was the way with the white brothers' counting.

As the caustic Sioux saying went, "He makes ten to lie down dead where one stumbled a little."

# 17

There was a hump-rib feast in Blunt & St. Clair's wagon corral that night that put a dimmer on any Kirby had sat to since leaving the Big Muddy and the Three Forks country.

The train had run into the same brand of Ciboleros that had hosted the Comanches, Sam swapping them five pounds of Dupont powder for three hundred of fresh-killed fat cow and choice sun-dried jerky. After watching the *boudin*-eating contest among the celebrating mule skinners and listening for the fifth time to old Sam's long-winded account of how he had pushed the mules after finding Kirby's saddle and rifle in the Jornada, and then his moccasin tracks mixed with the Comanches' at Lower Spring — how they had run into the six trappers from Blunt's Fort resting at Middle Spring following their escape from the Comanche trap, and how they had given them fresh mules and heard from them of Kirby's presence among Big Foot's band — how Popo, Don Pedro's *arriero*, still traveling with Sam, in charge of the mule herd, had come across a brother-in-law among the Ciboleros, and found out for Sam that Kirby had been alive and well four days ago — how yesterday they had found the white horse herders hiding out on Rabbit Ear Creek and had gotten their story of the Comanche horse-lift along with Kirby's part in it — how the train had just corralled on the Canadian, not even getting the cookfires laid yet, when they had all heard the Comanche yells ricocheting up the trail, Kirby begged off.

After all, damn it, him and the women had done some riding! His plaintive voice let the happy oldster know it, too. "Fer the luvva Pete, Sam! I ain't slept in three days. Ain't had a bath fer a solid week. Ain't seed my gal since Arkansaw Crossin'!"

Sam looked up at him, simian face puckered in a fifty-year-old persimmon that only Kirby Randolph could recognize as mother love. "Kirby, son, I'm jest thet gratified to find ye I cain't leave go of ye. And I got to tell ye somethin', boy. I reckon old Sam loves ye ever bit as strong as thet cuddly gal yonder."

Kirby caught the water-glint in the squinted eyes, felt the tremble in the wrinkled hand clutching his shoulder. He was quiet a minute before he answered, working meantime to swallow the lump in his own throat. When he had gotten it down, he patted the old man's arm. "Sure, Sam. Ain't I allus allowed ye're the best mother a boy ever had?"

"Ye go to hell," gruffed his companion, removing his arm from the scout's shoulder to fight the cookfire smoke away from his smarting gaze. "Yonder's the gal. And from the look in them slanchwise eyes of her'n, ye ain't goin' to need a mother no more. I'm resignin' h'yar and now. I done reared ye up but it's high time ye left home."

"Ye got thet right, old hoss." The young mountain man's parting look ran over the white-haired trapper warmly. "But I got a new job fer ye. Soon as Aurélie and me kin ketch us a padre in Santy Fee, thet is. From the time we corner us thet black-robe, ye kin start bein' the gal's mother-in-law."

Sam's answering snort went unchallenged as Kirby stepped quickly around the fire, his long arms extended to the waiting Aurélie. "Come on, honey." His slow grin eased the invitation, teasingly. "It appears to me thet hair of yer'n needs braid-in' agin." Then as the girl came eagerly to her feet, moving smilingly to meet him, he added in a murmur meant only for the two of them. "This h'yar Canadian water is colder then the Arkansaw but I allow the sand is as warm."

Walking with him, her slim body nestling to the prison of his sinewy arm, the fading glow of the cookfires flicker-lighting their way around the river bend, Aurélie put her cheek to his breast, wrinkled her nose up at him, the long sigh of content lacing the edges of her smile.

The too-quiet midnight built rumblingly into

one of the blazingly beautiful electrical storms typical of that section of the trail. Aurélie and Kirby, snug and dry beneath their borrowed blankets and buffalo robes, came awake to lie and watch the garish flare of the lightning chain its crazy way across the blackened skybelly, and to listen to the drumfire bounce of the hailstones rattling off the stretched canvas spine of the Conestoga above them.

Refreshed as only the very young can be by a scant three hours' sleep, the pair lay like truant children half the night through; hand to hand, head to head, blinking to the stab of the lightning, flinching to the crash of the thunder, talking in guarded voices of the trail ahead. Aurélie, proudly superior in her knowledge of the remaining way to Santa Fe, spun away the familiar miles for the enchanted Kirby, her clinging lips breaking the description at every landmark to brush the scout's swart cheek or linger briefly against his willing ear.

When she had finished, Kirby nodded thoughtfully, the retreating storm grumbling under his low words, his dark face illumined by more than the fitful lightning flashes. "Sure, Aurélie gal. It sounds like a tolerably smooth haul the way ye tell it. But me, I got an idee Santy Fee ain't no trail's end fer me. Nor fer my kind."

"How do you mean that, Kirby?" Aurélie's question mirrored her quick anxiety.

"Like I said it." The scout's words stepped

carefully into the silence. "Thar ain't no end of the trail fer a High Plains man. Not so long as he kin wrop his shins around a good hoss. And still see to run a line of tracks."

"Kirby, are you trying to tell me you still want to go on alone?"

The gaunt scout's great hand found her slim one, closed quickly over it, his low laugh cementing the warm pressure. "Wait up a minute, Aurélie gal. Yer answer's out yonder, thar." Before she could speak, he was gone, slipping away through the dark toward the distant bobbing tinkle that marked the position of Popo's bell mare and the rest of the night-foraging wagon herd. Listening intently, she heard the muffled tones of the old *arriero's* purring Spanish, the good sound of Kirby's rare laugh, the lonely whistle of a nighthawk.

After that, silence.

Presently her anxious ear picked up another sound, the popping crunch of a shod horse walking on hailstones. Before she could make anything of that, a departing lightning flicker disclosed the looming forms of Kirby and Bluebell.

Tying the tall Spanish mare to the wagon tongue, the scout ducked back under the Conestoga's bed and rolled into the warm blankets alongside the puzzled Aurélie. "Thar's yer answer, gal," he muttered, gruffly. "Tied hard and fast. Jest like ye wanted."

Aurélie's mouth dropped as far as her eyes

opened. "Kirby! *Wasicun!* You don't mean it!"

"Hell I don't," shrugged the scout, indifferently. "Ye're a *Shacun,* ain't ye? And this h'yar wagon's yer temporary tipi, ain't it?"

"Yes. Oh, yes — !"

"And thet's my mare, ain't she?"

"Oh, Kirby, Kirby — !"

"And she's tied out thar, ain't she? Fer Pete's sake, gal. Ye been away from yer mother's people too long."

"Kirby, Kirby! I love you, man!" The girl's slim arms came around the mountain man's sun-brown neck, the tear-wet crush of her lashes burning his shoulder. Presently she looked up, the old snow-bright smile flashing through the tears. "*Wasicun,* I'm going out there and feed that pony, right now!"

"No ye ain't," contradicted the scout. "The cussed mare can wait, Injun law or no Injun law. Right now it's me thet's hungry."

"And me that's sleepy," murmured the girl, sinking happily into the warm robes. "Lie down, *Wasicun.* Here, where you belong. By your woman's side."

"I'm down," sighed Kirby gratefully, feeling the soft warmth of her move into the lean cradle of his shoulder, closing his eyes to the drowsy fragrance of her stealing its sleepy way up and around him with her reaching arms. "And this time, honey gal," his trailing words slowed with the easing rhythm of his breathing, "I allow I'll stay down. A long, long time —"

There was quiet then in the oak-wheeled wagon-bed lodge of Kirby Randolph and Aurélie St. Clair. Quiet then, and for a long time after the last of the muttering thunder had tiptoed its growling way across the starlit crests of the distant Sangres.